THE CHINESE JAR MYSTERY

THE CHINESE JAR MYSTERY

John Stephen Strange

RAMBLE HOUSE

First published in 1934 (GB)
Published 2007 by Ramble House

ISBN 13: 978-1-60543-015-7

ISBN 10: 1-60543-015-3

Preparation: Gavin L. O'Keefe

THE CHINESE JAR MYSTERY

THE PERSONS OF THE STORY

THE GAUNT FAMILY

Mrs. Hetty Gaunt—head of the Gaunt dynasty, the unbending matriarch.
Waterman Gaunt III—her eldest son.
Mrs. Astrid Ingersoll—Waterman Gaunt's exotic mistress.
Edgar Gaunt—the liquor-sodden second son, married to
Elvira Gaunt—the heiress who hates her mother-in-law.
Nancy Gaunt—the lovely eldest daughter.
Carey Gaunt—the youngest son, weak, frightened, resentful.
Susan Gaunt—the youngest daughter, rebellious, headstrong.
Daniel Minton—Hetty Gaunt's nephew, head of the great Gaunt steamship lines.

THE GAUNT SERVANTS

Perkins—the butler.
Mrs. Perkins—the cook.
Reeves—Waterman Gaunt's valet.
Maggie—Hetty Gaunt's maid.
Maud—parlourmaid.
Gertrude—chambermaid.
Annie—kitchenmaid.
Hobson—chauffeur.
Captain M'Neil—skipper of the *Buccaneer*, the Gaunt yacht.

THE POLICE

Sergeant Potter—of the New London Police.
Collins—Potter's assistant.
Constable Bartlett—of Stone Haven.
Detective-Sergeant Hennessey—of the New York Police.

OTHER CHARACTERS

Otis Avery—the Gaunt family lawyer.
Rex Olsen—Astrid Ingersoll's brother.
Dr. Matthew Ryder—New York physician and Nancy Gaunt's lover.
Dr. Eben Blake—the local doctor.
Jimmy West—the young lawyer in love with Susan.
Tony Farelli—the lobster fisherman who has attracted Susan's attention.
Melvin Saunders—Waterman Gaunt's secretary.
Lucetta Brown—owner of the Stone Haven notion store, and Hetty Gaunt's lifelong friend.
Sol Atkins—antique dealer and undertaker, who discovered the first murder.

Out of these people, the great dynasty of the Gaunts and the men and women their lives touch and affect, the web of murder is spun. Among them is one who deals out death, and others whom murder will strike; one suddenly, in silence and darkness, one in the presence of many people, one . . .

Take up on the pages that follow the trail Sergeant Potter must trace with the menace of sudden death all around him, with the shadow of the curse of the Gaunts lying across a strange and complex case.

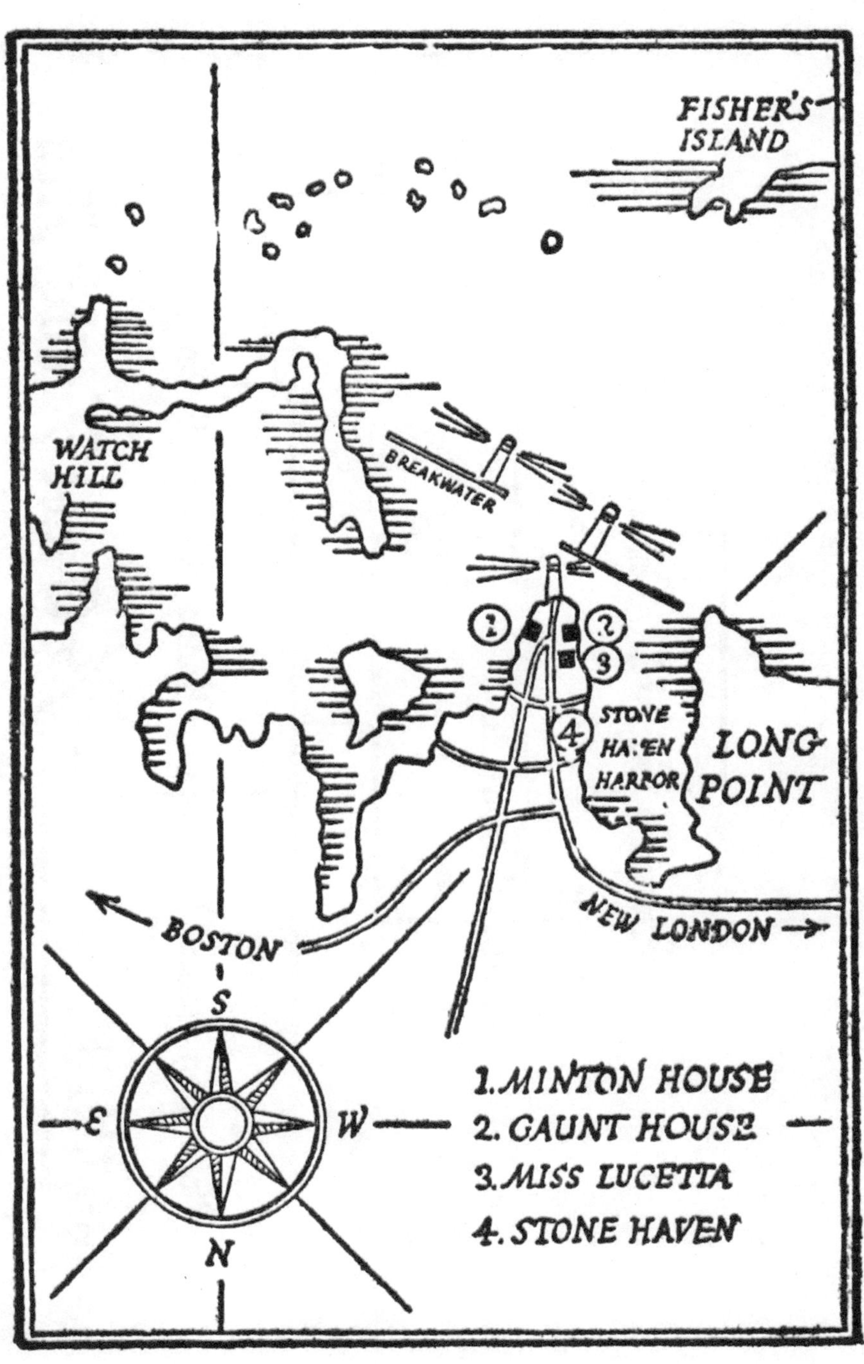
FISHER'S ISLAND
WATCH HILL
BREAKWATER
STONE HAVEN HARBOR
LONG POINT
BOSTON
NEW LONDON
S
E
W
N
1. MINTON HOUSE
2. GAUNT HOUSE
3. MISS LUCETTA
4. STONE HAVEN

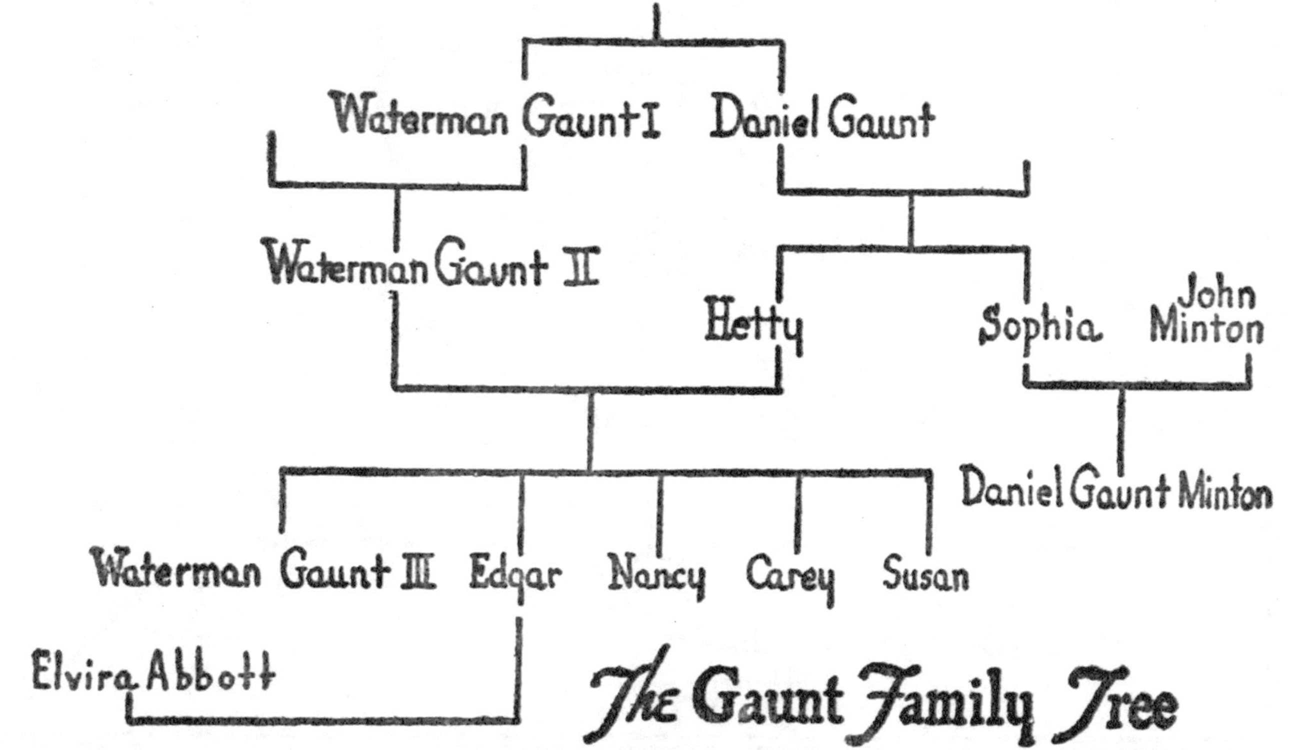

Waterman Gaunt I
Daniel Gaunt
Waterman Gaunt II
Hetty
Sophia
John Minton
Daniel Gaunt Minton
Waterman Gaunt III
Edgar
Nancy
Carey
Susan
Elvira Abbott
The Gaunt Family Tree

CHAPTER I

BEHIND the black hawthorn jar stood a tradition of death. Before it came into the possession of the Gaunts, before the "curse of the Gaunts" had ever been heard of, the shadow of death had fallen across the jar. Thousands of sea miles away, on the other side of the globe, Chinese superstition had filled it, under the red wax seal, with the uneasy ghosts of the dead.

It stood on the ornate white marble mantel in the library of the old Gaunt house in Stone Haven. It had stood there since 1855 when the first Waterman Gaunt had retired from the sea and built the house. He had brought the black hawthorn with him from China, where, as captain of the *Seabird*, he had, during the hazardous 'forties, made a fortune in the opium trade.

It was a beautiful example of a porcelain now very rare and valuable, thirty inches high with a black ground on which was traced a delicate pattern of white hawthorn blossoms and pale green leaves. The mouth of the jar was closed with a flat porcelain stopper sealed with red wax. The wax had run down the sides in places, so that it looked a little as though the jar was sealed with clotted blood. The suggestion was not inappropriate.

It stood in its place of honour between the crystal candelabra for nearly eighty years, dusted by generations of suitably awe-stricken parlourmaids and cherished by generations of half-credulous, half-derisive Gaunts, until that horrible night in August when Susan Gaunt, in a passion of hysterical tears, dashed it from its pedestal to shatter in a thousand fragments on the hearth.

Afterwards, when the madness had abated and the memory of those three terrible days had softened, she regretted the destruction of the jar as an act of superstitious vandalism, and yet—

Looking back when the play was all over, when the last bloody scene had been spoken and the curtain had rung down, it is hard to say that any event would have fallen out differently if the supernatural explanation had, after all, been the true one, and the "curse of the Gaunts," held in check for a while by the sinister seal on the black hawthorn jar, had, in fact, burst its restraining bonds to bring tragedy upon the second and third generation.

The roots of the story strike deep into the past, to the heyday of the American sailing ships in the 'forties and 'fifties, when the fast-sailing Yankee opium clippers, skippered by hard-bitten Yankee captains, raced from Calcutta to Woosung with a contraband cargo of chests filled with round balls of Benares or cakes of Patna opium.

It was a hazardous trade, involving not only the usual perils of wind and weather and Chinese pirates that faced those who plied the China Sea, but the danger of the government war junks, intent on suppressing the contraband traffic. But the trade was extremely profitable. The clippers commonly paid for themselves twice over on their maiden voyage, and huge fortunes were made in a few years for their owners and skippers, who were often part owners as well.

The first Waterman Gaunt, Susan's grandfather, had made a fortune in this trade and retired at thirty-five, built his elegant house at Stone Haven, married, and settled down to be a pillar of the church and the very epitome of respectability.

It was a decided change for him. Known all over the seven seas as one of the ablest skippers afloat, holder of two records for the run from Calcutta to Canton, he was also notorious, even in a brutal age, for his brutality and his unscrupulous dealings. His retirement from the sea was not entirely voluntary. Even his owners, who had stood by him through ten years of lurid episodes, were forced to abandon him when he was tried, on his return from his last voyage in 1854, for the murder of an old seaman, a member of his crew, and acquitted only because two of the witnesses changed their testimony at the last minute either because of fear or because they had been bribed.

A picturesque character, and no less picturesque in his death than in his life.

Finding time heavy on his hands in Stone Haven, his house once built and his son, Waterman Gaunt II, about to be born, he amused himself with an affair with a pretty woman in another big house across the street, the wife of his brother, Captain Daniel Gaunt, then homeward-bound from San Francisco.

The story of Daniel's unexpected return, his discovery of his wife's infidelity and his brother's perfidy, was the village scandal of the day. The rest of the story is only surmise, but it was accepted as gospel by Waterman Gaunt's contemporaries, although never proven, and there is no reason to suppose that it strayed far from the facts.

The story goes that Daniel Gaunt slipped a pistol into the capacious pocket of his frock coat one foggy evening, stepped across the village street, walked round through the garden of the big house opposite, keeping to the gravelled path where footprints would not show, discovered his brother sitting at the wide teakwood desk in the library facing the black hawthorn jar on the mantel beyond, and quietly and expertly shot him in the back. Certainly, when the servants came running, they found his heavy body slumped forward on the desk, spilling blood on the scattered papers.

It was in those days of excitement and confusion that the legend of the "curse of the Gaunts" took shape and substance. It was recalled that misfortune always followed fortunes made in the opium trade. Daniel Gaunt, questioned half-heartedly by the police and cleared in a formal statement, produced for public inspection—whether with the idea of self-extenuation or in a spirit of sardonic humour—a letter written by his brother to himself and thenceforth carefully preserved in the family archives: a letter written a year or two before the event just narrated, soon after Waterman Gaunt's enforced retirement.

". . . I have brought back some excellent porcelains, among other things a very fine black hawthorn, presented to me by that rascally Louis Chen whom you will remember. He came aboard one day in Woosung with half a dozen clerks loaded down with silks and knick-knacks, among other things this black hawthorn—a beauty. I noticed that the top was sealed with red wax and I asked him about it. The villain had the impudence to say that he knew of the belief held by Yankee seamen that a curse followed a fortune made in the opium trade, but that I need never fear it. In accordance with a custom which had prevailed in his family for generations, he had caused the ghosts of my enemies to be sealed into this jar. As long as the seal remained unbroken, judgment for my sins could never reach me.

"I was minded to kick the rascal overboard for his impudence, but I'd had a good look at the jar, so I swallowed my anger and thanked him. I had every intention of breaking the seal to see what he really had put inside, for from the feel of the thing you could tell there was something, but with one thing and another and the bad voyage home, it was not done. And then those damned humanitarians in Boston jumped me when we docked and would have had my neck in good earnest in that wretched Shipley matter—a bad dog he was, and better dead—if some of the witnesses had not been open to a little argument. I'll confess that since that episode I've had more respect for Louis Chen's magic. I've given the jar the place of honour in my new house—very elegant—and I have left the seal alone. Perhaps some day my curiosity will get the best of me. Between you and me, I wonder, sometimes, whether Louis Chen counted on that. I don't think it would break that old devil's heart if the seal was broken and the ghosts got loose and finished me."

Well, it was not the ghosts of Louis Chen that finished Waterman Gaunt. Or was it? Did there come a day when his curiosity could no longer be resisted? Did he break the seal and loose the curse? Who knows? One wonders whether the little Chinaman—friendly or malicious after all these years, who shall say?—would have been pleased or horrified at the trail of misfortune that followed his gift of the black hawthorn jar.

Susan Gaunt lay on the small of her back on the old horsehair sofa between the library windows, smoking nervously, and listening to the raised, angry voices in the next room. Carey was a fool to cross swords with their mother, she reflected grimly. Nothing ever came of it but a headache. She held the whip hand, and she had no scruples about using it. None of the Gaunts had any scruples: violent, wilful egoists—all of them. And her mother was a Gaunt by birth as well as marriage—a daughter of that Daniel Gaunt who, according to popular belief, had killed Susan's grandfather. Susan flung to her feet and paced the length of the room and back, nervously. As for Carey pitting his weak bitterness against his mother's anger—just because he wanted to go to France to travel. Surely he could wait a year—two years. But she knew that that was not really what he wanted. He was trying blindly, stupidly to save his soul alive—to get out from under his mother's domination before it was too late. Unaccustomed tears of pity and rage stung Susan's eyelids but she sniffed defiantly, readjusting her accustomed armour of light cynicism.

She heard the opening and closing of the other door which led from the study into the drawing-room. There was a momentary pause and then the door she had been watching was flung open and Carey came in.

Susan grinned at him.

"Been catching it, I take it," she said lightly.

"She's docked my allowance for the quarter."

"What for?"

"Because I wouldn't tell her why I went to New York."

"Then she doesn't know?"

"That I'd reserved a passage on the *Belgravia*? No."

"That's something."

"What good does it do? I can't use it."

"She'd have docked you for a year if she'd known."

Carey said nothing. After a moment, Susan's attention, drawn by his silence, swung to his face. It was not a handsome face in spite of fine eyes and a well modelled, intelligent forehead, for the chin was weak and sloping and the mouth irresolute. Just now it was bloodless, the veins at the temples blue and knotted. Even Susan was startled.

"Don't, Carey, you take it too hard."

"I'm twenty-five, Sue."

"Poor lad, I know it."

"And last week was the first time I ever went anywhere without my mother knowing where I was going and why. It was worth a thousand."

Susan giggled nervously.

"I'd have given that much just to see your face."

"I said, 'I'm going to New York—now.' And mother said, 'What for?' And I said, 'On private business.' And just walked out and got in my car and left." A faint look of satisfaction loosened the tension in his white face.

"So this quarter you don't go anywhere and cadge your cigarettes from me," said Susan lightly. She sat on the edge of the desk and laid her hand on her brother's. "You can't hate anyone like that, and live," she said softly. "You must wear your hate with a difference—like me. You must lie and slip out the back door."

"No!" cried Carey.

"Yes!" said Susan.

"I won't be like Wat and Edgar—cadging for favours."

"Nobody asked you," said Susan scornfully, "to be like Wat and Edgar."

"And I can't submit, like Nancy."

"No," said Susan.

"What can I do, Sue?" The question was the cry of the weak to the strong and she heard it as such. She stroked his hand gently.

"Wait," she whispered. "Meet fire with fire, and—wait. It can't be long. Mother has an incurable illness."

He stared at her in white-lipped horror. Susan reached for another cigarette. She lit it carefully and followed the smoke with thoughtful eyes.

"It's a funny thing," said Susan, "but I think—in my own odd fashion—I'm fonder of Mother than any of you, for the very reason that I admit to myself it would be swell for all of us if she just dropped dead one fine day. It sort of—clears the decks, so to speak. Once admit that and you've got perspective enough to see that she's a damn fascinatin' woman. Smart as hell, tenacious as the grave, and proud as Lucifer. Not one of us can hold a candle to her. She's the sort of person it's an honour to hate."

"You don't hate her."

"I do. I hate her like poison because she's ruined all our lives, or tried to. But it's a healthy hatred because I admit it and I'm proud of it and I mean to beat her at her own game with any weapons I can. Now your hate keeps you meagre and thin, waters your blood and eats your liver."

"I don't hate her," whispered Carey miserably.

"Liar! Ever since she said she'd stop your allowance if you went to Paris you've been sick with hatred. As for her darling eldest son, pride and prop of her declining years, the handsome repository of the Gaunt traditions, ever since she busted up his love's young dream of a thirty-room cottage with Christine Hemingway, if Wat had had the guts of an oyster he'd have stuck a knife in her ribs. Edgar's not the man to take anything but liquor very seriously, but he's never got over the fight she put up to save him from Elvira."

"I should think he'd look back on that with gratitude," muttered Carey with a crooked smile.

Susan giggled.

"Maybe. But Mamma's tactics were hardly of an endearing sort. Of course, Elvira chokes every time she thinks of her darling mother-in-law. We're a unanimous family in that respect, if no other."

"Nancy doesn't hate Mother."

Susan wrinkled her pretty brow perplexedly.

"Funny! I can't think why. She's really got more reason than any of us."

Carey flung to his feet miserably.

"Why in heaven's name did Father have to leave us this way? Why did he have to leave us all under Mother's thumb? We were all of age. Even you, Susan, had been twenty-one for several months when he died. Why couldn't he have left us independent? It's unthinkable that he should have left everything in Mother's hands, unconditionally."

"That will was made twenty years ago, Carey."

"I know it, but why didn't he make another later? He must have known he was going to die, he'd been ill for months. I'll never forgive him—never!"

Susan took up a pencil from the desk and turned it over and over in her fingers, staring at it.

"If he'd lived another twelve hours—he'd have left another will," she said softly.

Carey stared at her. "What do you mean?"

"What I say. He outlined a new will to Mr. Avery after dinner the night he died. He was to sign it the next morning."

"How do you know?"

"Because I went into the room when they were talking about it. I asked Mr. Avery afterwards and he said Father had never signed the will."

She looked across at her brother with a strange, closed expression. Unconsciously they lowered their voices. "What were the terms of the will?"

"I don't know," said Susan wearily. "What does it matter, since it wasn't signed? Anyway, Mr. Avery wouldn't tell me." Her eyes fell again to the pencil in her fingers. "Carey," she said almost in a whisper, "has it ever crossed your mind to wonder why Father died just then—just particularly on that particular night?"

"What are you driving at?"

"Oh," said Susan lightly but softly, and her scared eyes met her brother's for a minute and then looked away. "I'm not suggesting that murder runs in families, but after all we're a violent lot. Grandfather was murdered, and I've just wondered from time to time—strictly *entre nous*—whether by any chance Father was murdered, too."

CHAPTER II

THE next afternoon, which was a Friday in the middle of August, Waterman Gaunt III stood on the bridge of his steam yacht, the *Buccaneer*, and watched the Connecticut coastline lift over the horizon, a thin black line swimming in the light of the sun, which lay for a moment like a ball on the edge of the world and then sank abruptly out of sight. He leaned on the rail, smoking jerkily and flinging one half-smoked cigarette after another into the sea.

This was an hour he loved: His father and grandfather had used the sea for their own purposes, hard, practical purposes which had brought them immense gain; but Waterman Gaunt III loved the sea, ineffectually, uselessly, but as deeply, perhaps, as his checked and thwarted nature was capable of loving anything. It was his refuge from the annoyances and humiliations of life ashore. For while he had inherited none of the crude genius of his domineering grandfather, the first Waterman Gaunt, and none of the shrewd, cold competency of his father, Waterman Gaunt II, he had all their angry arrogance; turned bitter and sour by lack of capacity to support it, and he did not suffer the circumstances of his life gracefully. At forty, he was a bitter, brooding man, given to periods of depression alternated by futile, angry efforts to assert an authority he had never possessed. Only on his yacht did he find peace. It was his asylum.

But on this particular afternoon he did not look like a man in need of refuge. Captain M'Neil, glancing sidewise at the owner's face, wondered what had got into him. The usual brooding look was noticeably absent. There was a glint in the eyes and a line about the narrow, handsome mouth that the old seaman, who had sailed for the Gaunts for forty years, had never seen before. He was curious. His eyes turned frequently to the half-averted face.

"He looks like the Old Man, be damned if he don't," he said to himself in surprise.

To their left Montauk Point slid slowly past and presently Waterman, shading his eyes, could make out the line of Fisher's Island and far away to the right the crescent beach and jutting headland of Watch Hill. Just ahead lay Stone Haven harbour. An hour would see them in, and by that time it would be twilight. He stood erect, squaring his shoulders with a movement that reminded M'Neil again, startingly, of his father.

"A good run," he said pleasantly, and his eyes swept the sea to the eastward. A new, startled look came into them. "Fog!" he said.

M'Neil nodded. "Yes, sir. Been coming up the last half hour. We'll beat it in all right."

Waterman's eyes narrowed. From edge to edge of the sea astern the gray wall stretched. It was like a woman with wide skirts marching upon them, kicking long frills of mist ahead of her. The light caught the mist and silvered it, but behind this beguiling veil the fog advanced, black, shadowed with ominous purple, silent.

"We've got to beat it in," said Waterman curtly. "Fog or no fog, I've got to be in Stone Haven tonight."

"Yes, sir," said M'Neil.

Melvin Saunders, Waterman's secretary, came along the deck, staring back over his shoulder at the fog. He was perhaps thirty, with an ugly, pleasant, competent face, the mouth heavily lined and bracketed with humour and good sense. His eyes seemed to measure in turn the distance between the yacht and the fog and, on the other hand, the distance ahead between the yacht and the harbour.

He glanced up, saw his employer, and stopped.

"Mrs. Ingersoll is worrying about the cocktails," he said pleasantly. "I am deputed to find you."

With a last look along the horizon, Waterman Gaunt descended the short ladder to the deck and went aft. In the blue shadow of the awninged after-deck he found Astrid Ingersoll. She was wearing a pair of flaring corduroy pyjamas and she stood with her bare, sun-browned back turned to him, staring at the fog. Hearing his footsteps on the deck she turned and curled herself up with a swift feline motion on the cushioned seat that followed the line of the after-rail.

"Something gone wrong with the show?" she asked, a little nervously. "Have they got the wrong backdrop up, or what? Or does the scene call for lightning flashes and kettledrums?" She glanced shrewdly at Waterman, who laughed.

"Hardly!" he retorted. "Don't you recognise it? Fog! The suave, stealthy approach, and soft music." He lifted the big cocktail shaker from the wicker tea table and shook it experimentally. "Soft music!" he repeated, and smiled at her.

She was an odd little creature, worth any man's attention, small and very slender, with a round, sophisticated face, burned very brown and innocent of make-up except for the small scarlet bow of her lips. Her brown hair, worn in a long bob that curled behind her ears, was only a shade or two darker than the brown satin of her back and shoulders, and the bare feet in the white espadrilles were brown.

"Fog!" She shivered lightly, reaching a thin hand for the glass Waterman offered her, and helping herself to a paper-thin sandwich. "Your man makes the most heavenly stuff, Wat. But I won't stand a fog horn, I'd rather be run down."

"You needn't. We'll be inside Stone Haven breakwater before that hits us." He sat down beside her. "Where's your brother?"

"Asleep, I suppose. Rex usually is." She drank her cocktail sombrely. "What did you do with Saunders?"

"Up talking with M'Neil, I suppose," said Waterman carelessly. "A young man of tact."

"So that leaves us all alone, doesn't it?" she said with acid sweetness.

"Alone on the bosom of the deep," Waterman laughed. "Have another?"

She nodded without speaking and while he refilled their glasses, she took a cigarette from a thin gold case on the cushion beside her, lighted it, and drawing her sandalled feet up on the seat, turned away from him, leaning her chin on the rail and smoking sullenly.

She felt his hands on her bare back and shoulders. She did not move. After a moment they fell away and his choked voice said, "Astrid—you're lovely."

Then she flung her cigarette into the sea and turned. "What's the idea—going ashore to-night and leaving me here?"

He shrugged, turning his back on her, and tossed off the contents of his glass. After a minute he sat down in a big wicker chair, facing her, and smiled.

"I told you I have business to discuss—with my lawyer. You'd be bored."

"That's nothing to what I'll be shut up here—in the fog—with Rex."

"I'll leave Saunders to amuse you."

"And Captain M'Neil, I dare say."

He looked at her curiously. She went on:

"The man loathes me," she said with a sort of surprised amusement. "His Scotch conscience is perpetually shouting in his ear, 'Scarlet woman!' Odd how terms go out! Do you suppose there are any scarlet women any more?"

"A few, I should think," said Waterman dryly.

"No, no. I mean that peculiar blend of sentiment and hypocrisy. As dead as 'Camille'! The moral of which is that I think I'll go ashore to-night and meet your family."

Waterman Gaunt laughed softly. "My dear girl, if you have the remotest idea of marrying me—"

Astrid studied the tip of her sandal carefully, her lips curved in a secret smile.

"You will not only stay aboard but you take dashed good care my mother's binoculars don't spot you from the shore," finished Waterman grimly. "You re not the first girl I've tried to marry."

"I'd rather be the last," said Astrid, looking up under her lashes.

Waterman chuckled.

"Don't be an idiot and spoil it all. Look here!" He drew his chair nearer and spoke softly, the hidden triumph breaking through the careful reserve of his face. "With any luck, I expect to get things pretty well settled to-night—if you'll lie low like a good girl and not joggle my elbow. God, if you knew! Well, well, if I can pull it off to-night, with a little care everything should go all right. It won't be long, I promise you."

"It had better," said Astrid sullenly, "not be long."

Waterman whitened.

"What does that mean?" he murmured.

"It means, dear heart, that I'm not the waiting kind." There was an odd, breathless pause.

"If you want time," said Astrid grudgingly, "we could be married secretly."

"Too dangerous. Mother would almost certainly learn of it."

Astrid said nothing. Her laugh was as insulting as a blow across the face.

"She has power to cut me off without a penny," said Waterman icily.

The stored-up exasperation of weeks rushed to Astrid's lips.

"Of all the damned crazy wills I ever heard of. Your father must have been insane."

"I have often thought so," said Waterman grimly.

As though in answer to a cue, the outflung vanguard of the fog came upon them—a light mist that seemed to flatten the sea as it came, bringing a far-flung silence. It wrapped itself about them, chill, forbidding, and spread forward along the deck, wrapped itself around the figure of Melvin Saunders as he came aft from the bridge. The two under the awning did not see him.

"But there it is," said Waterman Gaunt flatly. "Father left everything to her, unconditionally. If she takes a notion to do it, she can cut me out absolutely. Comic, isn't it? Of course, I might be able to break the will, but it's risky. My darling brothers and sisters would fight it and—"

He stopped. She was looking at him with a curious intensity.

"So your mother doesn't want you to marry," she drawled.

He shrugged. "Apparently not. Afraid of competition, I suppose."

"But she does not object to an—er—irregular ménage?"

The man's eyes wavered only for an instant. He smiled ruefully. "If it isn't forced on her notice. After all, she is a woman of the world."

Astrid's eyes never left his face.

"What a good little mamma's boy it is," she said.

Suddenly she threw back her head and laughed, a wild, ungoverned laughter that came startingly in the silence. "God! That's funny!" Tears of laughter ran down her face. She saw Melvin Saunders standing uneasily by the cabin. Still laughing, she pointed a brown finger at Waterman Gaunt.

"He's a scream!" she cried breathlessly. Suddenly she stopped laughing. For a moment she sat quite still, leaning towards Waterman, her lips parted, panting softly.

Melvin Saunders thought she looked like a sleek, handsome cat, toying with the mouse whose back she has broken. "I came to tell you," he said to his employer, "Captain M'Neil says we'll make it all right. We're passing the breakwater."

Gaunt rose heavily and went to the rail. Through the mist he could see the low black line of the breakwater with the beacon at the tip. As they watched the light came on and began to blink rapidly. Above the smooth, soft hum of the engine they heard the melancholy clang of the bellbuoy marking the channel. A moment later the light fell astern. They had entered the harbour. Ahead they could see the long, narrow point on which lay the village of Stone Haven, embowered in trees. Already the mist lay over it, twining about the slender church spires that rose above the green, lying more heavily along the piers and fish shanties on the shore. Waterman Gaunt's eyes saw only one thing. The big white house at the end of the point, set in a terraced garden, bounded by a gray sea wall.

It was a huge old house, built in the worst Victorian manner, square and tall, with a mansard roof and a cupola, ornate and solid and respectable. The first Waterman Gaunt had built it in 1855 when he retired from the sea. It had been originally a cocoa-brown, but the second Waterman Gaunt had painted it white. Whitewashed the family skeleton, Susan said. It stood squarely on its green terraces, ugly as only houses of that type are ugly, yet possessed of a curious blunt dignity, a tasteless elegance, an inexplicable charm. So it had stood and watched the clippers come and go, lovely under clouds of canvas, stepping between the breakwater and the point, for Stone Haven had once been a flourishing shipbuilding town as the decayed dry-docks in the inner harbour testified. Now it watched with equal indifference the humbler traffic of the fishing boats, blunt, stubby, chugging lobster boats, the shark fisheries with their protruding bows tipped with a frail-looking half circle of steel where the man with the harpoon balanced himself over the flying sand.

Waterman Gaunt III watched it with a curious tightening of the heart. He hated it, hated its snug complacency, its unassailable assurance. Yet he knew it to be the rock about which the fluid meaninglessness of his life swirled. Away from it he was nothing. Here he might suffer but at least he was alive.

Astrid Ingersoll watched his face. She was troubled. She could have bitten her sharp tongue out for her outburst. She was a shrewd woman and she knew Waterman Gaunt very well. Saunders had gone forward again. She crossed to Waterman's side and laid her hand on his. "I'm sorry, Wat," she said softly. "I didn't mean a word of it."

For a moment she thought he had not heard. She watched his face, filled with bitter brooding. There was no longer any triumph in it. The fog swept in and covered them, covered the white house and the town. They heard M'Neil's voice issuing sharp orders and the rattle of the anchor chains.

"Wat!" she whispered again.

His arms went round her with hungry passion. She believed again, as she had believed before, that she could have her way with him.

But at eight o'clock he ordered out the boat and, after a short conference with Melvin Saunders, went ashore.

CHAPTER III

THE Michitiquock Club stood on a rounded hill five miles from Stone Haven. It was well back from the shore, but on a clear night one could look from its wide veranda across terraced lawns and shrubbery and the green meadows of Little Point to the Sound. The club itself was a handsome white house with square pillars supporting the overhanging roof. The only entrance for members was through the wide doorway behind these pillars, at which doorway there were, invariably, two handsomely uniformed doormen in attendance.

In spite of the commanding view from its windows, the Michitiquock Club boasted a singularly private situation. There was no point from which it could be seen nearer than the distant meadows of Little Point. Although it was only three hundred yards back from the highroad, it was entirely invisible from that point of vantage except in dead of winter when it was officially closed. Its only approach was by a wide gravelled driveway that curved between heavily masking shrubbery from an unpretentious gateway distinguished only by a miniature gatehouse and an iron scrollwork gate marked "Private." You could pass it every day for a year and hardly notice it was there. At this gate also there was a uniformed attendant who opened the gate obligingly when you blew your horn and immediately telephoned your description to the club if he was not familiar with your face and credentials.

The most curious thing about the Michitiquock clubhouse was the number of stairways. There was the main stairway carpeted in red plush which led up from the big hall near the desk to an upper corridor from which opened several private dining-rooms and the ladies' lounge. There was the service stairway at the back, which also led to this upper corridor. There were stairs in each wing leading to the offices of the staff. But if you were favourably known to the club secretary, you could, by penetrating through his private sanctum into an unsuspected, closet-like hall, ascend an enclosed, winding stair that ended in a green baize door. This in turn gave upon a narrow hall lined with mirrors in which the visitor encountered still another uniformed attendant, who, assured of his bona fides, would swing aside one of the long mirrors and admit him into an upper rear room, carpeted in crimson plush and decorated with pale green damask and white-and-gold directoire panelling. In this room were card tables. At the far end was a roulette wheel. Behind the seat of the croupier was an inconspicuous door concealed by the panelling which opened on still another stairway descending to a side door, heavily banked in shrubbery.

In a smaller room adjoining and connected by means of a wide arch was a mahogany bar with a row of high, slender chairs in front of it.

On this particular Friday evening in early August, the evening on which Waterman Gaunt's yacht had steamed into Stone Haven harbour, in spite of the fog that lay heavy on the roads, the big room and the adjacent bar were crowded. A casual glance revealed that something exciting was going on. There was a double circle of spectators around the roulette table and from time to time a little burst of excited comment came from them and eddied about the room, from table to table, and was caught up and repeated by the group in front of the bar. In the midst of the excitement, about eleven o'clock, a young man in an immaculate dinner coat entered from the hall and stood for a moment surveying the scene with surprise. He had an odd, puckered-up humorous face, very freckled, and crinkly blond hair. He pursed his lips in a soundless whistle and moved languidly over to the bar. The bartender greeted him like an old friend.

" 'Evening, Mr. West."

"Hullo, Jake. Make it rye." Jimmy West's eyes returned curiously to the group at the end far of the room. "What's the huddle? Somebody breaking the bank?"

"They say Mr. Edgar Gaunt is hitting it lucky, sir. Been winning steadily this last hour."

"No. You don't say so! Edgar! The old bucko!" He tossed off his drink. "Coals to Newcastle," he said sadly. "Ain't it the truth, Jake? To him that hath—"

"Ah!" nodded Jake sympathetically. "True enough, sir." He was small and brisk with the blank, expressionless eyes of the speakeasy bartender.

He deftly pocketed the money young West dropped on the bar and turned to serve another customer.

West strolled over to the scene of the excitement.

He tapped the shoulder of a plump girl in green on the edge of the circle. "My turn," he said softly.

She glanced up and smiled.

"Hullo, Jimmy. Can you beat it? He's won on seven five times running. He's betting on everything—day of the month, the number on his house in Cambridge, the figures of his automobile licence—he can't lose. Everything turns up lucky."

"They taught me in college to see for myself," said Jimmy smiling down at her.

She moved aside, letting him squeeze into her place. "Seeing it's you."

He craned his neck to look between the heads in front of him.

Edgar Gaunt was sitting on the far side of the green, felt-covered table, a pile of greenbacks in front of him, his eyes on the spinning wheel. He was a flabby. man, large, with a general effect of looseness. His chin was pendulent and his full lips seemed always to hang half open. He was actually two years younger than Waterman Gaunt, but he looked older. His hair was thin and already graying.

Now his face wore a look of smug satisfaction. He was clearly half drunk and had some difficulty in placing his counters accurately. He paid no attention to his audience. He seemed aloof from his surroundings, wrapped in the delicious intoxication of the successful gambler.

"My word!" muttered West over his shoulder to the girl in green. "He looks like Buddha on a spree."

A titter ran through the group around them, a titter merged in a sudden chorus of exclamations. "Done it again, by gad! Lucky devil!"

"I must go and tell Susan," said Jimmy to the girl in green. "This is rich!"

From inside the circle a sharp, soft cry came.

"Let me out, please."

The crowd parted to permit the passage of a brown-haired, brown-faced young woman, in a white crepe dress, and closed again behind her. Jimmy's good-natured eyes took in the extreme pallor of the face under the brown sunburn and the fact that she swayed as she walked.

"Going downstairs?" he asked, slipping a hand under her elbow. "So am I."

She stopped with a shiver and looked at him blankly for a minute. Then she smiled wanly.

"Hullo," she said. "I don't know you."

"My hard luck," deprecated Jimmy, tucking her hand under his arm. "You're the girl I've been looking for. We're going to go places and do things."

"N-not to-night, feller."

"Now," said West firmly. "We're throwing a party downstairs. Daniel Minton says it's his birthday, although it seems improbable, but we're celebrating on the chance."

"Daniel—Minton?" He saw her mouth grow suddenly pinched under her make-up. "Daniel Gaunt Minton?"

"Yes. Do you know him?"

She shook her head and glanced about the room, almost fearfully, he thought.

"Are any of—of the Gaunts here?"

He chuckled. "Whole shooting-match. Susan, Carey, and Nancy downstairs with Edgar's wife, Elvira. That was Edgar Gaunt who was raking in the cash at the roulette table."

She looked at him for a moment incredulously. Then she began to laugh, a strident, hysterical sound. "Oh, God! That's too funny!"

The laughter stopped as suddenly as it had begun. She stood very still, swaying on her feet.

"I'm not going downstairs. I'm going through to—to the dressing-room."

He looked at her desperate eyes and quivering mouth. "Bad idea! You've too much make-up on already. Here, wait a minute, Jake will fix us up." He led her over to the bar. "Make it two rye, Jake."

"Scotch," said the girl drearily, and leaned against the bar.

"Atta girl," said Jimmy approvingly. "I always like 'em to come up fighting." He put the glass into her hand. "Drink it up," he said. "Good medicine."

She drank, and gradually a faint colour seeped back into her face. "Now we'll have another," he said firmly. They had it.

"That's enough," said the girl in white. "When I have too much, I cry." She laid her hand for a minute on his arm. "Thanks, feller."

"Always happy to oblige," said West cheerily. "You're all right?"

"I'm half tight," said the girl, "if that's what you mean." Her eyes dwelt on her empty glass. "Funny stuff," she said. "Deludes you into thinking the world's a tolerable place."

"Good old world," said Jimmy. "Have another."

"All right." They had it.

"Trouble is," said the girl, "it's only tolerable when you're drunk."

"Poor kid!" said Jimmy.

"Oh, of course," she said with a large gesture, "it doesn't have to be liquor. It can be love—or gambling—racing, when your shirt's on the horse. But liquor stands by you when all else fails."

"East or West, liquor's best," said Jimmy solemnly. "That's what I say. Cocktails all round before dinner and we'd have no more wars. Have another!"

She sat turning her empty glass between her brown fingers.

"I'd better go, hadn't I? Do you know my brother?"

"I'd like to," said Jimmy, "if he's like you."

"Name is Olsen—Rex Olsen. He's round somewhere. Has a beard."

"No!" said Jimmy with lively surprise.

"Fact! He's an artist—so he says. Paints ships—when he isn't asleep. He's round somewhere."

"I'll find him."

"I'll be in the lounge." She looked at him and quickly looked away. " 'Night, feller."

"Change your mind and join the party," begged Jimmy.

"With the Gaunts? Boy, I know when I've had enough," she finished cryptically. " 'Night."

He held the door for her and stood looking after her while she crossed the mirrored hall. The attendant unlocked a door on the far side and let her through. Jimmy scratched his curly head perplexedly. Then, settling his jacket carefully, he went downstairs two at a time.

The dining-room of the Michitiquock Club occupied fully half of the ground floor. It was a handsome room with gold-coloured walls and white, early-nineteenth-century woodwork. A gray carpet covered the floor except for a large oblong of waxed boards in the centre, left bare for dancing. At one end was a raised platform occupied by a very good jazz band. Earlier in the evening the tables round the dancing floor had been crowded, but now a good many of the diners had gone upstairs to the card tables and the bar. Jimmy West, coming hastily into the room, had no difficulty in locating his party.

Susan and Carey were dancing, moving with a lovely grace, the easy harmony of people who have danced together for years. West's eyes lingered on them appreciatively. Susan certainly had an air, he reflected. Not pretty exactly. Her features were cut in too firm and vigorous a mould. But her eyes were lovely, and her figure in a sheath-like golden gown, that swayed into suave folds when she moved, was enchanting. "She has line, if you know what I mean," said Jimmy to his alter ego. And he sighed, for he had been pursuing her vainly for two years.

Elvira Gaunt, Edgar's wife, was also dancing, with an elderly man who hopped grotesquely and wore a look of painful concentration. She was plainly bored to death and as West entered she smiled at him provocatively. He knew she was asking him to cut in, but he avoided her glance. He could not bear Elvira. She was smooth and plump, with a faded, blonde prettiness and hard blue eyes. Carefully made up and corseted, she still believed that she did not look her age, and maintained a kittenish playfulness of manner which Jimmy characterised to himself as "pretty awful." He looked hastily for his host.

Daniel Minton was sitting with his cousin, Nancy Gaunt, at a big round table on the far edge of the dancing floor. They were talking earnestly together. Minton with his elbow on the table, sitting sidewise on his chair, seemed to surround them both with an invisible wall of privacy that defied intrusion. So obvious was his intention that West hesitated, awaiting a break in their conversation. He stood by the door, hands in his pockets, watching the dancers, his eyes drawn irresistibly back to the pair in the far corner.

Jimmy West was something of a philosopher in his own light-hearted fashion, much given to speculation about things and people, and Daniel Gaunt Minton fascinated him. He was perfectly aware of the scandalous tales that were current about the two branches of the Gaunt family and it amused him to speculate on the present relations between them. Two generations back, Daniel's grandfather, Daniel Gaunt, had shot and killed his brother, Nancy's grandfather, Waterman Gaunt—or so public opinion believed. And in the next generation, Hetty Gaunt, daughter of the murderer, had married Waterman Gaunt II, son of the man he had killed. There had been an enormous scandal. Yet that marriage had produced Nancy, with the calm, kind eyes. How stupid to make a fuss about anything. Rancour, like every other emotion, died out in time. What remained of the quarrel between Hetty and her sister Sophia which had so shaken the town? For years they did not speak because Sophia had insisted on marrying John Minton, the village druggist. And now Sophia was dead and her son was courting Hetty's daughter. Fascinatin' thing—life: richly woven in a thousand colours. Fascinatin' thing—heredity: not all physical, by a long shot; although the physical part was extraordinary. Take Minton, now, his stocky build, his heaviness which just escaped corpulence, his rather flashy good looks, his blunt hands so unlike the aristocratic slenderness of the Gaunts', were all a direct inheritance from his father, old John Minton, who was the son of a local fisherman and had owned the village drug store. Yet Daniel Gaunt Minton was unmistakably a Gaunt. The deep-set eyes under the bushy brows, the line of his rather heavy mouth, more than anything the assured carriage of his rather heavy body betrayed and labelled him infallibly. Unlike as he was, superficially, to the slender, pale woman beside him with her fine-cut features and air of sweet detachment, there was no mistaking their relationship. They might have been brother and sister.

Odd, reflected Jimmy West, that all that turbulent history should reduce itself to this simple sum: Daniel Gaunt's grandson making love to the granddaughter of Waterman Gaunt. How they would turn in their graves, those old-timers. And yet, perhaps not. There was something very accommodating about the moral fibre of the

Gaunts. They were realists, all of them, with the possible exception—his eyes flew again to the face of the woman at the table—of Nancy. Nancy was so sweet, so secret, one did not know. She had the air of one who goes quietly her own way without troubling to explain herself. What was her attitude toward Cousin Daniel? Would she marry him and so consolidate the family fortune? One could not tell. One could not, from her attitude of kind detachment, hazard a guess.

The music came to an abrupt end on a swirl of inconclusive dissonances. The dancers returned to their tables and Jimmy West crossed the room.

"I say," he said cheerily, "any of you seen a man with a beard?"

"Yes," said Daniel, "if you mean Rex Olsen." His voice was big and heavy, like his frame. He leaned back in his chair and looked around the room. "He was dancing a few minutes ago. Must have gone out."

"I saw him go up the stairs a minute ago," said Susan. "Why?"

"His sister isn't well—wants him to take her home. I said I'd find him."

"His sister?" repeated Daniel with a startled glance.

"Good Lord!" gulped Susan. "That's Wat's lady friend, isn't it?"

Nancy said nothing. Her clear eyes looked at Jimmy West, who was staring in a startled manner at Susan. "You don't mean Mrs. Ingersoll?"

"Why not? He hasn't any other sisters as far as I know."

"My God!" said Jimmy piously. "I—I never associated the names. But of course that's who it is. She didn't want to meet the Gaunts."

"What's she doing here?" asked Nancy wonderingly.

"Playing roulette," said Jimmy grimly. "She didn't say, but if you ask me, she'd lost something rather fancy."

"Where's she staying?" asked Daniel Minton. He rose to place Susan's chair for her.

"Search me," said Jimmy. There was excitement in his eye. "By Jove, the old boy's got taste. She's a stunner. I'll go up and see if Olsen's found her." He grinned at Elvira as he turned away. "By the way, Edgar's breaking the bank. He had a wad big enough to choke a horse when I came down." He hurried away.

The Gaunts looked at each other.

"Funny that she should come here," said Susan thoughtfully.

"After all, why not?" said Daniel Minton. "Olsen drives up every once in a while."

"Do you suppose Wat—" Carey did not finish his sentence.

They had already forgotten Edgar. This was not unusual. Everyone forgot Edgar.

When Edgar Gaunt came downstairs an hour later, he found that the rest of his party had gone home. A marked change had come over him. His elation had left him. His florid face was pale and there were blue rings under his eyes and around his mouth. His heavy body seemed to weigh forward, like the body of a fat old man. He walked uncertainly. No one spoke to him. The eyes that followed him were filled with the secret satisfaction reserved for the misfortunes of the wealthy, overlaid with a little unwilling pity.

He got his hat from the coat-room attendant and stood turning it for a minute in his hands uncertainly, looking about him in surprise as though he could not remember where he was. Then he seemed to pull himself together and went out, crossed the misty roadway, got into his car, and drove away.

"Looks as if he'd lost his shirt, poor devil," said one of the doormen in a low voice.

The other laughed. "Edgar Gaunt? He's got so many shirts he can't count 'em."

CHAPTER IV

About fifty yards from the old Gaunt house, just on the other side of the wrought-iron fence that surrounded the garden, was the neat little white clapboard house where Miss Lucetta Brown lived alone. She was a pretty creature, plump and elderly, with pretty white hair that curled girlishly around a pretty, fresh face. She owned the village dry-goods store and had been a neighbour of the Gaunts all her life. Curiously enough she came as near to being an intimate friend as old Mrs. Gaunt ever had. Like most strong, masterful women, Hetty Gaunt was essentially a lonely soul and the simple-hearted, unquestioning admiration and devotion offered to her by Lucetta Brown filled a profound need of which she was herself only half aware. They had been girls together—intimates all their lives. When Hetty's children were born Miss Lucetta had been in the house, managing things, answering letters, taking charge. When the children were sick or the servants left it was always Miss Lucetta who was sent for. Quiet and unexacting and useful, she would move about the house, soothing, smoothing the rough surfaces.

To Miss Lucetta, Hetty Gaunt was the symbol of romance. She saw in her friend all the decisive, dramatic qualities so lacking in her own character. It seemed to her that in Hetty's life were to be found all the colour and glamour that had somehow been left out of her own. She watched the comings and goings at the big house across the fence with a never-failing interest. She followed the detailed history of the Gaunts day by day as a person might peruse page by page the chapters of a fascinating novel. She knew more about the Gaunts than the Gaunts knew about themselves. But she never told what she knew. She had for all the Gaunts—for Hetty first and for her children afterwards—an instinctive and undeviating loyalty. That that loyalty was destined to involve her in a situation strange and horrible beyond her power to imagine was not as yet known to her.

She had no premonition of what the day was to bring when she came out of her back door on the morning following the arrival of Waterman's yacht in the harbour, which is to say on Saturday. She locked her door and glanced at the little watch attached by its black ribbon bracelet to her wrist. Precisely ten minutes of eight as usual. She went to the rail of her little porch and peered down into her narrow strip of garden, drawing long breaths of the sweet, salty air.

The fog had come in overnight. She had watched it come like a moving wall over the edge of the sea, erasing one after another the twinkling lights on the point, creeping upon the town, invading each dim street and filling it with a strange new quality of silence. In its wake had come the low, distant shriek of fog horns and a new accent on the melancholy clang of bellbuoys marking the channel.

She loved the fog, although it made her a little melancholy. More than anything else it seemed to bring her the very scent and essence of the sea which she had loved all her life. She looked across at the big house opposite, wreathed, beautifully, in fog; at the dim figures moving on the terrace. For a moment she watched them, debating whether she should go across and inquire for Mrs. Gaunt. But she did not go. Glancing at her watch again she saw that ten minutes had passed. She was late. Clucking her tongue reproachfully she hurried off up the street.

There were very few customers in the shop that morning. Only Mrs. Sloane from across the street who came in for a spool of scarlet thread and Maybelle Clark who wanted a pair of number seven knitting needles. That was all. No one would go out in such fog unless it was important. And that was why she was able to tell Sergeant Potter so accurately exactly what time it was—eleven o'clock to the minute—when Sarah Hoyt threw open the door of the shop and rushed in, all white and shaking, and said that Mrs. Gaunt was dying.

Sarah had been taking eggs to Mrs. Gaunt for years, and this morning she had come in in spite of the fog, as usual. She had been in the kitchen talking to Nancy Gaunt, who had just paid her for the eggs, when someone had called out from upstairs. They couldn't hear what he said—it was Edgar Gaunt's voice, she thought—but he sounded frightened. Nancy had run upstairs and she and

Hannah Perkins, the cook, had gone out in the front hall. A minute later Carey came rushing downstairs and they could hear him at the telephone sending a telegram to Dr. Ryder in New York. He had said his mother was dying.

Miss Lucetta Brown had locked up her shop and gone straight to the Gaunt house to see if there was anything she could do. Hannah Perkins had opened the door for her and had told her that Mrs. Gaunt was dead.

That afternoon the train from New York drew into the New London station slowly, with ringing of bells, feeling its way through the fog. It seemed endowed with an animal caution, picking its way delicately, like a cat, on the wet tracks. Or like a tiger, Carey Gaunt thought, with his heart hammering in his side. "Tiger, tiger, burning bright . . ." A red glare hung in the fog above the engine; there was a quick, deep panting as it crept past him; then it stopped, crouching, ready to spring, and silence swept in on every side. One was poignantly aware of the warning cry of a distant fog horn and the desolate ringing of bell-buoys at the river's mouth.

For a moment the boy was gripped with a sort of paralysis of horror. All this had happened before some time, some place. He remembered the night when his father had died, and he was gripped with a crushing, inexplicable nightmare of doom. The "curse of the Gaunts"! Absurd! Absurd! They had been old and had died. If that was a curse, it was a curse common to mankind. And yet—

On that night, too, he had run away from the house where his father lay dead, and Matthew Ryder had come and found him down on the rocks beyond the light, and had taken him home and put him to bed. Good old Matthew!

Doors were flung open and figures began to emerge from the coaches; blurred, featureless shapes carrying grotesque bundles. Carey started, awake, suddenly filled with fear that he might miss the man he had come to meet. He began to run cautiously along the slippery platform, his wet raincoat flapping about his knees, his face turned up towards the dim line of windows beside him. The Pullmans would be at the rear. What a confounded idiot!

He collided with a figure that loomed suddenly around a baggage truck walking rapidly in the opposite direction, and drew himself up with a gasp that was half a sob.

"Sorry!" And then he broke off to stand staring, filled with an immeasurable sense of relief. "Oh!" he said. "It's you!"

The man said nothing but: "Hello, Carey." And then he stood smiling a little, warm and kind, holding a suitcase in one hand and a small black Boston bag in the other. He was perhaps thirty-five or forty, of middle height and strong, stocky build. His face was square and strong, with keen eyes under prominent brows—a responsible face. The boy was horrified to feel tears press under his lids.

"She's dead," he blurted out. And then, to cover the tears, he began to laugh unnaturally. "I dashed downstairs to telephone the telegram to you and when I got back she was dead. Funny, wasn't it? All in a minute everything gone!"

Dr. Ryder set his bags on the wet platform and put his hands on the boy's shoulders with a bruising pressure.

"Stop it!" he said sternly. "Stop it! What in the devil's name did your sister let you come over for? I should have thought Nancy had more sense."

Carey stopped laughing but the gray, drawn mask was hardly more reassuring than the convulsed, comic one.

"Let me?" he repeated. "She couldn't stop me. Not even dear Edgar could stop me. Though he tried to. Said it wasn't fitting, with Mother just dead. Fitting! I told him it was more fitting than sitting around squabbling about who would get the dining-room chairs.

"Carey!"

"Can you believe it? Nancy was trying to get us to swallow some food—we hadn't had any lunch—and Elvira said of course Nancy would be closing the house and she'd hardly want the dining-room set in town—"

The boy choked suddenly and the tears ran down his cheeks. Matthew Ryder picked up his bags again.

"Where's your car?"

Carey blew his nose and pulled his cap down over his eyes. "Out here somewhere," he muttered, and turned away into the fog.

Following him, Dr. Ryder shivered slightly. Even though it was August, this chill, deep-sea fog struck into the bones. But as he made this excuse to himself Matthew Ryder knew it was something more chill and subtle than fog that caused the deep, uneasy presentiment that had weighed on his spirit ever since he had received Carey's incoherent telegram. All the way up in the train he had been thinking of Nancy Gaunt and of what her mother's death would mean to her. A loosening of the pack? He did not know. Undoubtedly Mrs. Gaunt had abused Nancy's good-nature, made use of her devotion, tyrannised over her, and yet in a way she had protected her, too, defended her against her precious brood of brothers and sisters. He had known them all for years and he had no illusions about them.

Dr. Ryder had frowned irritably at the Connecticut countryside scudding past the car windows. He was putting it badly; making it sound as though Nancy was weak, to be bamboozled and handled. Not weak—strong—the strongest person he knew; strong and sane and beautiful, allowing herself to be used and abused and tyrannised over because she chose to do so, because she loved and desired to serve. Well, the service was over now. And with that thought a deep, warm joy invaded him. Surely his waiting was over, too.

Often as he had traversed this road in the last five years—across the long bridge over the Thames with the wide river below and the wide arms of the harbour stretching out into the Sound, through hilly Groton with its precipitous streets, and out on to the shore road with its vanishing glimpses of the sea, he had never lost his first lifting sense of delight in it. To-day, with his nerves drawn taut, with that heightened sense of life one feels in the presence of death, he thought he had never seen anything so beautiful. Here and there the fog rolled in on them, forcing them to a crawling pace, turning the trees along the road to delicate patterns of lace-like branches and then lifting suddenly, showing them pastel vistas of long points reaching out into blue water, or pale sea marshes glittering with wet. A fairy road, full of the poetry of his long love for Nancy Gaunt, sharp with the pain of long denial, bitter-sweet with delight of looked-for meetings. For all his shrewd and clever mind that had brought him so young into prominence in his profession, at heart

Matthew Ryder remained simple and direct, and poetry was possible to him.

They drove for some miles without speaking, but when they had passed Massassoit, its worn, white doorways gleaming at them through the mist, as under a veil half lifted, the doctor glanced sideways at Carey and saw the boy's drawn face had relaxed. He said gently: "Good of you to come for me."

"No," said Carey, and he paled again, paper-white. "I wanted to get away—and I wanted to ask you a question." Suddenly he drew the car to the roadside, put on the brake, and turned to his friend. His eyes blazed with a look the doctor did not like. "It's fashionable to doubt everything now. Do we doubt too much, Matthew?"

Ryder said gravely: "I don't follow you."

"We're so smart. We no longer believe that a righteous God visits punishment on evildoers unto the third and fourth generation. We think, if we can escape the law courts, we can escape the consequence of our sins. Do you believe we can?"

"No," said Matthew Ryder. "We make our own hells. There can be no question of that."

"And you think there's nothing else?"

Ryder looked at him closely.

"I don't follow you."

"You think there's no outside force that exacts vengeance? Quietly, inexorably, in an unbelieving world? My God, Matthew, I believe I'm going mad."

The boy's head went down on his arms, crossed on the steering wheel. Matthew Ryder laid his arm over the bent shoulders.

"The curse that follows fortunes made in the opium trade—the 'curse of the Gaunts,' " he said gently. "Eh? My dear fellow, a nursery tale to frighten children."

"My grandfather was murdered," said the boy stubbornly. "My father and mother—"

"Died of diseases that are well known and, unfortunately, sufficiently common."

"You believe that?"

"I know it. I've been attending them for a long time, Carey—first your father and then your mother. I've been expecting this to happen—this year—next year—any time."

"Oh, my God!" Carey put his hands to his head with a frantic gesture, profoundly disturbing.

"What's the matter, Carey?"

The boy looked at his friend. For a moment Ryder had the impression that he was about to tell him something. Afterwards, when the presentiment that had overshadowed him all afternoon had become a terrible reality, he remembered vividly that dramatic little pause, that curious look of longing and despair. But no words came. Carey started the engine and threw off the brake. After they had driven for some minutes he muttered:

"Talking through my hat as usual. This business has thrown me off, rather. You'll have to forgive me."

"Perhaps you'd better tell me how it happened."

The prosaic suggestion seemed to stagger Carey.

"I don't know," he said uneasily. "At least, it's all so confused. Mother's been well—perfectly fine ever since she got over that last attack—July, wasn't it?"

"Yes, July."

"When you came up. Well, she's been better than in years, I should say. I looked into her room about nine and she was sitting up in bed eating her breakfast, as chipper as a grig, talking to Wat. He came in last night on the *Buccaneer*. She was saying, if the fog lifted, she wanted Wat to take her out to the yacht."

Carey paused and licked his dry lips. Ryder prompted him:

"Well? And then?"

"Susan and I went swimming off the wharf about an hour later. We usually go to the club but it was so foggy we decided it would be too much trouble to get there, so we went in off our own wharf instead. It was high tide and all right. When we came in we went up the back stairs to our rooms to take a shower and dress. I was just tying my necktie when Edgar yelled out—a sort of funny frightened howl. I ran out into the hall and there he was in the door of Mother's room, sort of gesticulating and calling. He looked terribly funny," he added. "You know how Edgar is when he's excited."

Glancing at him, Ryder saw the boy's lips quivering. He waited a moment. "Well?"

"Well, while I stood gaping like an idiot, Nancy came running up the back stairs and pushed past Edgar into

Mother's room and then I ran in too. We all ran in, and Mother was lying on the floor in her dressing gown, all twisted up and queer. We all lost our heads except Nancy. We began to talk all at once and carry on generally. Nancy made us lift Mother on to the bed and then she got her medicine and told us all to get out. Edgar grabbed my arm and pulled me into the hall.

" 'Go telegraph Matthew,' he said. 'Tell him to come quick.'

"I got downstairs somehow and sent the telegram. Funny. I can hardly remember anything about that. But I remember going upstairs again, and standing in the doorway and Nancy looking at me with a strange, blank sort of look and saying: 'She's dead, Carey.' Just quiet, like that. 'She's dead, Carey.' And then she just sat there, sort of patting her hands together gently as though she didn't know what to do next.

"I remember saying like an ass: 'What ought we to do?' And then she said in that same funny, conversational tone, as though we'd been discussing the weather: 'I don't know.' "

"I don't like it," Dr. Ryder said.

"No," agreed Carey. "It was awful. I can't tell you how ghastly I felt."

"Oh—you!" The doctor's voice was full of a profound impatience. Carey took the implied rebuke with unwonted humility.

"I know," he said. "We're all beasts about Nancy. But she was all right again in a minute. Wat had telephoned Dr. Palmer and when he came she was quite herself again. She got him to tell her what to do. He had Atkins come over and she made all the arrangements about the funeral and everything herself. She's all right."

"All right!" thought Matthew Ryder. Quite herself again. Taking care of everything; holding them all up in her strong hands.

"There's something about a certificate," said Carey uneasily. "Palmer said he'd talk to the coroner about it—or perhaps you could give it, since you've been attending Mother. He said there was some technicality—"

"It will be all right," said Ryder absently. He was hardly listening.

"But the coroner," insisted Carey. "I don't see—"

"It will be all right," repeated the doctor irritably.

Carey opened his mouth to speak again and closed it without speaking. They turned into the main street of Stone Haven.

It ran down the narrow point with the village on each side of it—old white houses with fanlights over the doors set in little gardens full of the gorgeous bloom of seaside dahlias. The little cross street ran abruptly into the harbours on either side where swaying sailboats, wreathed in mist, rode lazily at anchor. At the farther end, the main street itself ran down to the sea, and here they stopped, drawing up in front of the doorway of the old Gaunt house.

It loomed above them in the mist, huge and white and silent, its terraced gardens falling away to the shingle behind it. For a moment they saw it complete, its white doorway, its curtained windows, the high, wrought-iron fence sentinelled with dahlia blooms, the sloping garden behind, flanked by the low sea wall, the little wharf with its moored dinghy, the slender sailboat at anchor beyond. Then the curtain of fog rolled in again, drowning it from view, bringing with it an intense silence and the mournful voice of the bellbuoys.

The doctor's hand shook as he opened the car door and got out. Perhaps something of Carey's mood had communicated itself to him. He lifted out his bags and followed the boy who pushed open the front door and entered, calling softly:

"Nancy! Nancy!"

Edgar came out of the dining-room, his bald spot gleaming in the half light, a glass in his hand and the aroma of alcohol about him.

"Well!" he said. "Well, well! Glad to see you! How about a snifter?"

Ryder paid no attention. He caught a glimpse of Elvira, sitting in the drawing-room talking to a sorry-looking female in black, their faces turned blankly towards the opening door. And then he heard a step in the upper hall and Nancy stood above him, looking down. He surrendered his bags to Perkins, who came forward to receive them, and went up to her.

CHAPTER V

MRS. GAUNT'S room was on the west side of the house and its windows looked down across the garden and the sea wall at the bay. It was a big, old-fashioned room with a heavy turned cornice running round the walls under the high, elaborately decorated ceiling. It was furnished depressingly in black walnut, heavily carved, ornate, yet possessed of a certain ugly dignity that was curiously suggestive of the dignity of the ugly old lady who had been its occupant. Like her it had a curious charm, a grim power, a latent vitality in spite of its puce-coloured hangings and carpet, the fog pressing bleak and gray against the windows, the huge, funereal bed with the headboard not unlike a carved tombstone.

On this bed she lay, a small, stocky figure grimly dead. The wide mouth was folded tight together, the heavy-lidded eyes were firmly shut as though she defied the world to disturb her rest. Even in death she emanated the force of character that had made her, living, the tyrant of her home.

Matthew Ryder looked down at her gravely. Then he looked up at the girl standing on the other side of the bed, and for the first time was struck by Nancy's likeness to her mother. Under the fair, smooth flesh the same bony structure, shown faintly now by lines of fatigue and strain. And for the first time something of the same grim look, a folding of the lips, an expression of the eyes under the lovely, heavy lids. She was not looking at him, but at the face on the pillow. He had a strange feeling that in some silent way the two were communing together. Then Nancy looked up at him, slowly, gravely. How tired she was—how inexpressibly tired. Not beautiful now; pinched and white; even her clear gray eyes opaque with a look he could not read; the very droop of her shining black hair announcing fatigue; yet he had never been so moved by her, so drawn to her.

"Don't look at me like that," she muttered with lips that scarcely moved. "You'll make me cry—and I mustn't cry."

"It would do you good," he said gently.

"No!" She spoke stolidly, flatly. "What is to be done now? What is this about a death certificate?"

"A mere formality. In cases of sudden death where there is no doctor in attendance."

"But you've been attending Mother."

"I haven't seen her for a month. It's only a formality, my dear. I'll call the medical examiner at once. He may want to see your mother."

"But when Father died—"

"I had seen your father within a few hours."

"Will it mean an—autopsy?"

"Certainly not. I can certify the cause of death."

She drew a sudden breath of relief, sharply audible in the silent room.

"Mother hated illness so. She ignored it as much as she could. She thought it was indelicate. She would have hated—"

Suddenly her control snapped. She put out her hands blindly.

"Matthew, what am I to do?"

He went around the end of the bed to her.

"Nothing," he said. "You are to do nothing more. You have done your job."

She laid her head on his shoulder and wept.

On his way downstairs Matthew Ryder paused for a moment on the shadowy landing to collect himself. He was shaken, his nerves curiously tense. The house seemed wrapped in cotton wool. No sound but the melancholy clang of the bellbuoy penetrated from the outside world, and the rhythmic distant cry of the fog horn. It was so still that he could distinctly hear the crackle of the fire on the hearth in the drawing-room below. And then, directly beneath him, he heard a door open softly, a whispered ejaculation, and the sound of a breathless struggle.

"Let me go! What do you think you're doing?"

The answer came also in a whisper.

"You're not going out, Susan. Don't be a fool!"

"I'll go where I please and you can mind your own business."

There was a pause, and then Carey's voice, low and tense: "You're going to meet that Portuguese!"

"Well, what if I am?" The girl's low voice shook with passionate anger. "He's a better man than you are, Carey

Gaunt. And if I'm not to see him in the house I'll see him outside, and you can all be damned."

"Not to-night—not to-night, Susan, you're out of your head."

"I'm not, but I would have been if it had gone on much longer. I'm sick of this snivelling and lying. We're all glad she's dead, aren't we? Wat's tickled pink. He thinks he'll be his own boss now. And Elvira's always hated Mother, so Edgar's delighted. And you'll be free now to leave Stone Haven and do what you please. Don't be a rotten fraud, Carey."

"Nancy's not glad."

For a minute Susan did not answer. Then she said in a puzzled voice: "No, she's not glad. I don't know why. She had more reason than any of us."

"She loved Mother."

"Love!" The young voice was full of scorn. "What's love to us Gaunts? It's not in any of us."

"How can you be so hard, Sue?"

"Hard? We're all hard—and greedy, and cruel. So are you, my fine fellow, but you're weak, too, so you're more confusing than the rest of us."

"Susan!"

"Did I hurt his little feelings? Know the truth, my boy, and the truth will make you free. We have it on the best authority."

"That's blasphemous, Sue!"

"Oh, my God! What's happened to you? I don't know you any more. Afraid of your shadow, aren't you? Let me go."

"I won't! Take your coat off and—"

A tall, dark figure appeared in the lighted drawing-room door. Waterman Gaunt's harsh voice broke through the murmur of their wrangling.

"What are you two quarrelling about?"

Susan came out from the shadow of the stairway, fumbling with the buttons of her long raincoat, her eyes both scared and defiant. Carey followed her sullenly. "She's going out to meet that Portuguese, Tony Farelli—"

"Take your coat off," said Waterman Gaunt coldly, "and come into the drawing-room. You're not going anywhere to-night."

For a moment Susan looked as though she would defy him. But at that instant the old-fashioned door bell jangled. With a furious look at her oldest brother she threw off her coat and walked past him into the drawing-room as Perkins came through the rear hall to open the door.

In the twilight outside two dim figures loomed in the swathing fog. One Ryder recognised as Sol Atkins, the local undertaker and dealer in antique furniture. The other was a stranger to him. He went down the stairs to meet them.

As he crossed the hall Waterman Gaunt was shaking hands with the stranger, a slight, elderly man with gray hair, worn rather long, and a kindly habitually anxious-looking face. Gaunt turned to introduce him as Ryder came up.

"This is Dr. Blake, from Massassoit," he said. "He's our county medical examiner."

Dr. Blake shook hands cordially.

"I'm glad to meet you, Dr. Ryder. Atkins here, explained the difficulties to me and we thought it would save time and be more convenient for everybody if I just came along to meet you."

"Good of you," said Gaunt stiffly, "but I'm damned if I can see why it's necessary. Dr. Ryder's been taking care of Mrs. Gaunt. Certainly he can say what was the matter with her."

"Certainly," agreed Dr. Blake, smiling. "It's just a yard of red tape. We can fix it up in five minutes. I'll have to see Mrs. Gaunt, of course.

Waterman opened his mouth to protest. Ryder saw his face flush heavily, angrily. But he said nothing. He turned on his heel and went into the drawing-room.

Dr. Blake, as good as his word, made no difficulty about the certificate, and the formalities were quickly over. When they came downstairs again Ryder accompanied the medical examiner to his car. The fog was thicker than ever. The narrow street that ended a few yards beyond the front door was completely hidden. Only a red blur of a street lamp indicated the way back through Stone Haven.

"You'll have a wretched drive," said Ryder. "Better stay over till morning."

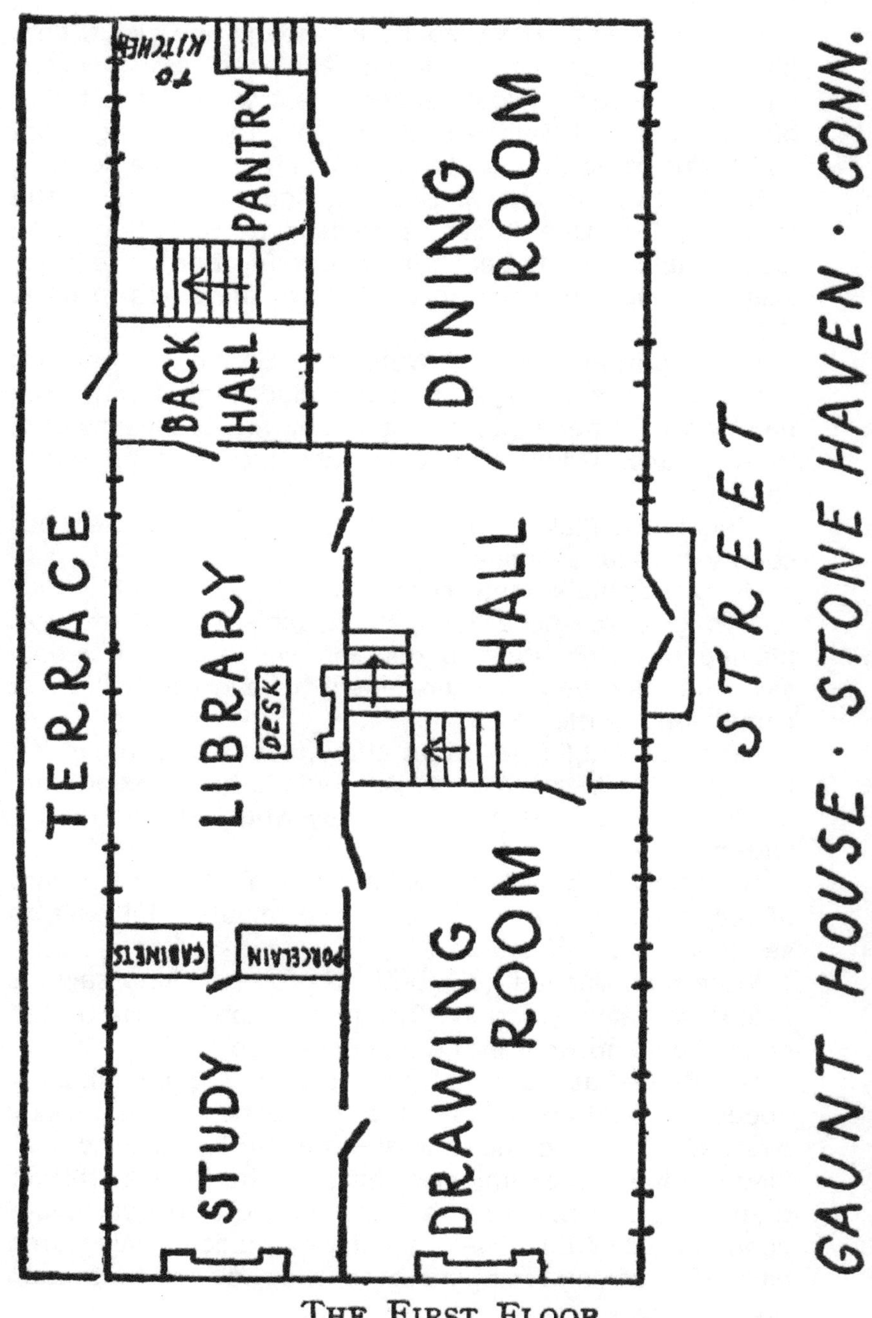

THE FIRST FLOOR

"Thanks, but I have a patient to see to-night. I'll make it somehow." He stood for a moment with his foot on the step of his car. "Funny thing, isn't it? Old Cap'n Gaunt—and now her—dropping dead like that."

"They were cousins, you know. Maybe some congenital tendency—"

Dr. Blake did not answer. He stared into the fog perplexedly.

"Not much medical science can do, is there? Sometimes I think I get behind the times up here—hard to keep in touch, you know. It bothers me." His benevolent, worried-looking face turned briefly towards Ryder and then away again. "But you're marching right in the procession—up with the band, you might say—and you don't know."

"No, there's not much known about the effective treatment of cardio-vascular diseases—or most diseases, if you come to that," admitted Ryder ruefully.

Blake sighed.

"Well, pleased to have met you, Dr. Ryder. Step in if you come over to Massassoit." He looked up at the blind front of the house and shook his head. "Queer—darned queer. Well, so long!"

His car moved cautiously off into the fog and was immediately swallowed up. Ryder stared after it for a moment and then turned back to the house. He found himself shivering. Deuced chill, this fog. As he closed the door behind him, shutting in the light, the brooding house discovered that night had come.

CHAPTER VI

THE dining-room of the old Gaunt house was a huge, cavernous affair, cheerful enough in the daytime, for it was lighted by a wide bow window over the bay, but at night full of shadows that leaned against the circle of light around the table and seemed to listen at the shoulders of the diners. There was, of course, electric light in the house, but in this room it was never used. The only light came from two handsome silver candelabra, set one at each end of the long table.

Matthew Ryder, coming down in response to the summons of the old-fashioned Japanese gong, found Edgar Gaunt standing beside the massive sideboard, a bottle of Scotch in one hand and a glass in the other. To Ryder there was always something pathetic about Edgar. In spite of the sporting pose he loved to affect, in spite of the loud and fancy checks and fervent ties he loved to wear, in spite of his jovial manner, so quickly changing to petulance, he was never really jolly. He had married money in the person of the sleek, cat-like Elvira Abbott, and Ryder fancied she ran him ragged.

Just now he was comfortably lit, his heavy face flushed, his manner expansive. He waved the bottle at Ryder. "How about it?" he said. "Need a bracer—time like this."

"Thanks." Ryder poured himself a drink and stood sipping it thoughtfully. A good idea. He was needing it. A black depression was on him—a sense of impending disaster. Ridiculous! Nerves—at his age! Edgar Gaunt's voice recalled him to himself.

"Have another. You'll need it." The big man leaned confidentially close. "Daniel's back again."

"Daniel?" Ryder looked up vaguely.

"Our dear cousin, Daniel Gaunt Minton, dear Aunt Sophia's darling boy. You haven't seen him yet but you will. He came in yesterday. He has a passion for funerals," said Edgar spitefully. "Always on hand at the kill, so to speak, like a—a whatsis—"

"Buzzard," suggested Ryder dryly.

"Buzzard—that's the ticket. Wonderful thing—science," said Edgar admiringly. "That's Daniel all over—buzzard. He popped up this way when Father died, too. Always round for the family obsequies. S'pose he smells the family fortune drawing nearer and nearer."

"I should think that would hardly interest him very deeply," said Ryder placatingly. "He's got his mother's fortune, and I always understood that old Mr. Minton was pretty well fixed."

Edgar winked one eye elaborately.

"Daniel's tarred with the same brush as the rest of us. He's a Gaunt, and there never was a Gaunt yet whose mouth didn't water at the thought of a little loose cash lying round. And besides, old man Minton dropped a pile in the market before he died. Ask Wat."

"I'll take your word for it," said Ryder dryly.

"Ah, that's what I like," said Edgar admiringly. "High-minded. No prying into affairs that don't concern you, eh? Stern professional ethics."

"Don't be an ass," said Matthew Ryder irritably. "I don't know Daniel Minton well, of course, and I don't particularly like him, but after all, there are five of you between Daniel and the family fortune."

Edgar did not answer at once. Instead, he looked round to the door as if to make sure no one had come in while they were talking. Then he looked again with a curious air of speculation at Dr. Ryder. "Think so?" he said slowly. "I wouldn't be too sure of that if I were you. Not *too* sure."

"What the devil are you talking about?"

"I'm drunk," said Edgar solemnly. "Very drunk."

"What are you driving at?"

"You'll see," said Edgar with dignity. "None of my business, anyhow."

They were interrupted by a quick, light step in the hall and Susan appeared in the doorway. She wore an écru lace dinner gown and apple-green slippers. She made a ravishing picture as she came forward into the circle of light around the table, the light on her sleek dark hair, her lovely eyes flashing with anger. She came purposefully across the room towards them and took a glass from the tray on the sideboard.

"A drink Eddie dear. A stiff one."

Edgar made no move to relinquish the bottle. He looked at her disapprovingly.

"Haven't you any sense of decency?" he demanded truculently. "One would think that to-night you'd have better taste—"

Susan looked down complacently at her dress.

"It's excellent taste, as a matter of fact. Shrieks of Paris, doesn't it, Matthew? Boston's spoiled Eddie's flair for such things. Give me a drink—what I mean, a *drink*!"

Ryder filled her glass, suddenly aware of the taut nerves under the hard brilliance of her manner. She raised the tumbler with a flourish, laying her free hand on her brother's shoulder.

"A parting toast, my darlings! Weep for me, Eddie. I'm going to leave home."

"The hell you are!" said Edgar gloomily. His good humour was passing, leaving him truculent.

"You put it forcibly but you get the idea. The hell I am! Maggie's got my bag practically packed."

"Where are you going?"

"Wherever the fancy takes me, darling Eddie."

"We'll see about that."

"You will indeed," agreed Susan amiably, "and so will Wat—as I've just been telling him."

"We'll cut your allowance."

"Don't be an ass, Eddie. I'm of age—and I know as well as you do that Mother didn't leave any will."

"I should think you'd be ashamed, with Mother hardly dead—" There were voices at the door and Edgar broke off as the rest of the family came into the room. Ryder was surprised to feel a hard, strong little hand clasp itself on his arm and Susan's hard, breathless voice. She stood with her back to the others looking up at him. He saw her mouth contorted in a stiff smile and her eyes were full of tears. "For God's sake," she muttered with stiff lips, "say something funny. I'm going to cry."

"Drink," he said. "Drink fast. That will do it."

She nodded and gulped down the contents of her glass.

Daniel Minton came across the room. Absurdly enough, for Ryder knew he had never been a seaman, his gait suggested the rolling stride of the sea. There was something faintly nautical about his dark blue, double-breasted suit. "If he only wore ear-rings," thought Ryder amusedly.

But, after all, the diamond on his little finger made a fair substitute.

Minton's florid face was even more florid than usual. He grasped Ryder's hand earnestly and clapped him on the shoulder.

"This is a bad business," he said. "A bad business. Poor Aunt Hetty. I suppose nothing could have prevented it?"

Ryder shook his head, edging away from the hand on his shoulder. "Probably not."

"Ah," nodded Daniel solemnly. "The Gaunt Lines will feel it. She's not only been the heaviest stockholder but the guiding spirit since Uncle Wat died. Smart woman. This will mean a bad shake-up."

"Will it shake you out of your job, dear Daniel?" asked Susan sweetly.

Daniel smiled at her indulgently. "Hardly that, my dear. But it will mean reorganisation. It's fortunate the news didn't get out before the market closed. We'll have time to issue a statement before Monday. We must all stick together."

"Too bad," said Susan saucily. "My idea was for us all to fall apart as rapidly as possible."

Minton laughed. "You're a caution, Sue."

Dr. Ryder heard a voice at his elbow, and he turned to find Elvira beside him.

"Dear Matthew," she murmured. "So good of you to come. It's such a comfort to Nancy—to all of us—to have you here."

He resented her patronage, her air of owning the house and its occupants, as he always resented Elvira. She was one of those slow, deceptively gentle women. There was not a particle of kindness in her, but this was not immediately apparent, for she loved to be petted and made much of and went through the usual social gestures to bring about this desirable end. Her mother-in-law had seen through her pretty, effusive manner, and Elvira had never forgiven her. There had always been bad blood between them. But one could never have guessed it now. Discreetly dressed in suitable black, Elvira looked the picture of decorous grief.

"Such a shock to all of us," she murmured. "So well only this morning and now—it seems so strange."

"That's the way those things happen," said Ryder coldly. "It was bound to happen some time."

"But why now—why to-day, of all days?"

Matthew Ryder stared down at his empty glass, and then, becoming aware of it, set it on the sideboard. "One doesn't know. Some little shock, some trifling argument, nothing at all, for that matter—"

She said nothing, and glancing at her he caught a curious, speculative look in her shallow blue eyes that was gone even as he recognised it.

"I'm so sensitive to things," murmured Elvira. "Edgar's always lecturing me about it. He says I wear myself out."

"My dear lady," said Ryder. "I haven't the faintest idea what you are talking about."

"Oh, well," sighed Elvira, "I'm so relieved. Of course it's all right, since you say so. Dear Matthew! Always such a comfort."

She pressed his arm with a lingering gesture and turned away, leaving him with an imperfectly suppressed desire to strangle her. But at this moment a diversion occurred, for Nancy came in and they all turned towards the table.

Waterman Gaunt sat in his father's place at the table's end with Elvira at his right and Carey next her; then Daniel at the left of Mrs. Gaunt's empty chair. Ryder, watching Nancy, saw her glance down at it, hesitate and steady herself for a moment with her hand on the back.

"Let me sit there," he murmured under cover of the general conversation.

But she shook her head and slipped quietly into the empty chair. He sat down beside her, finding Susan at his right, between him and Edgar.

Glancing from face to face, Ryder was impressed with the extraordinary likeness between them. With the exception, of course, of Elvira, they all bore the Gaunt stamp. Even Edgar's flabby face and Carey's thin, sensitive one were marked by it. A dominant race, this, and like all dominant things, ruthless. He was roused from his abstraction by Waterman Gaunt's heavy voice.

"Say grace, Carey."

From long habit the boy bent his head, but he got no further than the phrase: "For what we are about to receive—" His voice broke. He threw back his head and looked savagely at his brother. There was an electric pause and then Susan's voice, honey-sweet, ironically finished the grace that had been spoken at their mother's table all their lives.

"The Lord make us thankful."

"Susan! Susan!" It was Nancy's voice, broken with entreaty and pain. She had half risen from her chair and was looking at her sister with tear-filled eyes. Susan turned on her with passion.

"Then you've got to make him—" She broke off, bending her head to hide the trembling of her lips. "I can't stand it."

Nancy looked around the table from face to face.

"I don't understand. What is the matter with all of you? Susan—that dress. Have you no hearts, any of you?"

"Humbug!" cried Susan stormily. "Not you, darling. You're just a little stupid, bless you! But the rest of us aren't stupid. We know what we are about to receive and we are duly thankful for it. Let us have honesty if we can't have decency."

"Let us have mercy!" cried Nancy Gaunt.

Ryder studied the girl at his right perplexedly. That she was labouring under some extraordinary excitement was obvious. This was not all bad humour, and certainly not bad taste. Nerves strained to the breaking-point. Her young eyes held an anguish he could not bear to see. Her mother's death? He doubted it, although, in her own way, Susan had undoubtedly been fond of her mother. Tony Farelli? He wondered. Was he making her miserable? Or was her family making her miserable because of him? Or was it—something else?

For a moment Susan's eyes clashed with her sister's; then she shrugged. Her excitement seemed to collapse like a pricked balloon. She bowed mockingly to left and right. "Apologies!" she cried. "Ladies and gentlemen, I forgot myself. Let us be decorous. Let us talk a little polite scandal." A twinkle replaced the anger in her fine eyes.

"We saw a friend of yours last night, Wat, at the Michitiquock Club—a Mrs. Ingersoll."

There was a moment of strained silence. Waterman's face, which had been flushed with irritation, drained slowly of colour.

"Too bad," said Daniel Minton, "that you didn't let us know you were coming. We'd have been glad to wait for you."

Again there was that strange intense silence in which one became aware of fog pressing against the black windows, blanketing all sound. "Perhaps," said Carey at last, "you had private business."

"Nothing much," said Waterman with a ponderous lightness. "One or two things to discuss with Mother."

There was a tinkle of broken glass. Edgar's hand, tightening about his wineglass, had shivered the stem. "By God! If I thought you had—" He leaned forward, his inflamed eyes on his brother's face.

"I wanted to talk to Mother," repeated Waterman with dignity, "about this proposed purchase of the Meridian Line. I felt the matter had been presented to her in an unfortunate light. After all, as president of the Gaunt Lines, I had a right to express my views to the majority stockholder." His voice rose to blustering violence. "I felt—I still feel—that undue influence had been exerted from certain quarters—" He glared down the table at Daniel Minton.

"My dear fellow!" Minton leaned forward, clearing the place before him with an impatient gesture of his right forearm. "Your mother had confidence in my judgment. I think she realised that as general manager of the Gaunt Lines, I had perhaps a clearer view of the actual situation— In any case I have her written consent to the purchase at the stipulated figure."

"Well, that consent is no good to you now."

"We shall see. We can take it to the Courts and find out."

Waterman threw himself back in his chair and thrust his napkin on to the table. There was in his gesture something pathetically suggestive of a spoiled child in a temper. "I am aware," he said icily, "that my parents preferred you to me."

"Rot!" said Daniel Minton good-humouredly. "Aunt Hetty couldn't bear the sight of me—really. She never really got over her quarrel with Mother, although she patched it up for policy's sake. But she was able to take good advice, even from a man she disliked. She was a damn shrewd woman. She could fight it out on equal terms with the best business man I ever knew."

"Thank you," said Waterman bitterly; "I don't require your approval of my mother."

Minton shrugged, glancing once at Nancy and than bestowing his undivided attention on rolling a little pellet of bread between his fingers.

"We'll see," cried Waterman violently, "whether in this case her judgment was as good as you are pleased to think it."

Minton said nothing. He continued to roll his bread pellet. The sight apparently infuriated his cousin. "I intend," he shouted, "to take over the management of the Gaunt Lines myself."

Again that odd silence during which the shocked walls echoed his defiance. Then Susan drawled sweetly: "Oh, yeah?"

Waterman turned on her. "Why not?"

"Because, darling Wat, we are all interested in preserving our inheritance. And between us—since Mother didn't leave any will—we'll control four-fifths of her stock. Which —correct me if I'm wrong, Cousin Daniel—will be a voting majority."

"Quite right," nodded Minton. "Your mother held seventy per cent. of the stock. And I hold twenty," he added as an afterthought, his eyes still fixed on his twirling fingers.

"And you see, dear brother," said Carey softly, "we all know you haven't sense enough to come in out of the rain."

Waterman rose from his chair. There was a curious quiver of excitement in his eyes. His mouth drew into a narrow line. Carey's glance turned for an instant from his brother's face to the portrait that hung behind him on the wall. Yes, for the moment, Wat looked like his grandfather. A little heavier, perhaps, a little looser, but the same face, the same look for an instant, an illusion of the same oppressive, dominating personality.

"I should be surprised," he said, "if Mother left no will."

Their faces, upturned to his, were suddenly changed to stone. Then Susan, too, was on her feet.

"Wat! You know she never made a will."

"I don't. And neither do you. She would hardly have discussed the matter with a child. Of course she made a will. Cousin Daniel has just been praising her business acumen. Do you think anyone with that much intelligence would fail to safeguard the interests she had in her care?"

"Look here, Wat!" said Edgar suddenly. "Are you trying to tell us that you know Mother made a will leaving you a controlling share of the stock?"

Waterman did not answer. He did not need to.

"Where is it?" demanded Edgar. His heavy face was almost purple. He looked on the verge of apoplexy.

Waterman shrugged.

"Mr. Avery was here last night," said Nancy softly. "Hannah Perkins told me so."

Carey threw back his head and began to laugh.

"That's rich! That's gorgeous! Wat comes in in the fog and waits till we've gone off on our party. Then he meets Avery here and between them they draw up Mother's will."

"And we might never have suspected," drawled Susan sweetly, "if Wat had just made sure his lady friend would not be bored while he was gone."

"I don't know what you mean," said Waterman.

Minton dropped his bread pellet and looked up at Waterman.

"I doubt if the Courts will uphold such a will," he said quietly, "made under such circumstances."

"I should hope not," said Elvira. It was the first time she had spoken and their eyes swung briefly to her face, pallid under the rouge. "After all we've put up with—"

"You can fight it," said Waterman, leaning forward, his hands on the table, his jaw for once aggressive, "and be damned to you!"

Into the silence that followed his challenge broke the voice of Perkins in the hall.

"The family are at dinner, sir. I'll tell Mr. Gaunt you're here."

There was the murmur of another voice and an instant later a man appeared in the doorway. He was thin and tall, with sparse black hair surmounting a smooth fresh-coloured face and he wore a carefully trimmed black beard.

"Hullo!" he said. His eyes passed for a moment over the odd tableau at the table, and the tense figures relaxed suddenly as though only now aware of the oddity of their positions. Then he turned to Waterman. "Sorry to intrude, old man," he said negligently, "but it's getting damn wet out there in the bay. Positively had to wring out my clothes before I put 'em on. Lousy, what?"

"Hullo, Rex." Edgar rose to the occasion with an extended hand. "Have a drink."

Perkins produced a glass and a bottle and drew an extra chair up to the table. Rex Olsen sat down.

"Astrid's fed up, what I mean," he drawled. "Don't mean to intrude, but can't blame her, what? Wondered if you could give us a shakedown here to-night, Miss Nancy, or had we better buzz back to town?"

"I didn't know—I thought—" stammered Nancy.

"We thought you'd already gone back," Susan jumped to the rescue, with an amused glance at Waterman's embarrassed face. "Of course you must spend the night."

"Of course," echoed Nancy. "Perkins, you'll tell Hannah—Mr. Olsen and his sister—"

Perkins withdrew discreetly.

Rex Olsen turned the brandy in his glass, sniffing it appreciatively. "Lots doing in the bay to-night," he said. He was smiling faintly behind his beard. "Furtive sound of muffled oars, lowered voices, what? Astrid is nervous."

"There's a lobster war on," said Carey. "Somebody's been looting the lobster pots and all the Portuguese are out." He looked at Susan.

"My word!" said Rex Olsen lightly. "Astrid *will* be nervous. I'd better send the boat back for her."

"Perkins will have seen to that," said Waterman shortly.

Olsen looked at him speculatively for a moment. Then he raised his glass.

"Here's how!" he said cheerfully, and drank.

About half-past ten that same evening Matthew Ryder was sitting in the deserted drawing-room over the dying fire with a book. He found himself considerably shaken by the events of the evening, however, and his attention wandered. He was aware of the restlessness of the house: footsteps upstairs, the low voices of Waterman, Daniel and Rex Olsen in the library. And then he became aware of a new sound: the tap of a finger nail on the window beside him. He leaned forward and drew back the already half-parted curtain.

Outside, close to the glass and half blurred by the fog he saw the pale, lugubrious face of Atkins, the undertaker. The man held one fat finger to his lips and beckoned, nodding towards the front door of the house. After a moment's hesitation Dr. Ryder went quietly out into the hall and opened the door. Atkins stood on the step, his coat collar turned up, his round face wet and white.

"Get your hat and come round to my place, Doctor," he whispered. "I want you to look at something."

The gathering, incoherent fears of the last few hours rose up about Dr. Ryder and engulfed him. He felt strangely light and dizzy. His impulse was to shut the door in the face of this disquieting visitor. But he could not. He stepped back into the hall, found his coat and hat and, without a word, went out with Atkins into the fog, quietly closing the door behind him.

As if by common consent the two men did not speak as they felt their way along the slippery street. At a few feet the fog hid them from each other and the doctor could only follow the sharp clap-clap of Atkins' footsteps as they preceded him, stumbling over an unexpected curbstone and slipping on the wet asphalt.

Fortunately they had not far to go. Atkins' undertaking establishment was only a block and a half up the narrow village street. It was housed in a wing built onto an old white clapboard building whose upper floor served him for living quarters and whose lower floor he used for an antique shop. He opened the door of this shop, switched on a light, and when the doctor had entered, closed and locked the door. Then he threw back his coat and mopped his wet face with his handkerchief.

The single, unshaded bulb threw a garish light over the long, low room casting distorted shadows that fled away towards the four corners. It threw into sharp relief the graceful lines of three handsome maple highboys against the far wall; it glowed deeply in the polished tops of mahogany tables and glinted in the blue depths of half a dozen pieces of Sandwich glass on a shelf in the window.

Matthew Ryder had been in this room a great many times before. He had bought a number of old pieces from

Atkins and was always interested in his new acquisitions. But to-night he did not look around him. He stood with his eyes on Atkins' face held in a sort of paralysis.

"Well?" he said at last.

Atkins thrust the handkerchief into his pocket and turned to him with an almost desperate air.

"Doctor, I've been walking up and down this room for two hours trying to make up my mind what I ought to do. I've known those people all their lives. Wat and I went to school together up street here when we were little fellers. I think Nancy's one of the best women on earth. I wouldn't bring trouble on her for the world."

"Trouble—on Nancy? repeated Ryder stiffly.

"And besides," added Atkins shrewdly, "I wouldn't want to run afoul of any of the Gaunts without I had good reason for what I did. But I can't take the responsibility of not seeing what I have seen. It looks bad, Doctor."

"What have you seen?"

"That's what I brought you here to show you. If you say it's nothing, that's all right with me. I won't ask no questions nor spread no talk about it, you can count on that, but I couldn't rest easy to let it pass."

Matthew Ryder felt cold and his head was dizzy and light with a sense of unreality. This was nightmare, not fact. This room with its sharp light and shadow; Atkins' round, pallid, lugubrious face, and behind that thin board door—what? Trouble for Nancy. He spoke and was surprised to find his voice comfortably commonplace.

"Well, let's see this thing—whatever it is."

He followed Atkins through the door into his office. Here the undertaker took a key from his pocket and opened a door at the back. He motioned Ryder to precede him.

Ryder obeyed his gesture with he knew not what of nameless dread. But all he saw was a bare, whitewashed room with a large cabinet on the far side and in the middle a long table on which lay a sheeted figure. Atkins hesitated, seemed about to speak, changed his mind, and without a word turned back a corner of the sheet.

The unshaded bulb over the table threw a garish light into Mrs. Gaunt's immobile face. But Dr. Ryder's eyes did not linger on it, they were drawn to a small black spot, high up under the left arm. For a moment he stared closely at it. Then he picked up a slender, pointed instrument from the table and scraped gently at the spot. It came away, followed by a slow crimson drop. Ryder laid down the instrument and for a minute leaned his hand on the table. For the first time in fifteen years he felt the giddy nausea that had overcome him when, as a medical student, he had witnessed his first operation. Atkins' eyes were fixed on his stony, pallid face. After a moment the fit passed, and Ryder slowly drew the sheet back in place.

"You are right, of course," he said. "There'll have to be an autopsy." He stared down at his hands and dusted them unseeingly together.

"Murder!" he said softly.

"Couldn't have been self-inflicted?" suggested Atkins diffidently.

"Too high—too far back—no strength," muttered Ryder. "Murder! Oh, God!"

"I'll phone Dr. Blake?" suggested Atkins.

Ryder nodded wearily.

CHAPTER VII

DETECTIVE-SERGEANT JED POTTER Of the New London police force tipped back his chair and elevated his feet to the varnished yellow top of the centre table in Dr. Blake's office in Massassoit.

"All right, Doc, if you say so," he said doubtfully. He clasped his large, bony hands behind his head and stared thoughtfully at the low, papered ceiling.

Dr. Blake drew absent-minded circles on the back of his prescription pad.

"It's an odd thing, certainly," he said at last. "I said as much to Dr. Ryder this evening. I said: 'It's a funny thing—old Cap'n Gaunt, and now her—dropping dead like that.' "

"And what did he say?"

"Said they were cousins."

"What's that got to do with it? I thought old Cap'n Gaunt died of a stroke."

"Well, so he did."

"And the old lady of heart failure."

"She did. A thing called coronary thrombosis, which means a sudden injury to the blood vessels of the heart just as a stroke means a sudden injury to the blood vessels of the brain. They both may develop from the same physical background, which is often inherited."

"And that's where their being cousins comes in."

"Yes."

"Well," said Potter, "it's queer all the same."

He removed his feet from the table, felt in the pockets of his somewhat baggy coat, took out pipe and tobacco and filled the bowl, tamping it down thoughtfully. "Know anything about Ryder?" he asked at last.

"Yes," said Blake. "Know a lot about him. He's a first-class man. He's an excellent reputation in the profession."

"You don't think," said Potter slowly, drawing at his pipe, "that he would have any motive for suppressing anything?"

There was a long silence. The clock on the mantel above the immaculate, unused fireplace ticked loudly. Dr.

Blake's pale, anxious-looking face turned towards his friend. He stopped drawing circles. His eyes wandered uneasily from one to another of the familiar objects in the prim little room: the thin-legged golden oak chairs, the carefully darned and patched lace curtains at the windows, the aspidistra on the centre table. Finally they returned to Potter's face: a craggy face, with a stubborn, tenacious mouth, an aggressive nose, broken and badly mended years before, and thoughtful eyes under a good forehead. Dr. Blake coughed softly. "I never thought of that. But surely—"

Potter brushed his temporising aside with a wave of his big hand.

"I've been thinking of it," he said. "I dropped in to see Ottis Avery this afternoon. Just curiosity you might call it. He tells me Mrs. Gaunt made a will last night. He says Waterman Gaunt wrote him from New York and asked him to go over to Mrs. Gaunt's at nine o'clock. Waterman was there when he got there—came up on his yacht. Avery drew up the will and Mrs. Gaunt signed it."

"Well," said Blake, "after all, she knew she might die any minute."

Potter paid no attention. He was struggling with his pipe. He applied a match to it and coaxed it lovingly. When he had got it going to his satisfaction he said dryly:

"Avery told me something even funnier. He said he drew a will up for Captain Gaunt. And it just happened that Captain Gaunt was dead the next morning too—died in the night, poor devil—had a stroke. The will hadn't been signed that time."

"Rubbish!" said Blake. "Why, Dr. Ryder was in the house—in and out of Cap'n Gaunt's room. He couldn't have been mistaken."

"Wasn't he in the house this time?"

"No; they wired him and he came up on the afternoon tram."

"Oh!" Potter's face wore the expression of a man who is revising his ideas. "Well," he said at last, "it's just my darned curiosity as usual. Get me into trouble some day. But I wish I knew—"

"Look here!" said Blake uneasily, "if you say so, I'll revoke that certificate and order an autopsy."

Potter laughed.

"I ain't that kind of a fool," he said. "Buck the Gaunts without a shred of evidence to go on? Think I want to commit suicide?"

The telephone at Blake's elbow shrilled suddenly. The doctor reached an automatic hand for it.

"Hello!" he said. "Yes, this is Dr. Blake. Yes, Dr. Ryder, I didn't . . . What?" He swung around in his desk chair, and looked at Potter. "Yes . . . yes . . . Just a minute, Detective-Sergeant Potter is here in my office now. You'd better tell him." He covered the mouthpiece with his hand. "It's Ryder. He's at Atkins' undertaking place. I guess you've got your evidence." He thrust the instrument into Potter's hands and made way for him at the desk. The room seemed to waver around him. The aspidistra on the centre table seemed for a moment very far away and then very near. He thought wonderingly that he had known the Gaunts all his life. Behind him he heard Potter's voice: "Yes—yes—yes." And the indistinguishable drone of Ryder's narrative, abruptly finished. Then he heard Potter say:

"Anybody know about this but you and Atkins? . . . Good. . . . Don't tell anyone, not anyone at all—till I get there. I want to be there when the news is broken, understand? . . . Thanks. . . . All right. . . . Thanks. . . . Sure, go on back to the house if you want to, I'll meet you there in an hour." He hung up and turned to Blake. "Grab your hat," he said. "We're on our way."

When at last Ryder made his way home, the fog had thickened. The old-fashioned kerosene lantern that Atkins had given him made only a globe of light around him, so that he felt like a goldfish in an illuminated bowl. The warnings of fog horns were insistent and seemed to carry an almost hysterical note of warning: "Take—care, take—care." He picked out a half-a-dozen different notes, ranging the coast in each direction as far as sound could carry. Behind him and above him the clock in the tower of the Congregational Church struck twelve.

A shiver ran through him and a sudden weakness. He leaned for a moment against a door-post and grimly counted the strokes. Through his mind trailed that verse of Housman's:

Strapped, noosed, nighing his hour,
He stood and counted them and cursed his luck,
And then the clock collected in the tower
Its strength, and struck.

He had a momentary, horrible image of an indistinguishable figure, strapped, noosed—Murder!

He stumbled on.

Presently a break in the pavement and a sudden faint increase of the pervasive water murmur that was the only sound near at hand told him he was passing a gap between two buildings, no doubt the entrance to Farelli's wharf where his fish market stood and his lobster pots were stored and overhauled. He stepped gingerly down into the roadway and was about to cross when a figure loomed suddenly out of the fog and was revealed in the circle of lantern light.

"Who's that?"

Ryder blinked stupidly at the apparition, recalling his mind from a great distance.

It was a slight, wiry man in a dark suit and a cloth cap pulled down over his eyes. His hands were in his pockets and there was a curious air of poised stillness in his attitude. For a moment he stared challengingly at Ryder. Then he took his hands out of his pockets, bringing a cigarette in one and a box of matches in the other. He gummed the cigarette onto his lower lip.

"Oh," he said, "you're Dr. Ryder. I thought you were someone else."

He lit the cigarette. By the flare of the match Ryder got a good look at his face, small and lean and hardbitten. He recognised him as the town constable. Ryder smiled halfheartedly.

"Looking for bootleggers?"

"Naw." Constable Bartlett spat thoughtfully into the street. "I leave that to the revenue boys. And they know better than to go nosing round a night like this. Nope, I got my own worries." He narrowed his eyes and looked at Ryder through the slits. "You staying at Gaunt's?"

"Yes."

"Heard about Mrs. Gaunt dying. Too bad."

Ryder nodded. His very bones ached with weariness. He moved to go on but Bartlett stopped him.

"I'm looking for Farelli," he said flatly. "Been tipped off he's aimin' to conduct some private warfare out in the Sound to-night. Ain't seen him, have you?"

"No," said Ryder. "It's not likely I would."

"You might," said Bartlett slowly. "Ain't seen him down at the house—at Gaunt's, have ye?"

"No," said Ryder crisply. "Why should I see him there?"

Bartlett detached the cigarette from his lip, looked at it and put it back.

"Town the size of this," he said dryly, "things get about. Mrs. Gaunt never liked Farelli—warned him off the place. She's dead now."

"Well?"

"Dr. Ryder, you're a good friend of all those folks. Course, people will gossip—town of this size—but if it should just happen that Susan Gaunt is sweet on this Farelli fellow, somebody ought to tell her—some friend of the family, for choice—to lay off him. He's bad medicine. He knifed someone last year and would have got in wrong only the guy got well. Unless my tip-off is all wrong, he's aimin' to knife another feller to-night. He was born to be hanged. Somebody ought to tell her."

"If there were any truth in the story," said Ryder levelly, "she certainly ought to be told."

"Ah," nodded Bartlett. "I thought you'd see it that way."

"But of course it's just a pack of lies."

"Ah," nodded Bartlett again. "That's what I thought." He turned away.

"Wait," said Ryder, with sudden mastering curiosity. "Who's Farelli going to knife?"

The constable shrugged. "They're always squabbling over their lobster pots and every once in a while somebody gets his. Feller from over New York waters cleaned out Farelli's catch yesterday. Thought I'd see him and tell him to cool off a bit. He's been making threats. Well, so long."

He stepped out of the circle of light and was instantly swallowed by the fog. Ryder heard him stumbling down the road between the two buildings towards the pier.

Weary as Ryder was, tired to the bone and sick at heart at what lay before him, he approached the house almost with dread. He put out his lantern at the door and closed his hand on the knob unwillingly. He found that the door was locked. Clearly they had not discovered his absence, and thinking he had gone to bed, had bolted the door. Well, no doubt the back door would be open. In this quiet village locking up was a formality that seldom extended beyond the front door. He vaulted the iron fence and walked round the house through the garden. He saw at once that he had been mistaken in thinking they had all gone to bed. The library windows were alight and he could see Edgar and Daniel Minton. As Ryder watched, they left the room together. Ryder strolled down through the garden.

It was much warmer than it had been early in the evening and the air was sweet with the sea smell and the damp scent of growing things. He passed through a little area of fragrance that clung around the blooming bushes of the monthly tea roses and came out on the grassy terrace behind the house. How peaceful it was—so quiet that he could hear the slithery rattle of pebbles below where the slow waves curled up and retreated on the shingle. He strolled down to the sea wall and leaned there.

The fog came and went, showing him glimpses of the bay, faintly illumined by a diffused light from the invisible moon; and then again shrouded everything in a heavy veil. He had a fleeting glimpse of the sailboat moored at the wharf below and of another boat, short and squat with a stumpy mast and low cabin, such as is used by the fishermen of the coast, at anchor beyond. It seemed to him that from time to time he caught the murmur of voices from this second boat, and an instant later he was sure of it, for he saw it again and this time there were two figures on her deck and one of them was drawing the dinghy alongside. He heard distinctly the whispered injunction: "Look out! Your dress is caught." And then a rustle, a caught breath, and a smothered laugh. "It would be awkward to explain a tumble into the bay."

Ryder had been on the point of going up to the house, but now he hesitated. Surely that couldn't be Susan! And then he remembered the struggle under the stairs and Susan's furious voice: "If I can't meet him in the house I'll meet him outside—" He stood where he was, waiting.

He could see nothing. The fog blew in again, heavy, stifling. But he could hear the slap of the dinghy's bow on the water, the smothered creak of oarlocks, the low voices. Then the boat bumped the wharf gently and for a moment there was no sound at all. Then a man's voice said:

"Well, so long. I'll be seeing you."

Crude as the words were, the voice was warm and resonant, conspicuously lacking in the flat tones of the Yankee.

"Tony—" said Susan softly, and paused.

The voices were directly below him. Ryder stood in an agony of indecision and annoyance. What a little idiot the child was. He supposed it was only natural for her to kick over the traces under the circumstances, but he wanted to shake her. A lobster fisherman, of all things! Heaven only knew what an ugly scandal might come of it. Apparently the gossip was already going round the village.

There was the splutter of a match in the fog below him and in its light, reflected by cupping palms, Ryder saw the explanation of Susan's madness—the face of a field god: straight black brows over limpid dark eyes, a beautiful mouth, sensuous yet delicate, a well-moulded face the colour of warm bronze, a young face, reckless but not vicious, undeniably charming. The doctor's annoyance abated somewhat. He stood where he was, frankly listening now. He heard Susan say softly:

"What's your hurry, Tony?"

"Business," said Tony lightly. "I've got to be out halfway to Block Island before dawn."

"And get yourself cosily landed in jail, if not worse," Susan sighed. The match went out.

"A man has to stand up for himself in this game," said Tony Farelli.

"The police—" suggested Susan in a small voice.

Farelli laughed shortly.

"I admit it's funny," said Susan.

"How'm I going to prove who steals my lobsters?" asked Tony. "You don't leave a lot of clues around in the middle of the sound. I know who does it, all right, but I can't prove it. I can take care of myself."

"I wish," said Susan almost in a whisper, "that I had your nerve."

There was a little silence filled with the dragging rattle of pebbles on the shingle beach.

"I don't get you," said Tony in a low voice.

"There's so much that I know," whispered Susan, "and can't prove."

"You take a tip from me, Susie, and stay off it."

"That's what I'm going to do," said Susan.

"I'm going to run away."

This time the silence prolonged itself painfully.

"You mean," said Tony at last, "you're going to leave Stone Haven?"

"Yes, as soon as the funeral's over."

"Well," said Tony, "that's a fast one. Why didn't you tell me when you first came out?"

"I meant to. I tried to," said Susan's small, miserable voice.

"Well!" said Tony Farelli. "Then I likely won't see you again."

"Not unless you want to," said Susan.

"Well, I don't. You can go and be damned."

"I probably will." Susan giggled suddenly. "You're a swell guy, Tony. Come see me in New York."

"Drive up to your door on the fish truck some day. Girlie, how about a ride?"

"I'll slap your face if you do," said Susan. "So long, Tony. I've got to go in."

"You should have gone in hours ago. So long."

"Oh, hell!" said Susan. "Don't get yourself cut up, Tony."

"Fat chance!" said Tony cheerfully. "So long."

There followed the light tap of a girl's slippers on the gravel, the swish of a skirt, and then the sound of a boat shoving off and the retreating creak of oarlocks. Ryder waited, leaning on the wall. He felt extraordinarily moved. It was not until he heard the first sputter of Tony's engine that he wondered if, by any chance, he should have attempted any interference. But he dismissed the idea as soon as it occurred to him. After all, Tony Farelli was not the sort of young man with whom one interfered. He lit and smoked a cigarette, listening to the put-put of the boat moving cautiously out of the harbour. Then he ground the stub under his heel and followed Susan quietly into the house.

In the hall he met Rex Olsen.

"Hullo!" said Olsen. "Thought you'd gone to bed hours ago."

"Been out in the garden," said Ryder heavily. "Needed some fresh air.

"The garden seems to be popular to-night," said Olsen dryly, and he looked at Ryder curiously.

The doctor turned away down the hall, wondering if his face betrayed him.

"Believe I'll have a nightcap," he said. And then he added unwillingly: "Join me?"

"Thanks," said Olsen, "I think I'll turn in if you don't mind." He was still studying Ryder curiously.

The doctor turned away down the hall, wondering if his face betrayed him.

"By the way, Miss Gaunt was looking for you a while back. Funny she missed you. She looked," he added casually, "out in the garden."

"I strolled along the road a bit," said Ryder. "Think she wanted anything special?"

"I guess not. Anyway, she's gone to bed now. Well, so long." With a last curious look at Ryder, Olsen went upstairs.

Ryder went into the dining-room and poured himself a drink from the bottle on the sideboard. The room was dark but there was enough light from the hall to see by. He stood in the dimness, sipping slowly, oppressed by a growing feeling of doom. The house was quiet, but he was aware of life in it: distant footsteps, the sound of a door opening and closing, far-away voices. His mind's eye peered forward with dread to the impending scene. How would they meet it? Would one of the group start from fancied security into horrible awareness of being the quarry in a murder chase?

What were they doing now? He was filled with a sudden overwhelming curiosity to know what they were about. No harm, at least, to find out if they were all in the house. He set down his empty glass and went upstairs.

The sitting-room at the end of the hall was dark and the closed door of the room next it, occupied by Elvira and Edgar, showed no line of light along the sill. All the other rooms, apparently, were still alight. Waterman's door stood open. He looked in. The bed had been turned down and the night things laid out, but the room was empty. Next door, however, he heard voices and while he still stood there hesitantly the door of Rex Olsen's room opened, and he caught a glimpse of Daniel Minton and Olsen sitting together with a bottle and glasses before Edgar lurched into the hall and shut the door behind him. He was hardly able to stand on his feet. Ryder had no wish to encounter him and stepped back into the shelter of Waterman's room. But Edgar did not go past the door to his own room as Ryder expected. He stopped in the doorway and stood glowering, his heavy head belligerently outthrust, his blood-shot eyes seeking from one object to another until they found Ryder. Plainly, in the soft light he mistook him for Waterman. His scowl deepened. "By God," he said, "if I thought you'd double-crossed us all, I'd—" He lifted his big hands and twisted them as though he held his brother's neck between them.

"Go to bed," said Ryder. "You don't know what you're doing." He put his hand on Edgar's arm and steered him along the hall to his own door. The big man had collapsed suddenly and went with him without protest, muttering to himself.

Turning away as Edgar went into his room and closed the door, Ryder saw Nancy standing behind him. She had evidently come out of the room that had been her mother's, for the door stood open, letting a flood of soft light into the dim hallway. She was wearing a white negligee that trailed and clung to the pile of the carpet and rose close around her throat in soft folds. He thought she looked like a beautiful ghost, her face pale under the shiny black hair. She came across the hall to him noiselessly, so swiftly and airily that she seemed to float almost without motion.

"What is it, Matthew? Oh, what is it?"

"Nothing," he said. "Edgar has had a drop too much. I sent him to bed." He hardly knew what he was saying. He was aware only of her upturned face, her eyes in which the look changed swiftly, her lips that suddenly gave themselves to his.

"Nancy," he whispered. "Oh, my love, soon!"

She did not answer, but her silence gave consent. After a moment she said gently:

"I must go now." He sighed and released her.

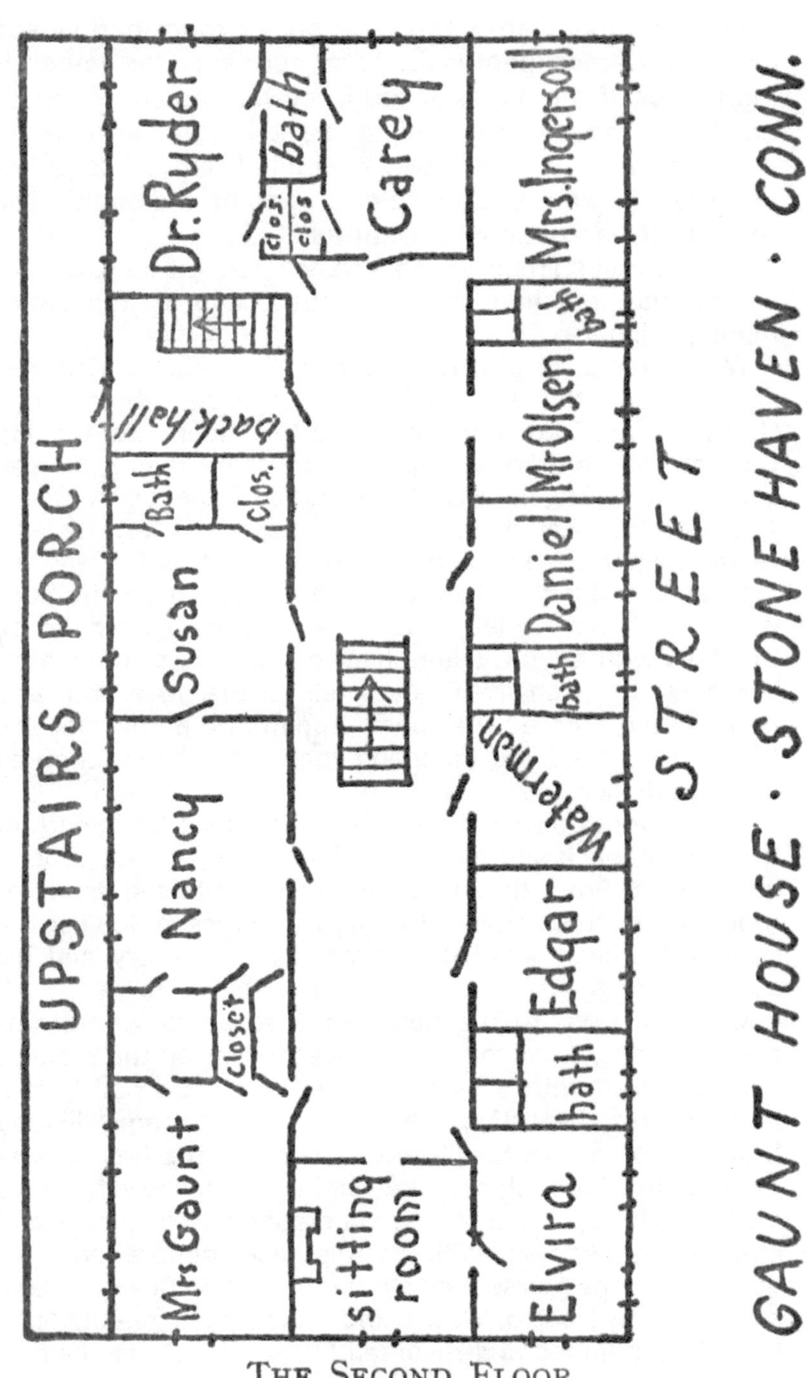

THE SECOND FLOOR

For a moment after the door of her room had closed on her he stood bemused. Then suddenly the impending horror of the night closed in on him again. He must go down and be prepared to meet Potter, who would arrive at any moment now. He pulled himself together and started for the stairs, glancing as he did so into the room that had been Mrs. Gaunt's.

The door still stood open as Nancy had left it. And what he saw through the open door caused him to stop a moment staring.

At the table desk in the window Waterman Gaunt was sitting facing the door. A lamp on the desk before him threw his face into sharp relief. He had clearly been going through his mother's papers, for there were several sorted piles ranged across the back of the desk. But it was the look on his face that arrested Ryder. He was reading what appeared to be a letter, and as he read his face assumed an expression of malicious triumph. Suddenly he threw the letter down, struck his open palm on the desk with a light, triumphant gesture, and threw himself back in his chair. His eyes fell on the open door and he rose and crossed the room. Apparently he did not see Ryder. He closed the door and the doctor heard the key turn in the lock.

Ryder went downstairs and began to pace the length of the library, back and forth, back and forth, a puzzled look on his face. From time to time he went into the drawing-room and peered out into the fog that pressed against the panes. But each time he returned to the library and his steady pacing.

Once he went to the hearth and stood for some moments staring up at the black hawthorn jar on the mantel, its top sealed with a grotesque red seal. It stood before him, sinister, beautiful, the symbol of the tragic destiny brought home with his ill-gotten gains by the first Waterman Gaunt from China. The curse that follows fortunes made in the opium trade—a superstition well known and credited by seamen. Well, in this case, generation after generation the curse had borne its dark flower, black hawthorn, symbol of death and worse than death. Matthew Ryder sighed and resumed his pacing. It was half an hour before Potter arrived. Ryder, hearing the soft shriek of his brakes, opened the door quietly. Potter came up the steps followed by two men in uniform.

"I've done what you asked," said Ryder, "but I feel like a traitor."

"Nonsense," said Potter briskly. "You've done no possible harm to anyone—except the murderer."

"It is—murder, then?"

"Not a doubt. I've just come from Atkins. Blake made, of course, only a hasty examination, but it was conclusive. He's taking the body to New London for an autopsy. You've told no one?"

"No one at all."

Potter nodded in a satisfied way. He turned to the taller of the two policemen.

"Jones, you stay here on the steps. Roberts will watch the back door. Keep out of sight, both of you, but no one is to leave the house. Now, where can we talk?"

Ryder led the way into the library and Potter followed him and closed the door.

"Now," he said, "tell me all you know about this. When did Mrs. Gaunt die?"

"I wasn't here," said Ryder, "but I'm told she died about eleven this morning."

"We can check that," said Potter. He sat down at the desk and flipped open a small notebook which he took from his pocket. "All right," he said. "Shoot!"

Ryder gave a brief account of his own connection with Mrs. Gaunt's death: his attendance on her from time to time, his arrival in response to Carey's telegram, his belief that the death was a natural one until Atkins had called his attention to the minute puncture under the left arm.

When he had finished, Potter nodded slowly two or three times. Then he said, with his curiously abstracted eyes on Ryder's face:

"I don't want to be offensive, Doctor—I'm asking for information—but wasn't it sort of funny your making a mistake like that?"

Ryder thrust his hand back through his hair.

"Well, no, he said ruefully. "I don't really think it was. I'd expected her to die at any time—that sort of illness almost invariably results in sudden snuffing out, with no apparent cause. That's one side of it. The other is that a wound of that sort—deep and extremely narrow—would not bleed externally. The mouth would close practically as soon as the instrument was withdrawn. There might have been a few drops of blood, but if that had been wiped away there would have been no further bleeding. It was really only an accident that Atkins noticed it."

Potter nodded again, slowly, abstractedly. He was silent so long that Ryder thought he had finished. Then he said unexpectedly:

"Dr. Ryder, do you think that you may also have made a mistake in the matter of Captain Gaunt's death?"

Ryder opened his mouth to speak and closed it again. His knees felt suddenly weak under him. He sat down. At last he said cautiously:

"I think it is possible."

Again a little pause and then Potter said with a curious finality: "I think it is probable. I am going to have the body exhumed."

Ryder went cold all over.

"It's preposterous," he muttered.

"Let us talk sense, Doctor. We are both practical men. This murder is a singularly bold affair, executed in broad daylight, in a houseful of people, any one of whom might at any moment have walked into the room. Isn't it at least reasonable to suppose that the murderer was familiar with the method of his crime and believed it safe from detection? After all, the ordinary layman couldn't be sure that there would be no outside bleeding from such a wound. Then we have the curious fact of the similarity between the two deaths: as far as I can learn, identical in almost every detail. That is very characteristic of habitual murderers."

Ryder flung himself out of his chair. He paced the length of the room and back. "Sergeant Potter," he said at last, "I am at a disadvantage with you, of course, because of my regrettable oversight in the case of Mrs. Gaunt's death."

"Not at all," said Potter, "I know your reputation, Doctor. Even before you told me so, I realised that your mistake was inevitable and had been so calculated by the murderer."

"Very well," said Ryder. "Then I wish to state as forcibly as I can that I believe Captain Gaunt's death was a natural one. I attended him during his illness. I was in the house when he died."

"Were you with him when he died?"

"No, but I had seen him an hour or so before. He died about two o'clock in the morning."

"Ah," said Potter swiftly. "You see! The first time, more caution. Who discovered the death?"

"Mrs. Gaunt and Nancy. They heard a sound in his room about two o'clock and went in. He was dead when they reached him. Nancy at once woke me. When I examined him he had been dead not more than five or ten minutes."

"And you believe he died a natural death?"

"I am certain of it."

Potter tapped his pencil thoughtfully against his teeth, his eyes on Dr. Ryder. At last he said:

"Just what was the matter with Captain Gaunt? I understand he'd been ill for about a year."

"That is correct. He had had a stroke which left him practically helpless—a right hemiplegia with motor aphasia."

"What does that mean?"

"His right side was paralysed, and his speech centres affected so that he was able to make sound but could not articulate."

"Was his mind affected?

"Not at all. And he could see and hear perfectly well."

"And had the use of his left arm and leg?"

"Exactly."

"He'd been bedridden for a year?"

"Practically so. His servant, Perkins, used to get him up in a wheel-chair for part of every day."

"And what, in your opinion, was the immediate cause of death?"

"A second stroke. It was to be expected at any time."

Potter nodded.

"You say Mrs. Gaunt discovered his death?"

"She and Nancy."

"She did not share his room?"

"No. He slept in the room next Mrs. Gaunt's—the one Nancy has now."

"Communicating?"

"Yes."

Potter made circles on the blotter with his pencil.

"Can you give me a list of the people who were in the house at the time?"

"Yes, I think so—the family, anyway. I can't tell about the domestic staff."

Porter nodded.

"I can check that," he said again. "Well?"

"Besides Mrs. Gaunt," said Ryder slowly, "all her children were here—as they are now—on vacation. It was about the same time of year. Waterman, Edgar and Elvira, his wife, Nancy, Susan, and Carey. Daniel Minton was here, too. Since old Mr. Minton's death the Minton house has been closed. Daniel stays here when he comes to Stone Haven."

"Anyone else?"

"Mr. Avery, the family lawyer, was here at dinner."

"And that's all?"

"As far as I can recollect," said Ryder slowly, "that's all."

"And which of those people were here this morning?"

"All of them—except Mr. Avery, of course. I can't say whether Waterman's secretary, Melvin Saunders, was here. I understand he's staying out on the yacht in the harbour, but he may have come ashore." He hesitated and added: "You realise when I say they were here, I mean they are staying in the house. I can't say where they were this morning. I wasn't here myself."

Potter tapped his pencil thoughtfully against his teeth. "Anyone else staying here?"

"To-night Rex Olsen and his sister, a Mrs. Ingersoll, are here. They came up with Waterman on the *Buccaneer*, yesterday, and spent last night on board."

"That's queer, isn't it?"

Ryder stirred uncomfortably. " I don't know much about them. You must ask Waterman Gaunt."

"I intend to," said Potter dryly. He leaned back and stared thoughtfully at the ceiling. "Any ideas, Doctor?"

"None," said Ryder abruptly.

Potter removed his gaze from the ceiling and turned it on Ryder's face. "Come, come," he said mildly. "you haven't been here long, but surely you must have some impression."

Ryder did not answer at once. At last he said:

"In weather like this it would not be difficult for an outsider to reach Mrs. Gaunt's room unobserved. The window opens on a long porch that runs all across the water side of the house. At the end, near Mrs. Gaunt's room, it is only four or five feet above the terrace. Any active person could climb up under cover of the fog."

"Dr. Ryder, do you really believe that?"

"I don't know what I believe," said Ryder. "I'm completely in the dark. I'm sure of only one thing and that is, that no member of the family could have had any hand in it."

"Do you know that Mrs. Gaunt made a will last night?"

"It was hinted at," admitted Ryder. "Nothing definite."

"When was that?"

Ryder, immersed in his own uneasy thoughts, missed the hidden eagerness in Potter's voice.

"At dinner, Waterman said something about his intention to take over the control of the Gaunt Lines now that his mother is dead, and there was an argument about it. He inferred that there was no use arguing, because his mother had left him the controlling stock."

There was a moment of intense silence. Ryder, suddenly aware of a new quality in the atmosphere, looked curiously at the detective. He was staring at his notebook with a look of complete astonishment as though he had never seen it before. Suddenly he got to his feet with an impatient gesture.

"I don't like this," he said softly. "We'd better get on with it. Could you go upstairs and make some excuse for them all to come down?"

"No," said Ryder. "I'm damned if I could. If you like, I'll go and tell them you're here and want to question them."

Potter leaned across the desk, an angry glint in his gray eyes.

"Don't be a fool, Doctor. This is murder we're dealing with—two murders—and unless we prevent it, three. It's no moment for delicate feelings."

Ryder stared at the detective, suddenly sick and breathless. "What do you mean?"

"Ask yourself, if the person who has killed twice in order to prevent the bulk of the Gaunt fortune from going to Waterman will hesitate at a third killing."

Ryder turned blindly towards the door.

"I'll tell them someone's here about the funeral—or something," he said vaguely, and was surprised to find his feet carrying him towards the stairs.

CHAPTER VIII

MEANWHILE in the big corner room upstairs where, for over forty years, Hetty Gaunt had lived, where she had borne her children, and where this morning she had died, Waterman Gaunt sat at his mother's desk with a sheet of letter paper spread out before him. His eyes were fixed on Mrs. Gaunt's delicate, copperplate script, but his mind was full of an incredulous triumph. Before him he saw the whole pattern of his life changing, taking shape, acquiring significance. The years of his subservience, his irresolution, were going—were already gone. He saw himself in the role so long played by the other Waterman Gaunts, the titular and actual head of the family, the master of his own fate. His heart beat heavily in his throat, his breath came heavy and deep, his face was twisted with sardonic triumph.

It was some time before that tapping at the locked door penetrated his absorption, but he heard it at last. He turned his head towards it, and a watchful look came into his eyes. He folded the letter and thrust it into his breast pocket. Then he crossed the room swiftly and listened at the door. The tapping came again, softly, as though someone were rapping soft fingertips against the wood. "Who is it?" he asked in a low voice.

The answer came, hardly more than a whisper:

"It's I—Astrid. I must speak to you."

He hesitated, a look of annoyance on his face. Then he turned the key and opened the door. When she had entered he closed and locked it again.

"Well?" he said, not too graciously.

She looked at him swiftly and looked away to hide the sudden unreasoning terror that gripped her by the throat. She crossed the room and helped herself to a cigarette from his open case which lay on the desk. His eyes followed morosely the slender figure in the smart black lounging suit, so fitted that it was like a sleek black skin under which the play of the muscles of her hips and back was plainly apparent. Her charm, usually so potent with him, only irritated him now. Like all weak, vain men, he liked to be catered to, and any challenge of his moods was intolerable to him. He followed her with rising anger. "Well?" he said again.

She lit her cigarette coolly, but he was too annoyed to notice how her hands shook. She was wishing desperately that she had not come but it was too late now. She must face it through.

"I had to see you," she murmured, raising limpid eyes to his. "It's been so long. I had to be sure you weren't angry with me."

"Angry with you?" he repeated with stubborn obtuseness.

"For sending Rex to ask you to—to let us come ashore."

"I think it was—tactless."

She laid her hand on his arm. "I couldn't stand it. Waiting out there hour after hour for a message from you—in that horrible fog—"

But in his present mood reproaches were more than he could bear.

"Why did you go to the club last night?" he demanded angrily. "You've got me in the devil of a mess. You were recognised, and now they've all caught on to the fact that I had a private session with mother and Mr. Avery. They're mad as hell about it and going to fight the will."

"I'm terribly sorry, Wat—for more reasons than one. But how was I to know they'd be there?"

"I asked you to lie low," he said doggedly, "but clearly my wishes don't mean very much to you."

She looked at him through the blue haze of her cigarette smoke and her odd, fascinating eyes narrowed. "Come," she said softly. "I've apologised. I'm sorry—very sorry if I've done anything to embarrass you. Now it's your turn."

"I fail to see," he said icily, "that I've any reason for apology."

She should have retreated and she knew it, but her own temper, never very securely under control, was rising at her throat.

"Why did you keep me hidden out there in the bay as though you were ashamed of me? After all, even if your fear of your mother was justified, it has been a good many hours since—such caution was necessary."

Waterman Gaunt fell back on the last resource of the weak.

"I suppose," he said, and his voice shook with rage, "you think it would have been good taste to bring you into my mother's house the instant she was dead."

She was so angry that her slender body shook and she was at the same time filled with a despairing knowledge of her own folly. But for the moment she did not care.

"I dare say," she said, "that you have persuaded yourself that you have a right to be ashamed of our relationship."

Waterman maintained a stubborn silence. Outside in the hall, Dr. Ryder, with his hand raised to knock on the door, paused suddenly, aware of her raised voice. So this was why Mrs. Ingersoll had not answered when he tapped on her door a moment since. He hesitated in embarrassment. Distinctly he heard her low, penetrating voice.

"Do not think that you can get away with this. I won't stand for it-and I have ways of defending myself."

As he knocked, Ryder heard Waterman Gaunt laugh with uneasy bravado.

Nancy went downstairs with Ryder, her arm linked in his. On the way down she stopped suddenly and leaned close to him.

"What is it?" she asked softly. "What is all this? There's something queer about it. Is it really about the funeral?"

He looked at her pale, strained face.

"No," he said. "Of course not. Detective Sergeant Potter, of the New London police, wants to question everyone in the house."

"Oh, my God!" She swayed as though she would faint and he put his arm round her, but she stiffened by an enormous effort of will power.

"What does he want to question us about?"

"Steady, old girl!" He held her upright in his strong, kind hands. "Have you got hold of yourself?"

"Yes." In a swirling world, the only solid steady thing was his face.

"The police have found out that your mother was murdered."

For a moment she said nothing. Then: "I see. I see." She put her hand vaguely to her face and took it away again. "We had better go down."

"I had instructions to tell no one. I think I had better tell Potter that I have told you."

"Very well."

"I shall also tell him that we are to be married."

"No!" said Nancy violently. "No, I won't let you involve yourself. Keep clear of us."

A sound below attracted Ryder. He looked down. Potter stood in the hall below, watching them. They went down.

"I have transgressed your orders in one particular," Ryder told Potter. "I have told Miss Gaunt why you wish to see us. You will understand why when I tell you that we are to be married. I could not let this news come to her from a stranger."

Potter looked from one face to another.

"Very well," he said. "You have told no one else?"

"No one." He stood aside to let them precede him into the library.

During the succeeding ten minutes Ryder, watching the detective, thought he observed under Potter's quiet manner a growing uneasiness. He seemed to listen for each approaching step, to glance hastily at each new figure that appeared in the doorway, and then to fall again to his uneasy contemplation of the notebook opened before him on the desk. Whom or what he was awaiting Ryder could not have said, but something of this tense uneasiness crept into his own attitude and he found himself listening and waiting too.

He was only half aware of the murmur of conversation about him, the surprised glances. He answered automatically the questions put to him, hardly aware of what he said. After what seemed an interminable time Potter came over to him.

"Where is Waterman Gaunt?" he asked, and suddenly Ryder knew with devastating clarity what was in the detective's mind.

"I don't know," he said, feeling suddenly quite sick. "He was in his mother's room when I went to call him."

"Did you see him?"

"No. I spoke to him through the door."

"Sure it was his voice?"

"Certain. He said he'd be down in a minute when he'd put some papers away."

"Everyone else here?"

Ryder glanced about the room. His eyes sought and found Mrs. Ingersoll, sitting in the far corner, smoking a cigarette in a long jade holder. He opened his mouth to say something and closed it again. It was no business of his. He checked over the people in the room.

Perkins the butler and his wife, Hannah the cook, stood near the hall door with the other servants: Reeves, Waterman's valet, four neat-looking maids, and an elderly man whom Ryder recognised as Hobson, who had been Mrs. Gaunt's chauffeur for many years. On the other side of the hearth, in the corner between the door into the drawing-room and the door between the porcelain cabinets that led into a little corner room used as a den, sat Elvira, looking rather scared, but keeping up a pretence of conversation with Daniel Minton who stood beside her. Edgar and Rex Olsen were talking to Mrs. Ingersoll, and Susan and Carey came in at this moment through the door from the back hall with a look of astonishment on their faces. "Yes," said Ryder, "they're all here—except Waterman."

Potter turned towards the hall door, outside which the uniformed figure of Jones was visible in the dim hallway. A moment later Ryder, fascinated, saw Jones go upstairs, two steps at a time. Potter came back and held a brief, low-voiced colloquy with Roberts who came to the window at his signal. The policeman came in, closed and locked the window behind him. By common consent the eyes of everyone in the room followed him in stupefied silence as he circled the room, closing and locking three of the four doors and dropping the keys into his pocket. The door into the hall he left open, blocking it with his broad, blue-coated figure.

Edgar swayed to his feet.

"Look here," he said thickly. "What is all this? Who are you? I've seen you somewhere—"

"I'm Detective-Sergeant Potter of the New London police force," snapped Potter. "When Mr. Waterman Gaunt arrives I shall have something to say to you all."

A murmur that was like a sigh ran round the room. Ryder, straining his ears, tried to follow the progress of the policeman upstairs but his footsteps were swallowed up in a sinister silence. The tension of his nerves was unbearable. His eyes again sought Astrid Ingersoll, noting the nervous jerking way in which the smoke rose from her cigarette. His mind was filled with a vague, horrible surmise. He wanted to rush upstairs, but his feet were rooted to the floor. And then suddenly, quite quietly, Waterman Gaunt walked into the room followed by Jones, who closed the hall door and took his place beside Roberts with his back against it.

The anticlimax was so great that Ryder laughed. The eyes of everyone present swung to him in surprise and then turned back to Waterman, whose brow darkened as he looked about the room.

"What's the meaning of this, Potter?" he demanded angrily. "To rout us all out in the middle of the night—" He flung himself down in the big desk chair that faced the fireplace and Potter across the wide, mahogany surface of the desk.

"I will tell you why I am here, Mr. Gaunt," said Potter. "I have ample authority. I am in charge of the investigation into the murder of your mother, Mrs. Hetty Gaunt."

One of the maids screamed and from the corner, near Ryder, came a strange moaning sound. It was Susan. She was staring at Potter and seemed unaware of the noise that came through her bloodless, parted lips. Carey shook her arm fiercely.

"Shut up, Sue." Abruptly the noise ceased. Waterman Gaunt spoke, and his voice sounded curious rather than horrified.

"How was she murdered?"

"She was stabbed under the left arm with a long, very thin instrument. There was practically no bleeding."

Waterman nodded slowly, surprisingly.

"The dagger in the black hawthorn jar," he said. The words fell like pebbles into a pool of silence. Potter caught up the implication eagerly.

"Do you know something about this?"

"I know—we all know—there was a dagger sealed into that black hawthorn jar on the mantel. It is called by some Chinese word which means 'the dagger that leaves no trace.' I found a reference to it to-night in a letter my mother began to Mr. Avery. I think, if you look, you will find that the seal on the jar is broken."

Following Waterman's eyes, Potter turned and lifted the black hawthorn jar from its place on the high mantel. He set it on the desk. It was at once apparent that Waterman was right. The red wax was chipped and broken and the seal came off easily in Potter's hand. He looked in and drew a sudden breath. "You're right, Mr. Gaunt." He took a clean handkerchief from his pocket and using it as a glove, thrust his hand into the opening of the jar. He drew out a long, wicked-looking instrument with a heavy, elaborate handle and a thin three-edged blade no bigger than a knitting needle and at least ten inches long.

"Who else knew of the existence of this dagger?" demanded Potter, glaring about the room.

There was no answer. Potter wrapped his handkerchief round the handle and laid the knife carefully on a clean sheet of paper on the desk. He drew forward his notebook and sat down.

"Now," he said, "we have something to go on. When was that seal broken? Can anyone give me any information on that point?"

"It was not broken a week ago," said Carey suddenly. "Susan and I were looking at the jar last Saturday and the seal was intact then."

There was a murmur near the hall door and Mrs. Perkins was heard to say: "Yes, speak up and tell him."

One of the maids took a doubtful step forward. It was Maud, the parlourmaid, a pretty, blonde girl with blue Irish eyes.

"It wasn't broken this morning, sir," she said in a quavering voice. "I always dust this room before the family is down, sir. I dusted the jar this morning as usual, and it was all right."

"You're certain of that?" snapped Potter.

"Certain sure, sir. I dusted the mantel too, of course. It was clean when I left it. And you can see for yourself, sir, there's bits of that wax on it now."

Potter rose, glanced at the mantelshelf, nodded, and sat down again.

"What time would that be?" he asked.

"Between seven-thirty and eight, sir."

"It was unopened later than that," said Susan suddenly. "I came into this room about eight-thirty—no one else was down—and found mother standing on the hearth in her nightgown and wrapper, trying to reach the jar. She was very small, as you know, and couldn't get hold of it very well. I lifted it down for her and put it on the desk."

"Well?"

"She examined it carefully and then—" Susan paused for a moment, breathless—"and then she said a queer thing. She said: 'I was right. This has been opened before. The seal has been broken and replaced. You can see the wax on top is a slightly different colour.' "

Ryder felt as though someone had laid a cold hand on the back of his neck. His hair stirred. As in a daze he heard Potter ask: "What happened then?"

"I put the jar back and mother went upstairs."

"It was still unopened?"

"Yes."

What happened in the next few minutes, swift as it was, was destined to remain forever on the photographic plates of Ryder's memory, an ineradicable picture that recurred at intervals in nightmares.

Waterman Gaunt brought his hand down on the desk before him with the light, triumphant gesture Ryder had seen him use in his mother's room upstairs. "By God," he said, "that clinches it." He thrust his hand into his breast pocket and drew out a folded sheet of letter paper. He began to open it. "This is a half-finished letter from my mother to Mr. Avery. I found it to-night thrust under the blotter on her desk. I think it will help—"

The sentence trailed off in a startled gasp. His face, a moment before visible in all its triumphant assurance, was blotted out. Someone had turned out the lights.

From the pandemonium that followed only two things emerged clearly and distinctly: a thin, strange scream, abruptly silent, and Potter's strident cry: "The switch, Jones—the switch!"

Then the lights came on again. Everyone was standing—Maud, the Irish girl who had testified about the hawthorn jar, absurdly enough on a chair, her skirts drawn up as though she feared a mouse. Only Waterman Gaunt remained seated, quite by himself in the middle of the big room, his head leaning at a curious angle on the desk in front of him, his long arms dragging towards the floor, and protruding from his broad back, between his wide shoulders, the heavy, ornate handle of the dagger from the black hawthorn vase.

CHAPTER IX

POTTER hurried round the desk and stooped over Waterman Gaunt. He straightened and looked swiftly round the circle of white faces. His glance settled on Ryder. "Have a look at him, Doctor," he said curtly. "I should say he was certainly dead."

A moment's examination confirmed Potter's opinion. Ryder nodded. "Instantaneous. Through the heart, I should say."

Potter stared thoughtfully down at the drooping body. He lifted the head slightly and slid an exploring hand under it. Then he looked under the desk.

"Jones," he ordered crisply, "call headquarters and have them send a policewoman over as fast as they can get her here. And we'll need Ellicott and Sims, too, and the usual squad. Then go to Atkins' and if Blake is still there, bring him here."

Jones disappeared.

Potter made a swift, careful examination of Waterman Gaunt's pockets, ranging the contents on the desk: handkerchiefs, a wallet full of crisp bills, some loose change, a key ring, three letters which the detective glanced at briefly. Nothing else. He returned to his place in front of the hearth.

"Now," said Potter, and he sat down again behind the desk, tilting the chair back and staring from one face to another, "whoever has that paper might as well produce it, because nobody is going to leave this room until it is found."

"What paper?" asked a quavering unidentified voice.

"The letter Mr. Gaunt was about to show me when he was killed." He waited. No one spoke.

"I have sent for a policewoman and a squad of experts from headquarters. When they arrive you will all be searched and detained while the room is searched, if the paper is not found on any of you. It would be better to save time and hand it over."

Again he paused and again no one answered his challenge.

After a moment, a whimpering, hysterical sound was heard in the far corner of the room. It came from Astrid Ingersoll. She stood clinging to her brother's arm, her face drained to a dreadful green pallor. Her jade cigarette-holder lay on the floor at her feet. Potter looked her up and down but said nothing. He again turned to his notebook.

"You will please all keep your places," he said. "I am going to note them down, in order." He looked round to his extreme left, where Elvira stood beside Daniel Minton. "Name, please?"

She gave it, in a quavering voice, and he went on round the circle, jotting down the names on a rough diagram before him. He wound up with Perkins, nearest to him on his right. "Now," he said briskly, "I want to know where the light switches are."

He looked at Perkins. "How many in this room?"

"Four, sir," said the butler. He seemed terribly shaken, and his voice quavered oddly. "One beside each door."

Potter glanced around again and put some finishing touches to his diagram.

"That makes it nice," he commented acidly. "There's not one of you who couldn't have reached a switch by moving a few feet."

He rose suddenly and crossed the room towards the door between the porcelain cabinets. He bent over and looked down at the floor. Every pair of eyes in the room followed him. He was staring at a thin spiral of smoke that rose from the Chinese rug. After a moment he picked up a half-smoked cigarette and studied it, holding it carefully between his fingers. It had left a charring spot on the rug which he crushed out with his foot. Then he walked across to Mrs. Ingersoll and looked down at the jade holder at her feet. She caught it up with a little exclamation.

"This cigarette was smoked in a holder," said Potter. "You're the only person who has used one since we've been in this room. What were you doing over near that door?"

"I—I got frightened when the lights went out," she gasped between stiff lips. "I—I forgot the door was locked and tried to get away."

"And then, when you found it was locked, you hurried back to the same place where you'd been when the lights went out?"

"I must have lost my head," she muttered resentfully.

Potter said nothing for a moment. Then he looked at Edgar Gaunt, who stood near. Edgar had plainly been shocked into soberness. His face wore a curious look of fright.

"Did Mrs. Ingersoll leave this chair before or after the lights went out?" Potter asked.

"I—I don't know," stammered Edgar. "Damn it all, it happened so confoundedly fast. We were moving back and forth—chatting—"

"Oh, you were moving back and forth. Who is 'we'?"

"Rex Olsen and I. I believe Mrs. Ingersoll did get up to look for an ash tray. Rex went to get her one—"

"Where is it?" demanded Potter.

Olsen glared at Edgar. "I didn't find one. I'd just turned to look for it when the lights went out."

"Turned towards the door perhaps," sneered Potter.

"No," said Olsen, "I went over towards that table near the window."

"Anyone see him?"

"I did," said Mrs. Ingersoll suddenly. "Of course I did. How stupid of me. It was all so sudden, I forgot for a moment."

Potter looked from her to Olsen and back again. Then he said abruptly: "Where was Edgar Gaunt?"

"How should I know?" said Olsen spitefully. "I had my back to him."

Potter transferred his glance to Astrid. She looked uncomfortably down at her clenched hands.

"I don't know. I was watching Rex."

Potter said nothing. He returned to the desk, stamped out the still glowing cigarette carefully, and slipped it into an envelope. On the envelope he wrote a few words and put it into his pocket. Then he turned to Elvira. She looked near collapse. Her face, usually a little florid, was marked with blue shadows. She looked ten years older than she had at dinner. "Where were you during this time?" asked Potter sharply.

She tried to speak, but no words came. She burst into tears. Daniel Minton; who stood beside her, patted her shoulder kindly.

"I can tell you where she was," he said to Potter. "When the lights went out she grabbed hold of my arm and held on to it like grim death. She was still holding on when they were turned up again."

The natural, human quality of his voice seemed to relieve the tension, to remove some of the overstrained horror of the situation. Everyone breathed more deeply. Potter continued to look at Elvira.

"Is that true?" he asked curtly.

She nodded, dabbing at her eyes with her handkerchief. Potter wrote something in his book. Then he looked at Nancy.

During all this excitement it seemed as though she had not moved. She looked like a stone figure in front of the sofa on which she had been sitting at the beginning of the inquiry. Ryder, who had returned to her side after his brief examination of Waterman's body, watched her anxiously. Potter addressed her coldly, but with more consideration than he had shown so far.

"You were nearer Mr. Gaunt than any of us," he said. "Did you see anything that might help us?"

"No—no, I think not," she said quietly. "I have been trying to recall, but it happened so quickly."

"Were you aware of any movement near you?"

"I was aware of movement everywhere. Everyone seemed to move forward."

"You did not leave your place?"

"I stood up; that was all."

"Can you tell me where Dr. Ryder was during this time?"

She looked briefly at Ryder, and then back at Potter. "He was standing beside me, just in front of the window."

"Where he is now?"

"Yes."

"How do you know?"

"I looked at him just before the lights went out. And he was there when they came on again."

"You have no way of knowing that he did not move in the meantime?"

Her eyes turned again to Ryder with a look of complete, luminous confidence.

"Why don't you ask him, Sergeant Potter?"

Ryder returned her look.

"You are quite right," he told her. "I was here, beside you, all the time the lights were out."

"Can anyone substantiate that?"

Susan spoke suddenly, for the first time.

"If you mean did he come over to this light switch, which is the only one he could have reached, he did not."

"How do you know?"

"I was standing with my back against it, as I am now. No one could have touched it without my knowledge. No one did touch it. That includes Carey," she added, glancing at her brother who stood beside her, and then looking again, with defiance, at Potter.

The detective's manner did not change by a hair's breadth.

"I suppose you did not touch it yourself?"

"I did not," said Susan dryly.

"Why didn't you? If you knew where the switch was—if you were standing right against it—why didn't you turn it on when I called for lights?"

"Must you have everything you ask for, dear Sergeant Potter?" purred Susan sweetly. "Besides, I was paralysed—couldn't move. Believe it or not."

"And I suppose you didn't move either?" said Potter acidly, looking at Carey Gaunt. The young man's face was pale, but he seemed to have recovered from the panic that had seized him earlier in the day.

"Your supposition is correct," said Carey coolly.

Potter turned a leaf of his notebook.

"Hobson?" he said.

The old man answered him with quiet dignity.

"I've been here right along, sir. I didn't notice anything."

Potter looked at the four maids, clinging together in the corner, and for the first time he smiled faintly.

"Did any of you turn the light off?"

They shook their collective heads with gasps of protest and horror.

"Or notice anything?" But they had nothing to contribute. Nor had Reeves, the valet, who was standing in the corner, looking rather sick.

Potter turned now to the last couple in the room: the butler and his stout pleasant-looking wife, who stood almost at the detective's elbow, between the fireplace and the hall door. After a quick glance, Potter swung his chair round so that he could look up into Perkins' face.

"Look here, man," he said, "what's wrong?"

Perkins was shaking from head to foot and his face was as white as paper. "I—I—I seen it done, sir," he gasped. And then, as though his control had snapped, his knees sagged, and he would have fallen if Mrs. Perkins had not held him up in her strong arms. Potter sprang to his feet and helped her lower her husband into the desk chair.

Potter turned to the policeman in the doorway.

"Go into the dining-room and get some whisky," he ordered, and when it was brought he poured a little into Perkins sagging mouth. The butler's colour came back slowly. He held himself upright and made a half-hearted attempt to rise.

"Sit where you are," said Potter. "Take your time. Now, what did you mean when you said you saw it done?"

"Lord help me, sir, I'll see it to my dying day," said Perkins with a shudder. "Mr. Gaunt was just between me and the window there. I could see him faint like when the light was out. The window was just a bit lighter than the room, you know, sir. And then I saw someone step up behind him and raise an arm like this, sir, and bring it down, and Mr. Waterman screamed. My God, sir, it was awful."

Sweat stood on Perkins' forehead. He took a handkerchief from his pocket and wiped it off.

"Which side did the person come from?" snapped Potter.

"Couldn't say, sir—just suddenly appeared, as you might say."

"Man or woman?"

"Couldn't be sure, sir. All very dim—"

Potter turned to Mrs. Perkins.

"Did you see anything?"

"I saw something move, sir—that's all."

At this moment Jones came in with Dr. Blake.

"The men are on their way, sir," he told Potter.

Dr. Blake stood nervously in the doorway, his hands twitching. Potter stepped forward, jerking his head towards the motionless figure in front of the desk.

"He's dead, all right," he said, "but you'd better have a look."

Blake made a hasty examination and then drew Potter out into the hall and conferred with him in low tones.

"I've got an ambulance here," he said. "Sent for it to get Mrs. Gaunt's body. We were just about to leave when Jones caught me. Want me to take him along too? Or do you want to wait?"

Potter thought a minute.

"I'll have to wait. I want some pictures."

"You're not going to keep them all there until Ellicott gets here?"

"Why not? I don't want to have to search two rooms." And he told Blake about the missing paper. The doctor's pale, worried-looking face creased into new folds of horror.

"Do you think it is as important as all that?"

"It was important enough to cost Waterman Gaunt his life," said Potter grimly. "No, no, I'm not taking chances. We'll finish this thing now. Three murders is enough."

"Three?" repeated Blake blankly. "You mean—"

"Old Captain Gaunt, of course. Not a doubt of it. I'll get an order to exhume in the morning. Want you to do an autopsy."

"Good God!" Dr. Blake passed an unsteady hand across his forehead. "Well, you're right. Of course you're right. I've always thought it was queer—damned queer."

He seemed about to say something else, but changed his mind. He gave a last worried glance into the library and went away.

Potter took up his stand in front of the fireplace.

"Make yourselves comfortable," he said with a grim smile. "We have quite a wait ahead of us."

CHAPTER X

IT seemed to Matthew Ryder that he could never forget a single detail of the horrible hour that followed: as if each sentence, each silence, were etched with acid on his memory. But, curiously enough, the only impression that really remained with him was the picture of the *Seabird* that hung over the mantel: the *Seabird*, the ship which, as a young man of twenty-five, the first Waterman Gaunt had commanded, and upon which, in the hazardous decade following 1845, he had made a fortune smuggling opium into China. In Ryder's mind that picture dominated the scene and gave it a sort of awful significance, as if this, indeed, was a final chapter of which that ancient history had been the beginning. And for that hour, at least, it seemed credible that a curse so begotten might bear this bloody fruit.

Ryder's eyes returned again and again to the picture. It was really more a diagram than a portrait: each rope, each spar, each canvas accurately in place, each wave held in suspended animation by a rigid stroke of the brush, each landmark minutely correct. Under it ran the inscription: "The *Seabird* entering Shanghai Harbour: Captain Waterman Gaunt."

Ryder had looked at that picture hundreds of times during the years he had been coming to this house, with interest, with amusement, but never with any sense of reality. Its very insistence on reality had taken it out of the realm of the familiar, had given it a quaintness that had overlaid it with a mist of romantic illusion, just as the extreme explicitness of the detailed story of Waterman Gaunt's career had contributed to the glamour of his legendary quality. For it is of the nature of legends to be explicit, just as it is of the nature of reality to be softened by atmosphere and mood, shrouded in subtleties, warped by the lights and shadows of partial knowledge.

Now for the first time Matthew Ryder sat stiff with the realisation that that was a real ship, that those ropes had been handled by real men; that upon those decks had taken place the battle with slant-eyed pirates in the China

Sea in which Gaunt had taken Wong, his servant, who had lived to serve him in this house, to come and go in this very room with its tall bookcases masking the walls, its long windows opening on the sea. In that ship had been transported the porcelains that filled the teakwood cabinets at the far end of this room: the black hawthorn vase that stood now on the desk, delivered of its deadly secret. In an iron safe in that very cabin had been brought home the boxes of silver bars and specie received in payment for the opium cargo—tainted money, blood-soaked, ghost-ridden, won by the brutalising of men, the sacrifice of life, by violence, brutality, unscrupulous fraud —and by magnificent seamanship, great courage, and daring.

Give the devil his due, reflected Matthew Ryder, staring at the picture with half-closed eyes. There had probably never been more splendid ships, more able captains than had plied in the opium trade. It gave one pause in formulating one's philosophy of social morality. Perhaps, after all—

His eyes slid from the picture on the wall to the great, flat-topped desk that stood in the centre of the room, facing the fire. Waterman Gaunt had come home, had made his farewells to that ship and that life, had built his house and begotten his son. And one foggy night he had died, sitting at that desk with a bullet in his back. This had actually happened. Someone had stood in one of those long windows behind him and had shot him in the back.

And now his grandson sat at that same desk, in that same chair, done to death. And the weapon that had killed him had been taken from that lovely, sinister black jar in which the "curse of the Gaunts" was supposed to be sealed. The curse of the Gaunts indeed!

Ryder's nerves twitched and shivered with an almost superstitious horror utterly foreign to his usual balanced, well-ordered mind. He tried to shake the mood from him. The weapon had been used because it was at hand. No doubt it had been used to kill old Mrs. Gaunt for the same reason. There was, of course, no possible connection between an eighty-year-old Chinese superstition and a series of particularly callous contemporary murders. Or was there? Did the events set in motion by the grandfather culminate naturally in the fate of his grandchildren? The room was heavy with the personality of the man for whom it had been built. The faces of his grandchildren, ranged white and strained around this new manifestation of horror, were deeply cut in his likeness. Was it too much to suppose that their souls, too, bore the impress of his ruthless nature? All, of course, except Nancy.

His eyes turned to her as to the one sane, wholesome thing in the room, and his heart went out to her. He would have saved her this at any cost, but he could not. He could not spare her one grief, one humiliation, one fear.

Potter, meanwhile, surveyed the row of faces before him with no illusions as to the difficulties of his task. A bunch of tough babies, and no mistake. It would take a can opener to get from them anything they did not want to tell. And there was plenty, he opined dryly, that they would not want to tell. On the other hand, he was well primed to tackle 'em. Under his acid, official exterior a deep rage was boiling. To pull a raw deal like that under his very nose! He would hear about it from headquarters—and he was itching to pass on his anticipated discomfort.

He tilted his chair back, hooking his thumbs aggressively in the armholes of his vest, shifting his stare deliberately from face to face.

"Now," he said, "let's have it! Anybody got any ideas to contribute?"

Get 'em fighting among themselves, he thought shrewdly, and we may learn something. He stared with calculated insolence at Elvira.

"You're Mrs. Edgar Gaunt, aren't you?"

She nodded, plucking nervously at her handkerchief.

"Speak up," said Potter sternly.

Daniel Minton broke in. "Look here, Potter. You can't get away with any third-degree methods here."

"Why not?" Potter's chair snapped upright, and he leaned forward across the desk. "Within a few minutes a man has been killed—stabbed in the back by one of the people in this room. There might have been some doubt about Mrs. Gaunt's murder, although not much, to be sure. But it was barely possible that she might have been killed by someone outside the family circle. But there's no doubt about this. Waterman Gaunt was killed by someone in this room. All windows and doors were locked except the door guarded by two of my men. No one entered this room or left it. The murderer is here among you. I mean to find him. I think," he added more mildly, "that those of you who are innocent would be the first to resent any lack of zeal on my part."

Minton shrugged. Carey spoke from the other side of the room. "Cousin Daniel just means," he said sweetly, "that he wants you to find the murderer, always remembering that there is a certain courtesy due to the Gaunts."

The boy's face was flushed and there was a reckless look in his eyes.

"Because you see," said Susan with the air of one helpfully imparting information, "we are one of the first families."

There was an electric silence. Potter smiled grimly. Minton's ears were purple. He sat down without a word. Potter returned to the charge.

"Which of you was the last to see Mrs. Gaunt alive—with the exception, shall we say, of the murderer?"

"I believe I was," said Nancy. "I went in a little after ten to see if I could help her dress. She said she didn't need me, however, so after a few minutes I went down to the kitchen to give Hannah the orders for the day."

"Do you know what time that was?"

"About ten-thirty, I think."

Hannah Perkins coughed discreetly.

"It was just ten-thirty, Miss Nancy," she said. "I thought it was getting late for the ordering and I'd just looked at the clock when you came down."

Potter made a note. "Was your mother still in bed when you left her?"

"No. She was moving about the room in her dressing gown. She had not yet started dressing."

"Did anyone else see her after that?"

No one spoke. They held their eyes on Potter's face as though they felt that even a casual glance would be an accusation.

"Who discovered her death?"

Edgar shifted uncomfortably in his chair.

"I did. But she wasn't dead when I found her. She was lying on the floor and when I bent over her she opened her eyes and tried to speak."

"Could you understand what she said?"

They hung breathless on his reply.

"No. I could see she was very bad. I went to the door and called Nancy."

"Just a moment before we go on. How did you happen to go into your mother's room just then?"

Edgar flushed dully and stared at the floor.

"There was something I wanted to see her about." Suddenly, as though at some awful thought, the colour drained from his face and he staggered to his feet. "My God!"

Potter did not move. "Well?"

"I'd been waiting for a chance to catch her alone all morning, but first Wat had sat with her while she was eating her breakfast, and just as he came out Nancy went in. I saw Nancy go downstairs—I was in the sitting-room—so I went along to knock at mother's door, but before I could knock I heard her talking to someone. It must have been—"

He broke off as though his voice had failed him.

"Did you hear any voice beside your mother's?"

"No."

"Could you hear what she was saying?"

"No. She seemed to be very angry—but mother was often angry."

"What makes you think she was angry?"

"Her voice was raised and she was talking very rapidly, as she does—did—when she was irritated."

"And yet you couldn't hear a word?"

"What do you think I am?" demanded Edgar belligerently. "Think I listen at keyholes?"

Potter paid no attention to his annoyance. For a moment he drummed with his fingers on the desk. Then he swung on Nancy.

"Are you prepared to swear there was no one in the room when you left?"

"Certainly. Mother was alone when I left her."

He turned on Edgar.

"And you are certain no one entered by the door?"

"Of course. I never took my eyes off it."

"Then how could anyone enter the room?"

"Easily," said Susan suddenly. "Either through Nancy's room, which communicates with Mother's, or from the upstairs porch which runs all across the back of the house. Anyone could have climbed up from the garden. It's only four or five feet from the terrace at the end near mother's window."

"Or entered it from one of the back bedroom windows," volunteered Elvira dryly.

"What rooms open on the porch?"

"Mine," said Nancy. "Susan's, next to mine, and then the guest room which Dr. Ryder now occupies. There is also an entrance from the upper hall."

"Where were you at this time?" Potter asked Susan.

"In my room, taking a shower. Carey and I had just come in from our swim."

"You saw no one on the porch?"

"No," said Susan sweetly. "But then you couldn't see your hand before your face because of the fog."

"Does your room communicate with your sister's?"

"Yes," said Susan brightly. "And the door wasn't locked. I could easily have gone through Nancy's room into mother's."

Potter's mouth was grim. "Did you?"

"No," said Susan flatly.

"And the guest room was unoccupied at that time?"

"Quite," nodded Susan.

"My room communicates with it," said Carey helpfully. "I could have gone through it out on to the porch quite easily. But I will forestall your natural question: I didn't." The edge of his voice was as sharp as a blade, but Potter seemed blandly unaware of it.

"Mrs. Ingersoll and Mr. Olsen had not yet arrived, I understand."

"Quite right," said Olsen easily "We were marooned on the *Buccaneer*, out in the harbour."

"But they could easily have come ashore in the fog," said Carey acidly, "and climbed on to the porch from the garden." His mocking eyes never left Potter's face. Mrs. Ingersoll shot him a venomous look.

"But we didn't," she said.

"You were on the *Buccaneer* at the time of Mrs. Gaunt's death?" suggested Potter placatingly.

She hesitated surprisingly, looking at her brother. And then, surprisingly, burst into hysterical tears. Olsen put his hand on her shoulder.

"I must protest against this inquisition," he said indignantly. "This situation is horrible beyond words for my sister. She was engaged to be married to Waterman Gaunt." The silence that ensued was broken only by a sharp, insulting laugh from Elvira. Olsen flushed darkly.

"The engagement was never announced because my sister understood that Mrs. Gaunt was fanatically opposed to her son's marriage. I believe this is general knowledge." He looked with some defiance about the room.

Susan laughed grimly.

"Elvira can tell you about that," she said acidly.

"I repeat my question, Mr. Olsen." Potter's voice was implacable. "Where were you and where was your sister at the time of Mrs. Gaunt's death?"

"We were in the yacht's dinghy, moored to the wharf at the bottom of the garden."

Every pair of eyes in the room swung to him in astonishment.

"Rex!" cried Mrs. Ingersoll despairingly.

"There's no use attempting to conceal it," said Olsen gently. "Melvin Saunders knows we were there. We came ashore when he came for the mail. We went first to the post office. Then Saunders came on here to see if Waterman wanted him. We went into several shops—Mrs. Ingersoll wanted to buy two or three little things and we were putting in time. When we couldn't think of anything else to do we went down through the garden and waited in the boat. After a while—a few minutes after eleven, it was—Saunders came down and said that Mrs. Gaunt had died suddenly, and he was needed ashore. So I rowed my sister back to the *Buccaneer*."

Mrs. Ingersoll's tears had ceased to flow. She sat with a wooden face staring before her.

Potter made a note in his black book. He anticipated an interesting interview with Melvin Saunders. Then he looked at Elvira. "We return to you, Mrs. Gaunt," he said with a grim smile. "May I ask you, with all courtesy, where you were when your mother-in-law was killed?"

Elvira's soft, smooth face was drawn and looked haggard under the make-up. "I was in my room across the hall, lying down. I had a bad headache."

"When did you go to your room?"

"I hadn't left it all morning. I breakfasted in bed, as usual, and afterwards felt too ill to get up."

"Did anyone come in during the morning?"

"Maggie brought my tray about nine and took it away about ten. No one else came near me," said Elvira tearfully.

"How could they," growled Edgar, "when you locked the door?"

There was an awkward pause while Elvira dabbed at her eyes with her handkerchief.

"Is there any way to leave your room except by the door into the hall?"

"There is also a door into the sitting-room."

"And you were in the sitting-room, Mr. Gaunt?"

Edgar nodded.

"For an hour before you went into your mother's room and found her dying?"

"At least that."

"And during that time your wife did not leave her room?"

"She did not."

"You are prepared to swear to it?"

Edgar grinned sardonically. "Certainly."

"So it seems, Mrs. Gaunt, that you have a fairly complete alibi—thanks to your husband," said Potter dryly.

"If you think Edgar would lie to shield me, you are mistaken," snapped Elvira sharply. "There is nothing noble about Edgar."

Susan laughed suddenly, hysterically. Carey laid a cautioning hand on her arm but she shook him off.

"So we return, Mr. Gaunt, to your reason for wanting so earnestly to see your mother in private. What was it?"

"I'm not obliged to answer that," said Edgar flatly, "and I won't."

"Then I'll answer it," said Susan suddenly.

Edgar turned on her furiously.

"Mind your own business, Sue."

"This is my business." The girl's face was bloodless. She was shaking.

"I'll tell you why Edgar wanted to see mother. It was probably partly cadging for money because he lost a pile at roulette last night. But the real reason was he wanted to find out if it was true, as we all believed, that she'd made a will leaving the control of the Gaunt Lines to Wat." She looked over her shoulder at Edgar's face. "Look at him and see if I'm not right."

Edgar was purple—inarticulate with rage and fright.

"And I'll tell you something more," said Susan to Potter. "If you can prove that she really made that will, you'll know why she was killed—and why someone stuck that dagger in Waterman's back just now."

She stood in the centre of the room, a slender fury, her eyes glowing darkly in her chalk-white face. Potter sat curiously still, his glance holding hers.

"I agree with you, he said. "I think it will not be difficult to prove that she made such a will."

Susan put her hand to her lips as though to quiet their trembling. When she spoke her voice jumped uncontrollably. "You seem to know a lot about us, Sergeant Potter. Do you know that my father also made a will the night he died?"

"Yes."

She drew a great breath. Suddenly Potter came round the desk and stood beside her. He looked at her with unexpected gentleness.

"I think, Miss Gaunt," he said, "if you know anything else, for your own safety, you'd better tell it now."

Carey, watching his sister with eyes hypnotised with terror, seemed to see her suddenly standing in a dark cloud that rose about her, waist-high, breast-high; shrouding at last her brave eyes and shining hair. Of course it wasn't a real cloud. Only this deadly faintness that overcame him at times. He put out his hand towards her vaguely.

"Susan," he muttered.

And then the cloud swirled and engulfed him too. He plunged forward into it and lay still.

CHAPTER XI

THERE was a moment of stupefied silence. Then Susan flung herself down beside her brother, raising his head in her arms. His lips were blue. She looked frantically around, seeking Dr. Ryder, her gaze full of a wild surmise. "He—he's not dead?"

Ryder's fingers were already on the boy's pulse.

"No," he said. "No, certainly not—fainted."

Someone thrust a glass of whisky into his hand, and he held it to Carey's lips. The boy's eyes were already fluttering. He gulped and coughed, looked up for a moment wildly at Susan, and closed his eyes again. Ryder stood up and looked at Potter.

"I've got to get him to bed," he said sternly. "I won't be responsible for him if he's not allowed to rest."

Potter returned the doctor's look with a level stare.

"No one leaves this room without being searched."

"Then search us and get it over with. I tell you the boy's got to have attention."

For a minute Potter's cold eyes bored into the doctor's angry ones. Then he nodded to Jones. Ryder turned and preceded the policeman into the hall. Presently Jones returned, and he and Roberts between them lifted Carey and carried him upstairs,

"I insist on going with him," cried Susan angrily.

"I'm sorry, Miss Gaunt."

Potter closed the door into the hall and stood with his back against it.

It was ten minutes before Ryder returned, accompanied by Jones. Roberts, he explained, had been left upstairs with Carey. Potter nodded.

"Think it was a genuine faint, do you?" he asked with a suggestion of a sneer.

"Certainly," said Ryder curtly. "Over-excitement and strain."

He turned his back with almost ostentatious deliberation on Potter and went across the room to Susan. "He'll be all right," he told her gently. "I've given him a sedative."

For a moment Potter watched him with a suggestion of a sardonic smile. Then he sat down again behind the desk and reverted to his notebook.

"To resume," he said grimly. "You have nothing more to tell me, Miss Susan?"

"Nothing " said Susan curtly.

"Very well, then." He drew a line across the page, leaned back, hooked his thumbs in the armholes of his vest, and looked appraisingly at Daniel Minton. "I have not heard anything from you, so far, Mr. Minton. Have you no ideas that might help me?"

"I have not," said Minton sharply. "I am extremely resentful of the tone of your inquiry."

"Come, come, Mr. Minton," said Potter smoothly. "Are you still insisting on your privileges as one of our first families?"

Minton flushed. He seemed on the point of an angry outburst, thought better of it, shrugged. For an instant he studied the detective thoughtfully. Then he laughed. "All right," he said. "You win. What do you want to know?"

"I understand you are general manager of the Gaunt Lines?"

"That is correct."

"And Mr. Waterman Gaunt was president?"

"Yes," said Minton. "He succeeded to that office after his father's death."

"Was he very active in the conduct of the company's business?"

"No," admitted Minton. "From the time of my uncle's first stroke the office had really become an honorary one. My uncle had been the guiding spirit of the company before that, but after his illness the active part of the business had fallen more and more into my hands, and my Cousin Waterman seemed to have little interest in assuming responsibility."

"But until his death your uncle, Captain Gaunt, retained the final authority?"

"Certainly. He held a voting majority of the stock. All important decisions were referred to him—even to the very day of his death. As a matter of fact, I had come up that very morning to consult him about a matter upon which the board wanted his opinion."

"How did it happen that you, rather than either of Captain Gaunt's older sons, succeeded him in authority?" Minton hesitated.

"That's an awkward question," he admitted.

"I'll answer it," broke in Edgar suddenly. "He was my father's right-hand man from the time he was twenty-five because he loved the business and studied it. I was too busy drinking, and Wat was more interested in women than in ships. Besides, although we've never been willing to admit it, Dan has the brains of the family and we all know it."

"Good Lord, Edgar!" protested Minton dryly. "You overcome me!

"Don't mention it," said Edgar with a venomous look. "I'm taking a turn at Susan's game of telling the truth."

Potter smiled secretly at his notebook.

"I understand, then, that on Captain Gaunt's death, the real authority passed to you?"

"No," said Minton. "I handled all ordinary matters, but the final decision in important affairs went to Aunt Hetty, Mrs. Gaunt. She was a remarkable woman, Sergeant Potter; shrewd and practical in the highest degree. I have never known a woman so little influenced by sentiment in her business judgment."

"Did she share what Mr. Gaunt declares to be the opinion of the rest of the family concerning your capacities?"

Minton smiled deprecatingly.

"I believe she did, as a matter of fact," he said. "Certainly she was always ready to hear my opinions, and usually acted on them. Not always. But when she ran counter to them it was for a good reason and not because of her personal dislike for me."

"So she disliked you personally?"

"Oh," said Minton with a surprised look. "I should certainly think so. After all, Aunt Hetty was a woman—or perhaps it would be fairer to say that she was, after all, human. She disliked my father and had had a serious quarrel with my mother for insisting, as she thought, in marrying beneath her. The quarrel was patched up years later, but the bitterness remained. She never quite forgave me for being my father's son."

"Do you think that feeling influenced her in giving Waterman Gaunt control of the Gaunt Lines in her will?"

Minton nodded. He took out a cigarette and lit it thoughtfully.

"I'll tell you what I think about that. I don't think that, during her lifetime, she could have borne to have Waterman in control. She was an extremely competent woman and, like all competent people, she was frightfully irked by incompetence. But she was also a mother—a relationship which upsets even the most perfectly balanced women. I think she was perfectly aware that Waterman had never had a square deal. I think she even felt a little guilty about it. I imagine her will—if, indeed, it turns out to be what we all seem to assume—was, in a way, a gesture of atonement. No doubt she intended to make it up to Waterman when she would no longer be here to be annoyed by the situation. I think, also, there was an element of belated revenge in it—revenge for the irritation I had caused her by filling a place which she must have felt belonged rightfully to her sons."

"Why do you say: 'if the will turns out to be what we assume'? Do you doubt that Mrs. Gaunt did, in fact, leave control to her oldest son?"

"No," said Minton. "I don't doubt it. Waterman certainly knew the contents of the will and from what he said only one conclusion is possible. I simply mean we have not seen the will yet. In fact, as far as anything we have absolutely been told goes, we do not know for certain that a will actually exists."

"It does exist," said Potter quietly. "Mr. Avery told me so."

"Then perhaps," said Minton dryly, "he completed his extraordinary behaviour by showing you the will."

"No," said Potter coolly, "he did not. For one reason, because he did not have it in his possession."

There was a moment of rather singular silence. The eyes of everyone in the room were on Potter's face.

"Why not?" asked Mrs. Ingersoll at last, and there was an oddly hysterical note in her voice. "Why wouldn't he have it? What was done with it?"

Their eyes swung curiously to Astrid's white face.

"Don't be an ass," said Olsen irritably. "The will's all right."

"What do you know about it?" Potter shot the question at him sternly. "What business is it of yours?"

Olsen looked slightly taken aback.

"None, of course. I just happened to be reading in Saunders' cabin when he returned to the yacht last night. He had a long envelope which he took from his pocket and locked up in a drawer in his desk. Afterwards, when I heard all that talk about the will, I assumed that was it."

"Oh! You assumed it?"

"As a matter of fact," admitted Olsen, "I knew it. Saunders laid the envelope on the desk while he unlocked the drawer and I saw the inscription on it. It said: 'My last will and testament,' and it was signed 'Hetty Gaunt.' "

"Well!" It was Elvira who spoke. Her exclamation conveyed rage, astonishment, contempt. But before she could go on Potter cut her short.

"Just a moment, Mrs. Gaunt." He returned to Daniel Minton. "I understand you to say that you had come up from New York on the day of Captain Gaunt's death?"

"Yes. I needed to consult him on a point of policy."

"You were in the house when he died?"

"Yes, certainly."

"And you came up again yesterday, and were in the house when Mrs. Gaunt died?"

"Again, yes."

"Does that not strike you as a coincidence?"

"A coincidence—certainly."

"And you were present to-night when Waterman Gaunt was killed?"

"Well, really," said Minton dryly, "why pick on me? We were all here. In fact, if I'm not mistaken, we were all in the house on all three occasions."

"Except Mrs. Ingersoll and Mr. Olsen."

"By all means, said Minton with an ironic smile, "let us except Mrs. Ingersoll and Mr. Olsen."

Potter dropped his badgering manner.

"What was your reason for wanting to consult Mrs. Gaunt yesterday?"

"We have been negotiating the purchase of the Meridian Line—a line which competes with our Central American traffic. The deal has come to the point where it must be completed or fall through—and we will never have the opportunity to buy at that price again. But Mrs. Gaunt hesitated. I learned that Waterman was against the deal, principally because I favoured it, and was trying to persuade his mother not to agree. Of course she could have blocked it if she'd wanted to, so I came up, saw her, and got her signature to the necessary papers." He paused and then added: "As a matter of fact, I would have come up yesterday anyway. It was my birthday and I'd promised the girls—Nancy and Susan and Elvira—a blow-out at the Michitiquock Club."

"This had been arranged beforehand?"

"Two weeks beforehand."

"Did Waterman Gaunt know about the plan?"

"Yes. I asked him to join us, but he said he was unable to do so."

"Yet he was here at the time."

Minton smiled.

"I imagine he thought it would be a good chance for an uninterrupted interview with his mother."

Potter nodded. He looked down at his notebook and then he looked up at Minton. "You realise your position I am sure, Mr. Minton," he said.

Minton looked a little puzzled. "You mean—"

"I mean that if Captain Gaunt had signed his will, if Mrs. Gaunt had signed hers—"

"But as I understand it, she did sign it."

"But you didn't know it."

"I see," said Minton slowly. "I see."

"You stood to lose a great deal."

Minton's hand shook a little as he crushed out his cigarette.

"But look here—there's not a member of the family who didn't stand to lose more than I did."

"Oh, yeah?" said Edgar with an ugly look.

Minton flushed again, darkly. His temper was slipping. "Yes," he snapped. "And if I remember correctly, you were quite put out about it at dinner. You seemed to think that Wat had double-crossed you."

Edgar subsided sullenly, his flabby face as pale as ashes. Minton swung round on Potter.

"Look here," he said, "you're wasting your time. I didn't kill my uncle, nor Mrs. Gaunt—nor Waterman either, for that matter. You have heard Mrs. Edgar Gaunt say that she had hold of my arm all the time the lights were out. I've given you all the help I can. I've answered all your questions fully. But I'll be damned if I'll be made the goat of this situation. I liked Aunt Hetty—which is more than can be said for any other member of her family except—" and his indignant voice and look softened suddenly— "except Nancy. Her devotion to her mother is not for me to speak of. But the rest of them hated her. Look at their faces."

There was an appalling moment when no one spoke. The silence was broken by Elvira. She said, in a low, almost cooing voice: "Why do you except Nancy? She's wanted to marry Dr. Ryder for five years—but she has had to nurse her father and then her mother instead. Perhaps she got tired of meeting Matthew under the rose."

There was a stunned silence. Potter, looking at Nancy, saw that she was as white as paper. Ryder got to his feet. "I think you've gone so far, Mrs. Gaunt, that you'd better go further and explain yourself," he said quietly.

"Perhaps," said Elvira, frightened but venomous, "she got tired of being your mistress."

Matthew Ryder's plain, pleasant face wore a look they had never seen on it before.

"That is a lie."

But Elvira had completely lost control of herself.

"There's a little inn beyond New London, called The Mariners. I stopped there one morning last mouth. Hobson was driving me to New Haven to do some shopping, and something went wrong with the car near this place. Hobson stopped at a roadside garage—and they said it would take an hour to fix the car, so I walked up to the inn, meaning to have a cup of coffee while I waited. We'd left here early and I was hungry. It was about nine o'clock then." She glared around at their hostile faces.

"It was quite a decent place—a sort of small hotel. But I didn't get my coffee. When I looked into the dining-room I saw Nancy and Matthew Ryder having breakfast together."

If she had let a bomb off in their midst they could not have been more startled. Matthew Ryder took Nancy's cold hand and held it in his.

"It's quite true," he said quietly. "We did have breakfast there together about a month ago. I had to see a patient in New Haven the night before, so when I had finished I called Nancy and asked her if she would run over early and meet me at The Mariners for breakfast. I hadn't time to get over here, for I had an appointment in New York at three. She met me about eight-thirty and we breakfasted together. I left her about ten, to drive to New York."

Elvira laughed insultingly.

"Did she meet you at eight-thirty that morning or at eight-thirty the night before?"

"At eight-thirty that morning," said Matthew Ryder quietly.

"It happens to be true," broke in Nancy softly. "But if it hadn't been true there could be nothing between us that I would be ashamed of. We love each other. We would have married a long time ago except that my first duty seemed to be to my mother."

Standing with her hand in her lover's, she looked at Potter, her face glowing with a new, inner radiance. Ryder tried to speak, but his throat contracted and he was seized with a great trembling.

Elvira sniffed audibly. "And I suppose you never felt any ill-will towards your mother for standing in the way of this great love of yours?"

"Why, no, I didn't," said Nancy quietly. As she said it it sounded like a bare statement of fact. But Potter, writing busily in his little book, hesitated a moment and then added a light question mark in the margin.

CHAPTER XII

IT was after four o'clock in the morning when Jed Potter, standing in the middle of the library, ran a desperate hand through his hair and swore softly and brilliantly. "The paper has to be here somewhere," he said. "I saw it in his hands with my own eyes. It was certainly not carried from the room. It's got to be here."

His corps of four assistants looked at him dejectedly. They had spent a busy two hours. With the assistance of Policewoman Perkins, they had searched every person who had been present in the library at the time of Waterman Gaunt's death, and when the family had retired, exhausted, to their rooms Potter and his cohorts had divided the library into segments and had subjected it to close and expert examination. The net result had been exactly nothing. Collins, a stout, red-faced man with a walrus moustache that made him look like the pictures of Ol' Bill, replaced the last book on the bookshelves and wiped his steaming forehead.

"I'll be doggoned if it's here," he said morosely. "Bet you the feller ate it."

"He'd have a job doing that," said Potter slowly. "It was that crisp, tough notepaper. If he'd had a chance to tear it up—but he didn't. He only had a minute, and besides, I'd have heard the paper tear." He stood thoughtfully in front of the fireplace, staring around him. "He only had a minute," he repeated thoughtfully. Suddenly he moved round the desk and took his place behind the chair where Waterman's body had rested. "The light wasn't out more than three minutes," he said slowly. "During that time the murderer had to cross the room from one of the light switches, get the dagger from the desk, kill Gaunt, and get rid of the letter." He looked about him with a puzzled frown. "It's probably in some perfectly obvious place."

"You've been reading too many detective stories," grumbled Collins. "Why don't you look on the chandelier?"

Potter was doing just that. He did not smile. He inspected the old-fashioned pewter chandelier gravely. He got a chair and stood on it and looked closer. It had been designed originally to hold kerosene lamps and the bowls were still in place, although they now held electric bulbs. He ran his hand over them carefully. Then he climbed down and gave his attention to the desk.

"He'd want to get rid of it at the earliest possible moment. Each second meant an additional risk of the light coming on."

"I've been all through the desk," said Collins gloomily.

Potter put his hand wearily over his eyes.

"I seem to remember something," he said. "I can't get it. Some sound." They waited. Suddenly Potter's head snapped back. "I've got it," he said, all trace of fatigue gone. "A click. A soft, sharp click. Quite near me. Now what could it have been?" He leaned over the desk again and suddenly he swore softly under his breath.

In the centre of the wide, polished mahogany stood a big, old-fashioned brass inkwell on a thick glass stand. It had a close-fitting hinged cover surmounted by a poised figure of Mercury. The whole thing measured perhaps eight inches from the desk to the tip of Mercury's winged cap. Potter raised the cover half an inch and closed it sharply. It made a soft, sharp click.

"That's it," he said. "What a dithering idiot! Look at the ink spilled all down the sides of it! The fellow must have had a beastly scare when he saw that. It's been shrieking at me for hours and I never stopped to think that any parlourmaid in a house like this would be fired for leaving an inkwell in that condition."

He took a pen from the rack and fished cautiously in the ink. Carefully he drew out a sodden mass and carefully spread it on the blotter.

"Well," he said, "there you are! And a precious lot of good it does us! Might as well have burned it."

He stood staring down at the sodden sheet from which all trace of writing had been soaked away, and his face was white and grim.

"Smart," he said. "Smart as hell. There's going to be more trouble." He looked across at Collins. "Look here," he said. "I'm not going to wait. Get a boat somewhere and go out to the *Buccaneer*. I want Melvin Saunders and I want Mrs. Gaunt's will, and I want them right away."

Collins groaned. "Why pick on me?" he grumbled. "I don't know one end of an oar from the other."

Potter went to the window and stuck his head out.

"Roberts!" he called softly.

Officer Roberts appeared out of the swathing fog.

"Yes, sir."

"There's probably a boat of some sort down at the wharf. Find it and take this landlubber out to the *Buccaneer*. If there isn't any boat, steal the first one you can find. Harvey will take your place out there till you get back."

Collins turned up his collar with a resigned air.

"Who says you have to join the Navy to see the world? Meet you in Davy Jones's locker," he said sadly, and disappeared into the fog.

Tony Farelli took a last swig of coffee from his thermos bottle, pushed in the cork and screwed the top in place. Then he uncrooked his knees from the spoke of the *Dora's* wheel, glanced at his compass, throttled down the engine to a low hum, and listened intently. Yes, that would be the bellbuoy opposite the breakwater—and high time, too. It was getting lighter than he liked. The murk about him that had been like the Stygian pit was dimly visible now. He could see the oily stir of water over the side. But after all, he reflected philosophically, the only good the light did him was to enable him to see that he couldn't see. For the fog was heavy as ever. It folded back a little to let his boat slip through and closed again behind him, secret and silent and chill. He looked at his watch. It was four-thirty. He lighted a cigarette and sat back comfortably, giving the engine a little more gas. It barked and spat, jerking its way forward slowly, cautiously. Tony smiled. His handsome young face wore a look of smirking satisfaction. A good night's work. By the time the gentleman from the New York side got out of the hospital, he would be more careful to recognise the red-and-black stripes on the wooden buoys that marked the location of Tony's lobster pots. "I betcha I've cured his colour blindness," remarked Tony to himself with a grin.

The *Dora* chugged slowly forward and Tony's eyes, apparently so careless, scanned the wall of fog ahead of him. He would be close in now—not many yards from the tip of the breakwater. Ah! there it was again—the clang of the buoy which Tony knew as well, and had known as long, as his mother's voice. A little to the left. He swung the wheel over and nosed his way past a gray mass, darker and thicker than the gray in which he moved, which he knew to be the end of the breakwater.

Again he shut the engine down and crept forward where, with one hand on the tiller rope, he crouched, staring into the fog. The *Dora* was barely crawling now, rolling a little on the oily surface of the harbour.

Suddenly something high and dark loomed above him. He jerked the rope in his hands and swung to starboard, narrowly escaping collision. As he swung past he could see, curving over him, the beautiful concave bow of the *Buccaneer*, and her name in slender gold letters. The water gurgled between them as the *Dora* righted herself and crept on.

Tony whistled softly and by a natural association of ideas his thoughts turned from his recent exploits to Susan. He would have a story to tell her. How she would laugh! And then he remembered that she was going away—that perhaps he would not see her again for a long time, and the fine edge of his triumph was dulled. He felt a sudden gnawing in the pit of his stomach. She was a good kid—a sweet one. He would not know whom to talk to when she was gone.

He crawled back into the cockpit and shut off the engine completely. He must be very near shore now. As the put-put died away he could hear the rattle of waves on the shingle. That meant he was opposite the Gaunt house, for the shingle stopped farther along. And then he heard another sound—the rhythmic splash of someone swimming, the gasping breath of someone swimming hard, almost at the point of exhaustion. He listened, unable to tell from which direction the sound came. And then it stopped and was succeeded by the crunch of someone walking cautiously on the shingle and then silence.

Tony pursed his lips in a soundless whistle. Something was up, but whatever it was he had no intention of getting mixed up in anything to-night. He couldn't be far from his own moorings now. He got out an oar and began sculling leisurely, watching the landmarks that loomed out of the mist.

It took him perhaps ten minutes to reach his moorings, but he did not anchor then. Something happened of so startling a nature that it disrupted not only his own life for the time being but the life of the whole town of Stone Haven.

Out on the harbour, in the direction from which he had just come, the silence was rent by a sudden detonation. The fog about him was turned for a moment into a sickening red glare; the surface of the bay rocked under him, so that he was almost pitched overboard. He stood appalled, clutching the rail and looking aft. A thin, high cry of anguish rose suddenly and spun itself out into silence. There was a red spot in the fog, growing momentarily more intense, and the roar and crackle of fire. Again he heard shouts from the bay—shouts taken up along the shore in answering cries, the banging of doors, the running of feet.

Tony worked frantically on his engine, getting her started. He knew what it was, right enough. There had been an explosion on the *Buccaneer*. By the look of it she was burning fast. He flung the wheel over furiously. The engine caught and he leapt to the tiller; swinging her round in a wide circle. He hung over the rail, watching the water as far as he could see. Someone had been aboard. Someone had been hurt. Perhaps there were others. He saw a piece of wreckage floating and shutting off his engine, drifted, listening.

He was very close to the fire now—as close in as he dared to go. The air was hot around him. He could see the *Buccaneer* clearly, set in a lurid halo of crimson fog. She seemed to be blazing from stem to stern. Gasoline fires acted that way, of course—incredibly fast. It hadn't been five minutes since the explosion. Now for the first time he remembered the unseen swimmer. What had he been doing in the bay at that hour? "By God!" whispered Tony, and struck his closed fist on the rail.

He shouted into the red twilight.

"*Buccaneer*, ahoy!"

Somewhere off to port a faint voice answered him.

"Help!"

He twirled the wheel and the *Dora* still had sufficient momentum to answer to her helm. He hung over the rail. "Where are you?"

The voice was much nearer now.

"Here! Almost under your bow."

He went forward with the oar in his hand and leaning over, saw a face below him. He thrust the oar down.

"Can you hold it?" he asked. "I'll pull you aft."

Two hands came up and grasped the oar. A moment later Tony was helping Melvin Saunders into the *Dora's* cockpit. He was clad only in pyjamas and there was a long red gash on his forehead from which the blood ran down into his right eye. "I'm all right," he said at once. "Look for the others."

Tony leaned over the rail.

"Ahoy!" he called. There was no answer. The roar of the flames drowned out every other sound. A piece of wreckage, which looked like a wicker deck chair, floated by.

"Who else was on board?" asked Tony.

"Captain M'Neil and two men."

"My God," said Tony.

Saunders joined him at the rail.

"They can't be gone." His teeth chattered so that he could hardly speak and he was shaking from head to foot. "I saw one of the crew just before you came. He was clinging to something—"

Other boats began to appear on the scene. They drew into the circle of light, converging on the burning yacht, the faces of the men in them showing crimson in the reflected glare. Tony shouted to them that there were three men overboard and they began to pull slowly around the *Buccaneer*, as close as they dared. Presently shouts announced the rescue of one survivor, and then another.

A light rowboat, pulling frantically from the direction of the Gaunt House, with Officers Robert at the oars and Collins in the stern, drew into the circle of light. Roberts leaned on his oars a moment and shouted at the nearest boat.

"Anybody found Melvin Saunders?"

The man in the boat pointed at the *Dora* and Roberts swung his craft about and pulled alongside. Collins looked up with relief into Saunders' white face. "What in God's name happened?"

"I don't know," said Saunders. "I was asleep. The explosion threw me out of my berth. Everything seemed to be instantly on fire. I ran for the rail and jumped for it."

"What about Mrs. Gaunt's will?" asked Collins.

"My God!" Saunders collapsed suddenly on the seat that circled the after-rail. "I never thought of it until this instant."

"You locked it in the desk in your cabin?"

"I did," said Saunders. "But if I'd remembered it, I wouldn't have had time to get it out. It was locked up and the key in my trousers pocket."

He stared at the burning yacht. The super-structure had practically disappeared. Only the hull remained—a black basket full of roaring red flowers.

Suddenly there was a loud report. Someone shouted: "The cable's parted." For the moment the audience at that sinister drama forgot everything else. They leaned on their oars, watching.

There was no wind but the tide had turned and was flowing out between the breakwater and the point. The doomed vessel felt the pull and urge under her keel. She seemed to right herself, swing slowly round, her nose turned towards the harbour's mouth, and with a slow, lovely grace, gaining speed as the current caught her, she began to drift sea-ward.

No one spoke. The least imaginative among them was stricken to silence. There was nothing they could do. They followed her without a word, waiting for the fireboat from New London.

Tony turned to Collins.

"What do you want me to do?" he asked.

"Get Saunders ashore, will you? I'll see about the other survivors, but Sergeant Potter wants to see him right away at the Gaunt house. Hell's broke loose there. Waterman Gaunt was murdered during the night."

CHAPTER XIII

STONE HAVEN was staggered by the disaster to the *Buccaneer*. A black pall of horror seemed to hang over the town. The explosion occurred just before five that Sunday morning, and from that time on it seemed as though every able-bodied man, woman, and child who was not in a boat on the harbour was gathered in the crowd that assembled on the rocks beyond the light to watch the burning craft.

She drifted slowly on the tide, beating back the fog with her furious upflung flames, like a desperate, dethroned queen going defiantly to her death, followed by her sorrowing retinue. When the fire-boat from New London reached her she had drifted beyond the breakwater and lay rolling in the trough of smooth, invisible waves, her superstructure gone, her hull a smouldering wreck. At eight o'clock, when the first man boarded her, there was little left of her but her shell, now half full of water, and barely able to support the weight of her blackened engine. He had brought a towline aboard and he climbed forward to affix it to her bow. For a moment, amidship, he disappeared from view. Then he appeared again, clinging to a half-burned remnant of the rail, his face pallid under its coating of grime.

"There's a man here," he shouted, and disappeared again.

And so it happened that the body of Captain M'Neil, who had sailed for the Gaunts for forty years, was placed on an improvised stretcher, covered with a length of canvas, and lowered carefully overside into a police launch, which bore it swiftly to the New London morgue.

The *Buccaneer* was towed back to her moorings and anchored, and a crew sent aboard to pump her out. There was still work for the experts there before she went to the junk pile.

The crowd went home to its belated Sunday breakfast, to be greeted with the news of the murder of Mrs. Gaunt and her son.

Church was but meagerly attended that day. People stood about on street corners and in the local drug stores talking in hushed voices as though in a house of mourning. They looked resentfully at the fog. There was something sinister in its padded silence. As the day wore on and it deepened instead of lightening, it began to share in the conversation with the murders, as though in some curious way it were an actor in the grim drama being played out in that silent house on the point.

People went and stood in the road and looked at the Gaunt house. They could not have said what they expected to see, but it drew them. Its blind face with curtained windows looming through the fog wore a closed, secret look. All day long a small shifting crowd stood before it, for the most part silent, exchanging occasional remarks with the uniformed policeman on the steps.

They observed and commented on the entrance of Otis Avery, the family lawyer, who arrived from New London as early as eight o'clock. They observed the coming and going of the county chief of police, whose arrival was heralded by a police siren shrilling down the quiet street. They watched with amused detachment the manoeuvres of a small army of reporters and newspaper photographers, who descended on the village by train and automobile in the course of the morning.

It being Sunday, Miss Lucetta Brown's notion and drygoods shop was, of course, closed. All day long she sat in her neat little front parlour receiving visitors: her weekday customers coming in to call; newspaper men; photographers who wanted to photograph her house; policemen who wanted to take her testimony.

In spite of her grief and distress, she was fluttered by all this attention. She looked even prettier than usual in her neat blue Sunday silk with her smooth cheeks pink and her blue eyes bright with excitement. The story had got about that she had been one of the first to know of Mrs. Gaunt's death. And, of course, she lived right next to the Gaunts. The excitement of her visitors mounted to fever pitch when it was learned that she had actually witnessed Mrs. Gaunt's will on the night before her death. Miss Lucetta, with some trepidation, told the story in great detail to Collins, whom Potter sent to interview her early in the afternoon.

"Waterman came across to my house himself," she said. "Real late, 'twas, about ten o'clock. Another five minutes and I'd have gone to bed. Said his mother had just written out a legal paper and they needed a witness, and would I go. 'Course I couldn't do anything else, being as I've known Hetty Gaunt all my life. So I put on my coat—the fog was in already and it was real chilly—and I went over.

"Hetty was in the library sitting at the big desk. And Mr. Avery was copying something out on a big sheet of paper. Just as I got there a funny thing happened."

She paused and looked at him doubtfully.

"Yes?" he prompted her. "Please tell me everything, exactly as it happened."

"Something *very* funny happened. The windows were all closed because Hetty hated fog—always has. Well, I'd no sooner got in the room than someone knocked on the window. Wat opened it and that secretary of his, Mr. Saunders, came in through the window.

" 'You're late,' says Waterman.

" 'Couldn't help it,' says Mr. Saunders. 'Can't see your hand in front of your face.'

" 'Well,' says Wat, pretty average snappy. 'Now that you're here, you can witness Mrs. Gaunt's signature to this paper.'

"Mr. Avery passed it over to Hetty.

" 'I think that's all right, Mrs. Gaunt.'

"She read it through and nodded. Then she commenced to laugh. It was weird," confessed Miss Lucetta. "You know what a little thing Hetty was. And there she set up in that great big chair with her feet off the floor, laughing and laughing.

"Mr. Avery looked at her kind of doubtful, like he wasn't sure he liked what was going on, but Wat grinned from ear to ear.

"Finally Mr. Avery said: 'Have you thought this over carefully, Mrs. Gaunt? You are certain this is what you want?'

" 'Yes,' she said, still laughing, 'this is exactly what I want.'

" 'I must insist on making it clear that I have drawn this up under protest,' Mr. Avery said, very solemn. 'I advise against it. I think it most unwise.'

"Wat glowered at him like he wanted to choke him. 'What business is it of yours?' he asked. You could see he was mad clean through.

" 'It's no business of mine any more,' says Avery. 'I wash my hands of it.'

"Hetty stopped laughing.

" 'I know what I'm doing,' she says.

"Mr. Avery bowed, stiff as a poker.

"Hetty looked at me.

" 'I wish I could tell you the joke, Lucetta,' she says, 'but you'll know soon enough.'

"Then she grabbed up a pen from the desk and wrote her name at the bottom of the paper. And then I wrote mine alongside it and Mr. Saunders, he wrote his. Then Hetty folded it up and put it in an envelope and wrote something on the back. Then she looked at Mr. Avery in a sort of funny, sly way.

" 'What do you advise me to do with it?' she asked him.

"I declare, for a minute he got real red in the face. He got his mouth all open to say something and then he didn't. Wat interrupted, sort of deadly polite.

" 'Since Mr. Avery has washed his hands of the matter, I'll take charge of it,' he says. 'Saunders can lock it up on the *Buccaneer* for to-night and we'll put it in your safe-deposit box later.'

"Hetty was willing. 'All right,' she said, and she gave him the envelope. 'It would be better not to leave it in the house.'

"And then she told us the paper was her last will and testament and asked us not to say anything about it till after she was dead."

Miss Lucetta wound up her story with a shiver.

"She didn't know, poor soul, how soon that would be—no, nor *how* it would be, either. We never know what the future holds in *this* world." And she sighed, her eyes suddenly filled with tears.

It was two o'clock in the afternoon when a new rumour began to go around the village. Old Captain Gaunt's body was to be exhumed—was being exhumed—had already been exhumed. Dr. Blake was doing an autopsy. It was thought he'd been murdered too. No one knew. He had been murdered. He hadn't been murdered. It was all a hoax staged by a tabloid newspaper. It wasn't a hoax. It was true. Old Captain Gaunt had been killed in the same way his wife and eldest son had been killed—with the dagger from the black hawthorn jar.

And now, for the first time, oddly enough, the history of the Gaunt family was dragged out from attics of memory into the light. People began to talk, with a smirk intended to cover half-credulity, of the "curse of the Gaunts." It was remembered that the first Waterman Gaunt had led a violent and sinful life, had broken every law of God and man, and had died, accused, by his brother's hand. And now it appeared that his son and his grandson had also died by violence. People shrugged their shoulders and old women said to each other: "Unto the third and fourth generation."

A delighted newspaper man got the tale from the owner of the village speakeasy, and the next morning the papers carried a lurid and colourful yarn, adorned with a picture of the *Seabird* reprinted from the official biography of the first Waterman Gaunt, along with a portrait of her Captain with side whiskers and a choker. The tale was embellished by an interview with the village ancient who was reported to have said that he remembered as a child being afraid to pass the Gaunt house at night for fear old Captain Gaunt's ghost would jump out and eat him. Actually, however, the rumours concerning the autopsy on the exhumed body of Waterman Gaunt II anticipated the reality. It was not until five o'clock that Sergeant Potter, called to the telephone, received Dr. Blake's official confirmation of his suspicion. He listened at some length to the doctor's remarks and then he said:

"So you think it's safe to say there's no reasonable doubt that he was murdered?"

"There's no doubt at all," snapped Blake with unusual brusqueness. "Of course, after two years, it's not as obvious as in the case of Mrs. Gaunt, but there's a lot of indirect evidence—quite conclusive. I'm making out a detailed medical report, but you may take that as final."

"Three little murders in a row," murmured Potter. "Not to mention that gasoline explosion on the *Buccaneer*. How sweet!"

"Good God!" cried Blake. "Was that deliberate?"

Potter had been talking to Tony Farelli. He frowned wearily at the mouthpiece of the telephone.

"Oh, I should think so," he said. "I've got a witness who heard someone swimming ashore to the Gaunt place about ten minutes before the yacht blew up."

"Did he see who it was?" asked Blake eagerly.

"Listen," said Potter patiently. "Get this into your head. Nobody's seen anybody; nobody's done anything; everybody's innocent as the babe unborn. Not five minutes after the explosion I had everyone in the house checked up and they were all in their rooms, in their night clothes, with no wet clothes or towels anywhere to be found. Talk about murder as a fine art! They've got it down to a science in this house. They're an able family. Perhaps if I wait long enough there'll only be one left and then I can nab him by a process of elimination."

"You're tired," said Blake soothingly. "You'll see it clearer in the morning."

"You're doggoned right, I'm tired," said Potter, "and I'm afraid to go to sleep for fear something else will happen."

He hung up with a sigh and stood for a moment staring unseeing at the telephone. Then with another sigh he opened the door of the telephone closet and went back to the library.

CHAPTER XIV

OTIS AVERY was standing in front of a crackling fire in the library. He was a stout man, almost bald, with a ruddy face and small, shrewd eyes. One knew that, rain or shine, he played golf every Saturday afternoon and all day Sunday. He affected a slightly English style of dress and dangled a pair of glasses on a black ribbon. He had been Mrs. Gaunt's lawyer and Captain Gaunt's before that, for many years.

Beside him, in a big, leather-covered chair, Melvin Saunders lounged exhaustedly. His ugly, pleasant face showed the marks of his experience. Horror lurked in the back of the gray eyes that stared so persistently into the fire. But he made no parade of his condition.

Up and down the length of the room, passing and repassing the gray oblongs of the fog-shrouded windows, Daniel Minton paced nervously.

They had been talking in the desultory fashion of men exhausted by a frightful ordeal. As Potter entered the room they started nervously, turning expectant, questioning eyes to him.

"Blake says there's no doubt of it," he said. "Captain Gaunt was murdered—same as the others. Signs of internal hæmorrhage, etc."

Avery stopped dangling his glasses and began to wipe them with meticulous care on a clean handkerchief. Saunders' lips set more tightly. Minton threw up his hands in a gesture of horror, dropped them again, and resumed his interrupted pacing. Potter sat down wearily and stared into the fire.

After a moment Minton came forward and, leaning on the desk, looked across at Avery.

"I appreciate that this is a devilish situation," he said, "and God knows I'm as sorry about Aunt Hetty and Wat as anybody—sorrier, maybe, because I didn't have to live with them. But my duty is clear—and yours, too, sir, if I may say so. We've got to save what we can out of the wreck. There'll be the devil to pay on the Street to-morrow. I'll have to be there in the morning—although heaven knows there's not much I can do."

"Sorry," said Potter, "but no one leaves Stone Haven until this affair is cleared up."

"You've no right to hold me," flared Minton angrily. "This is a damn serious matter."

"It is," said Potter grimly. "And you'll all stay here till it's settled. I'm sorry to inconvenience you, but if anyone makes a move to leave, I'll clap 'em into jail as a material witness."

Minton looked at the point of an explosion, but after a minute he shrugged and turned to Avery.

"Did you know that Aunt Hetty's been buying Meridian, too? We both got in early before there was any gossip about the merger. It's been skyrocketing—but there will be hell to pay to-morrow. Apparently it's got about all over the place that Aunt Hetty's will was burned up on the yacht."

"Lucetta Brown's been telling it," nodded Potter. "She'd given the story to the papers before I could stop it."

"The newspapers!" Minton groaned. "Where does this will business leave us, anyway?" Avery cleared his throat uneasily. "If it can be proved that Mrs. Gaunt's will was destroyed—"

"That should not be difficult," said Melvin Saunders. "I saw her sign it and put it in an envelope, which she sealed. She admitted in my presence that it was her last will and testament, and made a note to that effect on the envelope. Mr. Gaunt then put the envelope in my hands and instructed me to lock it up in my cabin on the yacht. I did so. Last night, when I went to bed, I looked to make sure it was still there. It was, with the seal unbroken. I did not remove it after the explosion. I didn't have time. And I understand everything on the yacht was destroyed."

"Could anyone have taken it from your cabin while you slept?" asked Potter.

"Impossible. I had locked the door when I went in. I had to unlock it when I went out. And the ports were too small for anyone to get in that way."

"Then," said Avery, "if the Courts accept your story, as I have no doubt will be the case, we are in the same position that we would have occupied if Mrs. Gaunt had made no will. The property will be divided equally among the next of kin, which, in this case, will be her children."

"Even though you drew her will and could swear to her intentions?" asked Potter.

"Even so," nodded Avery. "The point has, of course, arisen many times before, and in only one case that I can recall have the courts ruled otherwise. And in that case they permitted the rough draft of the lost will to be probated. There was, however, peculiar points about the circumstances—and there was no question of the will being contested, as, I take it, would undoubtedly happen in this case."

Melvin Saunders shook a cigarette from his pack, put it between his lips and lighted it. His face was grim. "This is going to be a serious blow to Mrs. Ingersoll," he said.

They all stared at him.

"How so?" asked Avery coldly.

"I sound vindictive," admitted Saunders, "but I'm not—although I don't like the lady. But I think you ought to know, for what it is worth, that Mr. Gaunt had his will drawn about a year ago, when I first came to him. In it, so he told me, he left the bulk of his estate to Mrs. Ingersoll."

Minton whistled softly. "How long has he been keeping her, do you know?"

"I never heard. I had an idea it was quite a recent arrangement at that time."

"Odd he should have told you about the will."

Melvin Saunders hesitated.

"I think," he said, frowning at the glowing tip of his cigarette, "he was trying to justify himself. He told me he expected to marry Mrs. Ingersoll as soon as it could be arranged. He was an odd chap. He was always afraid of being criticised."

"Do you think he really intended to marry Mrs. Ingersoll?" asked Potter.

"I think he did at the time. He seemed to be perfectly infatuated."

"But you think he weakened?"

"Towards the end," nodded Saunders. "After all, he'd found the current arrangement very pleasant and he didn't want to run the risk of his mother's displeasure. Recently they've had scenes. I gathered that he was putting her off. They had one, in fact, the afternoon we arrived here."

Potter pricked up his ears.

"Did you overhear it?"

"Yes, I did," said Saunders steadily. "In part. She was angry because he wouldn't take her ashore with him. That was why she dressed up as soon as he'd gone and made her brother take her to the Michitiquock Club."

"There's a rumour that she lost heavily."

"She did," said Saunders. "I went into the main cabin next morning and found her crying into her cantaloupe. She said she was going to commit suicide if Mr. Gaunt didn't come across."

"It's a funny thing," said Minton softly. "Rex Olsen asked Nancy to put them up here—just a few hours before the *Buccaneer* was blown up."

Saunders cocked an eyebrow at the fire.

"Apparently," said Avery, "you don't agree with that suggestion."

Saunders looked across at Potter.

"I see that Sergeant Potter agrees with me. It doesn't make sense. Why in the world would they want to destroy Mrs. Gaunt's will? If that will were probated, Mrs. Ingersoll would be one of the richest women in this part of the country. As it is, I suppose she won't get anything?" He looked inquiringly at Avery.

"If you are right about Waterman's will, she'll get his share," he said, "since Wat survived his mother."

"Still," insisted Saunders, "it doesn't make sense."

"I suppose," said Potter slowly, "it's not inevitably true that the same person blew up the yacht."

Mr. Avery again cleared his throat.

"I suggest," he said, "that it has not yet been demonstrated that the yacht was blown up at all—I mean, of course, deliberately. I am not a mechanic, but it seems to me that that would not be a very simple thing to do. It would require considerable technical knowledge."

"Not necessarily," said Minton. "After all, nowadays, practically everybody knows something about automobile engines—and a gas engine on a yacht is not very different. The principle remains the same."

Potter nodded, his eyes on Avery.

"Mr. Minton is quite right. Of course I'll have to have expert opinion, but I wouldn't count too much on finding that that explosion was an accident."

In the upstairs sitting-room Matthew Ryder sat with Nancy before the fire. A tea tray stood on a low table at her elbow, but they had finished their half-hearted pretence of drinking tea. The room was full of a bleak, blue half-light, warmed only by the ruddy glow of the fire.

Nancy seemed lost in a mournful reverie, her unseeing eyes on the flickering flames. Ryder studied her pale face anxiously. Her gallantry, in this unguarded moment, could not quite cover her exhaustion or her fear. Presently, with a sigh, he leaned forward and laid his hand on hers.

She spoke without looking up. "Will you have to go back to New York to-morrow?"

"No," he said. "I arranged that by telephone this afternoon. I will stay as long as you need me."

Her hand turned so that the palm clung to his. After a moment he bent and kissed it, and laid his cheek against it. "As far as I can see," he said at last, "there is nothing we can do but wait."

"My dear," she said without stirring, scarcely above a breath, "I am afraid."

He said nothing. He turned her hand in his, caressing it gently, his eyes on the long slender fingers.

"My mother—Wat—and now father!" whispered Nancy. "Oh, do you think they can be right about father? It's so long!"

"I'm afraid so." He felt her trembling.

"Matthew, I'm afraid!" she said again.

He looked at her in wonder and dismay. After a moment he said softly: "How long were you with Wat in your mother's room last night?"

"I went in about half-past ten. I saw the light. He was going through mother's papers. I stayed and helped him. She had an enormous amount of stuff stored in her closet and desk. I don't suppose she'd torn up a letter in forty years. We didn't even get through what was in the desk. I stayed until I heard your voice in the hall. I don't know what time it was."

"After twelve," said Ryder. "About half-past, I should think."

She turned her lovely eyes to him for the first time. "Why do you ask?"

"You weren't with Wat when he found that letter—the letter that was taken from him when he was killed?"

A faint flicker of the eyes told him that she understood the purport of his question.

"No," she said quietly.

"Nancy, for God's sake—" His voice shook and he hesitated a moment, steadying himself. "You don't know—you haven't the faintest idea—what was in that letter?"

There was a little pause while she studied his anguished face. Then her own lit faintly with such a smile as a mother might give to a frightened child.

"No," she said, "I don't know—in the way you mean. I didn't see the letter. I didn't know there was such a letter until Wat produced it—downstairs in the library."

"Oh thank God!" He hid his face from her, leaning his forehead on her hands.

"But of course," said Nancy, "I have an idea what was in it."

"Yes. Yes—of course." He got to his feet and stood before her, back to the fire. "That's obvious, I should think."

"It's not so very obvious," said Nancy, frowning doubtfully. "Mother must have found something—" She broke off with a desperate gesture. "Matthew, I don't know what to think. I've been going over it until I'm half crazy."

"I know, my dear, I know."

"No," cried Nancy with a strange look, "you don't know."

"Can you tell me?"

"Not even you."

Ryder looked down at her with kind, comprehending eyes.

"My dear, I believe—I believe with all my heart—that you distress yourself needlessly."

"You mean—"

"I mean that I do not believe that your mother killed your father."

Nancy went as white as the collar of her black dress. "How did you—"

"If Susan is right," Ryder went on gently, "and your mother expected to find that the black hawthorn jar had been opened and resealed—don't you see that clears her?

If she'd done it herself she wouldn't have needed to look. It means—it must mean—that she'd just discovered something that led her to connect the dagger in the jar with your father's death."

Nancy spoke with trembling lips.

"But how could she—a clue, after two years?"

"It's the only theory that explains the facts," said Ryder gently. "Wat said the paper was an unfinished letter from your mother to Mr. Avery and that it contained a reference to the dagger in the jar. Clearly it explained, in Waterman's mind, Mrs. Gaunt's death, too. She must have discovered something that would point, ultimately, to your father's murderer. Evidently the murderer thought so, anyway. Otherwise, why should he take the fearful risk of killing Wat as he did?"

Nancy put her hands to her face. "I wish I could think so. Matthew, I would—I would give so much if I could think so."

The despair in her voice almost broke his heart.

"Let me help you."

"Not even you—not now—not until I have decided what I must do."

She left him presently and Ryder went along the hall to his own room. He went in and closed the door behind him. The room was dim with a premature, foggy twilight. He took off his coat and threw himself down on the bed. He was dead tired. The awful night through which they had all passed, the strain and anxiety of the day culminating in this interview with Nancy, had told heavily on him. He lay on the bed like a stone, neither awake nor asleep, in a sort of suspended animation.

But presently fantastic patterns began to form and re-form before his eyes. Susan's face, full of gallant defiance: Carey's terrified look before he had plunged forward unconscious on the library floor. A bad business, that. Poor lad, it was more than probable he had his mother's heart. But what was it that had precipitated that attack? The long strain of the night? But there had been terror in the boy's face. Terror of something Susan was about to say?

Ryder shook the thought from him, tried to shake all thought from him. But a new picture rose into his consciousness. Astrid Ingersoll quarrelling with Waterman behind the closed door of his mother's room. What was it she had said? "I have ways of defending myself." What did she mean? What was the meaning of any of this ghastly business? And Nancy—Nancy's face white and anguished; Nancy's voice saying: "Matthew, I am afraid!" He sat up, unable to be still.

And suddenly he gasped and stared incredulously, for from where he sat he could see, silhouetted against the gray square of the window, the outline of a man sitting in a chair.

"Who's there?" he asked sharply.

The figure in the chair turned its head towards him. "I'm drunk," said Edgar's voice thickly. " 'xtremely drunk. Hope you don't mind."

"What are you doing there?"

"Watching. Couldn't see from my room—other side the house. Took the liberty. Hope you don't mind."

Dr. Ryder got up from the bed.

"What are you watching?"

Edgar chuckled thickly.

"Elvira. She thinks I don't know. Thinks I'm blind drunk. But that's where she's wrong. Smart woman-Elvira—but I'm smarter."

"What are you talking about?"

"Come here and I'll show you." He sat forward, peering out the window. "Almost too dark now, but the fog's lifting. There they are—down there."

Ryder saw that Edgar was right. There was a faint breeze stirring and the fog moved before it, gustily. Now and again it lifted a little, giving a brief glimpse of the garden and beyond the waters of the bay. Through one of these momentary vistas Ryder saw, down by the sea wall, two figures moving back and forth, side by side.

"There they are," repeated Edgar triumphantly.

"Who are they?"

"Elvira and her lover, Daniel Minton."

"You're drunk," said Ryder with disgust. "You don't know what you're saying."

"I'm drunk, all right," said Edgar, chuckling, "but I'm not *that* drunk. She thinks because she's got the whip hand—because the money's hers—she can do as she likes. But I'll show her."

"What do you mean the money's hers? You've plenty of your own, haven't you?"

"I have now," said Edgar cunningly.

"Your father gave you a lot when you married."

"Ran through it long ago," said Edgar sadly. "Terrible mistake. She's ridden me like a devil ever since. That," said Edgar solemnly, "is why I took to drink—in a serious way, I mean. Self-defence. But it's all over now. I'll be well fixed. I can snap my fingers at her—and I will. I'll divorce her."

"Because of Daniel? Don't be absurd. Suppose she does flirt a bit—"

"Flirt?" There was an ugly note in Edgar's laugh. "The thing I can't understand," he said after a minute, "is what *his* game is. Unless he wants to keep a second string to his bow in case you cut him out. Did you see his face last night when Nancy was going on about her devotion to you?"

Ryder went suddenly cold. "Please explain yourself," he said in a barely audible voice.

"Well, of course Nancy's his first choice. She'll be rather warmer than Elvira—now mother's dead. And she's years younger."

Ryder grasped his visitor by the shoulders and jerked him suddenly to his feet.

"Are you insinuating that Minton is bothering Nancy?" he asked harshly.

"Well," drawled Edgar, "you might call it bothering, although I'm not altogether sure that's the right word. After all, he's a handsome devil."

Ryder's hands relaxed and fell to his side.

"Get out," he said in a low voice.

"I beg your pardon?" said Edgar politely.

"Get out. Oh, get out. You're drunk."

"Yes," said Edgar in a surprised voice, "I believe I am. Talk too much. Beastly bad form. Apologise."

"Get out."

"Certainly, old fellow. Certainly. Show me the door and I'll go."

For a minute Ryder did not move. Then he led Edgar into the communicating bathroom, drew a basin of cold water, and bade him dip his head in it. After a few minutes of floundering Edgar emerged. Ryder had turned on the lights and he looked critically at Edgar's flushed face.

"That's better. Now listen to me. We'll forget what you've just told me. Forget it absolutely. And you'll stay sober—at least until the police are through with this case."

"Can't do it, old fellow," muttered Edgar. "Know you mean well, but—hang it all, Matthew, you know I can't."

"You've got to," said Ryder grimly. "If you spill that stuff to Potter, I believe he'll arrest you for your mother's murder."

Edgar blanched a dreadful blue-white.

"My God!" he muttered.

"You're to stay sober and forget about Elvira and her affairs—if she really has any, which I doubt."

"Yes, I will—by God, I will!"

"I'll have Hannah bring you up some coffee. Go on back to your room and clean up."

Edgar turned unsteadily towards the door.

"Good of you," he muttered. "Won't forget it. And don't you forget what I told you, either."

"Get out," said Ryder irritably.

Edgar went.

For ten minutes after he had gone Ryder stood in the window staring blindly out into the garden. Then he washed his face and brushed his hair and knocked on the door of Carey's room.

CHAPTER XV

SUSAN's voice bade him enter. He went in and found her sitting by her brother's bedside. She had been there most of the day. As she rose on his entrance Ryder was reminded, curiously enough, of a watch-dog crouching at his master's feet, sniffing suspiciously at each intruder. Not that Susan crouched. She stood quietly by the bed, watching him with doubtful eyes.

He sat down in the chair she had vacated and laid his fingers professionally on Carey's wrist.

"Feeling better?" he asked, smiling.

Carey's haggard eyes stared at him resentfully.

"I'm all right. I'm going to get up, I'll go crazy if I stay here any longer. I'd have been up hours ago but Susan made such a fuss I gave in. For heaven's sake, Matthew, let me out of this."

"To-morrow morning," said Ryder soothingly. "You can stick it till then. You don't want to keel over again, you know."

"But I can't stand it—lying here and thinking and nothing to do. Lying awake all night and thinking."

Ryder studied the drawn, tortured face curiously.

"You won't lie awake," he said quietly. "I'll give you something."

"I thought you said," accused Susan, "that he was not to be bothered."

"I did," said Ryder. "Who's been bothering him?"

"Potter was here for an hour this afternoon quizzing him. I'll admit he was very decent about it, but—"

"Decent!" interrupted Carey irritably. "It was plain as the nose on your face he thought this attack of mine was a put-up job and that I could tell him all about everything if I wanted to."

"You imagined it. Why should he think you could tell him anything—that is, anything more than the rest of us? He's been questioning everybody, of course."

"He seemed to think there was something funny in our bathing suits—Susan's and mine—being wet just after the

Buccaneer was blown up. They were hanging out on the rail on the upper porch, you know."

Ryder nodded. "We hung them there when we came in from swimming. Of course they were wet. How the devil would they be anything else, with a heavy fog all day?"

"Oh, shut up, Carey!" interrupted Susan, with exasperation. "We've been over that a million times."

"Well, I'm sick of being hounded about it. I'm sick of being treated as though I were a malingerer." He sat up in bed and glared at his sister. "You know perfectly well that Potter believes I killed mother and Wat. He spent twenty minutes trying to make me admit I knew there was a dagger in the jar."

Susan turned her pallid face entreatingly to Ryder.

"Can't you do anything for him? If he goes on this way, God only knows what will happen."

Ryder went through the connecting door into his own room. He came back in a moment with a bottle in his hand. He poured out two tablets and gave them to Carey. As he took them, the boy gave Ryder a curious look, penetrating, questioning, but he made no protest and said nothing more. A moment later Perkins knocked on the door and told Susan that Mr. West was downstairs and asked to see her. For a moment Susan hesitated; then she said: "Tell him I'm dressing, but that I'll be with him in a moment."

"I'll stay with Carey awhile," offered Ryder.

Susan thanked him and went along the hall to her own room.

Jimmy West stood in the drawing-room waiting for Susan. It had been ten minutes since she had sent down word that she was dressing, but would be with him in a few minutes. Knowing Susan, he had composed himself for a long wait in the deep easy chair by the fire, but he found that it did not do. He was too restless, too horribly upset. He jerked to his feet and began to prowl about the room, lighting cigarettes and throwing them, half-smoked, into the fire. His usually cheery face was creased with anxiety and distress. His usually immaculate collar was wilted. His crinkly blonde hair, usually slicked down in an ineffectual effort to eliminate the curl, showed a tendency to stand on end. He looked like a young man whose beloved has suddenly become involved in a more than ordinarily horrible murder mystery.

He watched the hands of the ormolu clock on the mantel move with incredible slowness from seven to half-past, and swore under his breath. The atmosphere of the room became insufferably close; the silence, broken only by the crackling of the fire, the ticking of the clock, and an occasional distant voice, seemed more than he could bear.

Ordinarily he loved this room. It had always seemed to him beautiful with the stiff, quaint charm of a bygone generation: soft green walls and heavy crimson curtains falling to the floor, elaborately looped across the top and held in place by preposterous wreaths of gilt rosebuds; white marble mantel, elaborately scrolled; a large mirror that reached from floor to ceiling, framed in ornate gold leaf. From the luxurious Turkey carpet on the floor to the elaborately decorated ceiling it was a perfect example of its period: elegant, a little pompous, a little ridiculous, wholly charming.

But to-night he hated it. It seemed like a prison to him—a pretty cage, confining his Susan's sky-loving wings. He wanted to lay about him to smash the Dresden figures on the mantel and the china dog on the hearth, and the round gilt foot-stools with their flowered tops.

Susan came in so quietly that he did not hear her.

"For Pete's sake, Jimmy, stand still, can't you? You give me the willies."

He turned and looked at her bright hostile eyes. He loved that white dress she was wearing. He thought, with a lover's bromidic enthusiasm, that she looked like an angel. So he growled irritably.

"Anybody'd think you were dressing for a ball, the time you took."

Susan glared at him with angry sweetness.

"I suppose you thought I'd be waiting all day on the doorstep till you got around to coming."

He wiped his forehead with a grimy handkerchief.

"Listen, Susan. I drove up to Boston yesterday. I didn't even know about your mother's death or—or anything—until this afternoon. And I've been coming hell-bent for leather ever since. I haven't even been home yet, as you see."

Susan looked him up and down and amusement began to crinkle round her eyes.

"I see. Don't they have newspapers in Boston any more?" she asked sweetly.

"When would I see any newspapers?" demanded Jimmy aggrievedly. "Tom Blount threw a bachelor party last night for Heinie. You know that. I didn't come to till three o'clock this afternoon."

"Oh!" said Susan blankly. "But you were supposed to usher at the wedding to-night."

"What are weddings to me?" said Jimmy lightly.

Susan's eyed filled. She searched unsuccessfully for a handkerchief.

"I've caught the damndest cold," she muttered irritably. And then suddenly she was in Jimmy West's arms and he was comforting her rapturously.

"Susie! Little Susie!"

"I'm as tall as you are," sobbed Susan stormily. "I hate you. I never cry—never!"

"It's good for you," said West soothingly, and he wiped her eyes with a grimy handkerchief. "It's good for any woman to weep on a manly bosom now and then. Restores their sense of inferiority so often regrettably absent these days."

"Jimmy, you're a fool. Don't you know this is serious?"

"I'm glad you think so. I've been trying to impress it on you for two years."

"Oh, you!" said Susan scornfully. "They've arrested Tony!"

"My God!" cried West, astounded. "For the murders?"

"No, you idiot, of course not. They've arrested him for knifing a man out on the Sound last night."

And she told him about Tony's punitive expedition. "They'd never have caught him except that he was decent enough to tell the police about hearing that man swim ashore from the *Buccaneer*. Of course he had to tell the whole story, so they arrested him and now they say he'll have to stay in jail till the man dies or gets well."

"Oh, he'll get well, all right," said Jimmy cheerfully. "Those fellows always do."

"Yes," agreed Susan reasonably. "But meanwhile Tony has to stay in jail—and anyway they'll probably charge him with assault, or something. I think," she added, "they're really more interested in him as a witness than anything else." She looked up at Jimmy with a submissive admiring look that roused his suspicions at once. "Couldn't you do something about it?"

"You have got a nerve," he said with grudging admiration. "Why should I get the blighter out of jail?"

"Because it would be such a decent thing to do," said Susan coolly. "You could do it if you wanted to."

"Yes," admitted Jimmy warily. "They'd probably let him out on bail—with a little persuasion."

He stared at her gravely. "Look here, darling, I want to ask you a plain question."

"All right." She was trembling a little, but he didn't notice.

"I know you think I'm a joke," he said painfully.

"No, I don't."

"I think you do, a little, *au fond*. But I'm terribly fond of you. That isn't a joke." He swallowed painfully. "Do you love Tony?"

"No," said Susan. "But I think he's a swell guy. I want him out of jail."

"Well," said Jimmy, "and you shall have him out of jail. Practically instantly, if you like. The banks are all closed, but I imagine they'll take my cheque."

"I imagine they will," said Susan, smiling. "Jimmy, you're an angel—really."

"I didn't know there was any doubt about it. 'Bye."

"Wait a minute!"

Try as she would, Susan could not stay the anxious glance over her shoulder, the frightened look into the hall. Jimmy was back at her side in an instant. He grasped her shoulders and forced her to look at him. He could feel her trembling now, could see the terror lurking at the back of her eyes.

"Susie, this doesn't involve you in any way? You're not in danger?" He spoke scarcely above his breath.

Susan smiled crookedly.

"Of course it involves me. Every one of us is involved. We all had motive to burn. Potter just hasn't decided which of us it is."

Jimmy looked her in the eye. "Is it just this general suspicion that's worrying you?"

"No," said Susan flatly.

"Got any evidence you want destroyed? If so, I'm your man."

"Is that why you rushed back from Boston?"

West nodded.

"Do you think I did it?" asked Susan.

"Don't be an ass!"

Susan drew a long breath. When she spoke it was under her breath. "Tell Tony I've got to see him—right away. You've got to arrange it somehow between you so that nobody'll know."

"Righto! Anything else?"

Susan managed a smile. "Not for the moment. You might drop in to-morrow. Perhaps I'll ask you to burn the papers then."

"Fine!" Finding himself so conveniently near, he kissed her in a matter-of-fact manner. " 'Bye," he said with outward calmness, and started for the door. But again she stopped him.

"Jimmy—"

He turned in the doorway, smiling.

"I don't think you're a joke—*au fond* or any other way. I think you're swell."

"Fine!" said Jimmy gayly. "See you later!" And he disappeared.

When he had gone Susan stood for a moment very still, forcing her shaking limbs to quietness, steadying her trembling lips. Then she went upstairs again and knocked on Carey's door.

CHAPTER XVI

AFTER supper that Sunday evening Potter interviewed the servants, one after the other, in the little corner room that opened out of the library. He had sent for Perkins first and explained his wishes.

"Yes, sir," said Perkins. "They're all ready. We've been expecting it."

"Oh, you've been expecting it?" repeated Potter, looking at him questioningly.

"I understand it's usual, sir."

His tone implied a certain reproof that Potter had neglected this obvious duty so long. The detective studied the butler's long, thin face with interest: an intelligent face it was. He fancied that not much escaped the shrewd eyes under the drooping lids. A dependable face, too; decent; the face of a man who would be loyal to his salt.

"I understand that you were Captain Gaunt's valet until his death?"

"Yes, sir. His manservant," Perkins corrected gently.

"You helped to take care of him during his illness?"

"Yes, sir. Dr. Ryder used to say he ought to have a nurse, but we managed very well."

"You were fond of Captain Gaunt, Perkins?'"

The butler looked a little shocked.

"I admired him, sir. He was a very just man."

"Did it ever occur to you that his death might not have been a natural one?"

"Never, sir. We knew that he might die at any time. I thought, like everyone else, that he had died in his sleep."

Potter nodded.

"Now about last Friday night. I understand that the whole family left here about eight o'clock to dine at the Michitiquock Club?"

"That is correct, sir. They all went except old Mrs. Gaunt."

"And Mr. Waterman Gaunt arrived about nine?"

"Yes, sir. I admitted him myself."

"Did you know up to that time that the *Buccaneer* was in the harbour?"

"I did not know it then, sir. It was very foggy, as you know, and no one saw her come in. I did not know how Mr. Gaunt had arrived until Reeves, his man, came ashore a little later with his luggage."

"Had you expected Mr. Gaunt that evening?"

"No, sir. Not until a few minutes before he arrived. Then Mrs. Gaunt rang for me in the library and told me to wait up until Mr. Gaunt arrived and then I could go to bed. She would not require me again that night."

"So his mother expected him?"

"Evidently, sir."

"Did you know of Mr. Avery's arrival?"

"Yes, sir. He arrived about ten minutes before Mr. Gaunt. I admitted him and showed him into the library."

"Do you think that the other members of the family knew Mr. Gaunt was expected?"

"I can't say, sir."

"And you've nothing further to contribute about what you saw last night when Mr. Gaunt was killed?"

The butler's face grew a shade paler.

"Nothing, sir."

"To your knowledge, did anyone know of the existence of the dagger in the black hawthorn jar?"

"No, sir. I would swear, sir, that no one in the house knew what was in the jar."

Potter looked at the man's immobile face with exasperation. He was sure he was holding back something—some suspicion—some knowledge. As well try to get information from an oyster—or a rock of his native New England granite. The detective shrugged. "Tell Reeves I'd like to see him, please."

"Yes, sir."

The valet was altogether a more hopeful proposition: dapper and quick, with a knowing eye. He'd been with Waterman Gaunt only six months but there seemed to be very little about his master's business that he hadn't learned in that time. And what he didn't know he was willing to guess. He described in lavish detail Astrid Ingersoll's modernistic penthouse apartment on Central Park West, her jewels and her clothes.

"Crazy about her, he was, Sergeant. Nothing too good for her. Used to wangle money from his mother."

"Did Mrs. Gaunt know about all this?"

Reeves winked elaborately.

"She made out she didn't, but she was smart as hell. I'll bet you she had it all figured out it was the easiest way to keep him happy."

"Think he intended to marry her?"

Reeves winked again.

"Maybe, along at first. But he was sitting pretty as it was. He'd have been a fool to marry her. She'd have been a hellion, once she had him where she wanted him—and her brother too. Those are a pair of tough babies, all right, Sergeant. Out for what they can get, and don't you forget it. Only way to keep 'em in hand was to keep 'em dangling."

"Know anything about Olsen?"

"Drinks like a fish and gambles like nobody's business."

"Anything crooked?"

"Not that I know—but I'm willing to guess."

"All right," Potter nodded curtly in dismissal. "Send that parlourmaid in—the one that testified about the jar last night."

"The good-looking one," said Reeves with another wink. "Maud." And he retired with the grin still on his face.

Maud, when she arrived a moment later, was clearly in a state of terror. Her pretty Irish eyes were red with weeping and her manner timid.

Potter smiled at her. "Sit down," he said. "I'm not going to eat you up."

"Oh, sir!" gasped Maud. She looked undecided whether to cry or giggle, but finally decided on the latter.

"I want you to help me," said Potter, drawing his chair nearer to her. "I'm sure you can if you will."

She stole a fearful look at him but seemed reassured by what she saw. Potter's craggy face could look very gentle when he chose.

"Y-yes, sir, said Maud doubtfully.

"I want you to tell me anything you can about this very sad business."

And now again, surprisingly, Maud began to cry.

"Oh. he didn't do it—I know he didn't."

"I'm sure you're right," said Potter, "but who is he?"

"Mr. Carey, sir. They're all saying he did it, but he didn't. He wouldn't hurt a fly. Always very kind and gentlemanly. And his mother treated him terrible. Always shouting at him. I hate to speak ill of the dead, sir, but she was a wicked, selfish old lady. It wouldn't have cost her much, with all she had."

"What wouldn't have cost her much?"

"To let him go to Paris, like he wanted. He writes something lovely, sir, and he wanted to study to be a writer. But she wouldn't let him."

"How do you know what he wants to do?"

"He—he—" Maud flushed crimson to the tips of her pretty ears. "He told me," she finished in a whisper.

Potter looked at the girl's honest, gentle face and he sighed.

"So he wanted to go to Paris and his mother wouldn't let him. Did they quarrel about it?"

"Yes, sir. That is—oh, I might as well tell you or someone else will. Yes, they did quarrel about it."

"When?"

"Oh, a lot of times. But he didn't do it, sir. He couldn't. He used to talk about how fine his mother was and how fond he was of her in spite of everything, and her devilling him so."

Potter dropped the subject. "How about Miss Susan? Did she get on well with her mother?"

The pretty mouth just now so soft and beseeching hardened into a grim line. Maud even went so far as to toss her head.

"Well," she said, "I'm not one to carry tales."

"I know she's a friend of Tony Farelli's," said Potter wearily.

"Friend!" exclaimed Maud, the parlourmaid, scornfully. "Slips out to meet him at all hours—doesn't care when she gets in. Why, Sergeant Potter,"—the honest Irish face was scandalised—"the night her mother lay dead, I heard her with him down in the garden after midnight. And she swears and drinks cocktails."

Potter had lost interest. "Ask Mrs. Perkins to come in, please," he said, "as you go out."

Maud cast an indignant look at him and flounced out of the room. Mrs. Perkins, the cook, was a stout, pleasant-faced woman of perhaps forty-five. Potter reflected, as he pulled forward a chair for her, that she would have made two of her husband. He studied her for a moment thoughtfully. There was good sense in her face, and kindness.

"Mrs. Perkins," he said at last, "I want you to help me on a difficult point. I assure you that what you tell me will remain confidential unless it turns out to have a bearing on the case."

"I'll tell you anything I can," she said readily. "Way I figure it, there's a poor old man and woman been done to death, not to mention their oldest son. It's not time to hold things back, as I told Perkins."

Potter nodded. "I've been told by a good many people," he said, "that Edgar Gaunt and his wife don't get on too well. Is that true?"

"Lands sakes, sir, that's no secret. They quarrel like cat and dog. Everybody knows it."

"What about?"

"Money, mostly. But lately there's been something else."

"Yes?"

She turned troubled eyes on him.

"I hate to say it, sir—particularly as I'm sure there's nothing in it."

"If there's nothing in it, it will go no further."

"Well," said Mrs. Perkins uncomfortably, "they had a quarrel last week—you could hear it out in the hall—about Mr. Minton. Maggie—that's Mrs. Gaunt's maid—told me. Said Mr. Edgar was accusing her of carrying on with his cousin Daniel."

"And you think there's nothing in it?"

"If there is, sir, it's all on her side, of that I'm sure," said Mrs. Perkins emphatically. "Mr. Minton is a real gentleman. Always very considerate and nice. Not at all the kind to go gallivanting after another man's wife."

"He's often here, is he?"

"Yes, sir. His father died last year and since then the old Minton house has been closed. He comes here to stay when he comes to Stone Haven."

"Get on well with his aunt and uncle?"

"Oh, yes, sir. They both depended a great deal on his judgment. Sometimes Mrs. Gaunt would be real sharp with him but that was just her way. He always was very nice to her."

Potter asked her a few more perfunctory questions and let her go. Maggie was the next on his list—a tall, rather severe-looking woman of middle age. She had been Mrs. Gaunt's maid, she told him, although really she had been maid to the young ladies, too, Miss Nancy and Miss Susan.

"I understand," said Potter, "that Miss Nancy was very devoted to her mother?"

"And her father, too," said Maggie warmly. "Ah, there's an angel, if I do say it. Sweet. She's nursed them both, and difficult as they were sometimes, never a cross word from her."

"She must have been a good deal tied down? Not able to get away very much?"

"Ah!" sighed Maggie sympathetically. "Hard on a young thing and Mrs. Gaunt that difficult sometimes, but she never complained. And she used to get out odd times, too. She has a car of her own—they all have, for that matter—and she used to get out and drive."

"Early in the morning?"

"Quite often early in the morning, sir, before her mother was awake."

"I've heard Mr. Minton was interested in her. Is that true?"

"You'd better ask him," said Maggie stiffly. "If he is, he'd better look elsewhere. There's nothing for him there."

"Going to marry Dr. Ryder, is she?"

Maggie looked at him sharply.

"What are you getting at?" she demanded. "You know it as well as I do."

"All right," said Potter. "We'll stop beating about the bush. Is it true she left the house early in the morning, about a month ago—the day Mrs. Edgar Gaunt went to New Haven to shop?"

"How should I know? I tell you she often drove out early."

"And yesterday morning—Saturday—did she drive out early then?"

Maggie turned white. "How should I know?"

"But you do know, don't you?"

"Well, what of it? Yes, she did."

"What time?"

"I don't know. I went in at eight o'clock with her tray and she'd gone."

"And when did she get back?"

"I saw her coming in about ten. She came into her room and took off her hat and I was there putting away some clothes that had just come from the cleaners'."

"What did she do then?"

"She asked if her mother was up. I said no; that Mr. Waterman was in there talking to her. So she went out into the hall. But just then Mr. Waterman came out of his mother's room, so Miss Nancy went in. I went downstairs after that."

"Did she tell you where she had been?"

"She did not."

"Maggie, did you see Miss Nancy come in on Friday night?"

Maggie shot a baleful glance at him.

"Certainly, sir," she said stiffly. "I always wait up for the young ladies."

"You are sure she went to bed?"

"Of course I'm sure. She gave me her dress to hang up and then she said she didn't need me any more. She was half undressed when I left her."

"Are you sure she didn't dress again when you had gone and go out?"

Maggie rose to her feet and stared down at Potter with a withering look of scorn.

"If you think Miss Nancy is that kind of a young lady, you ought to be ashamed of yourself. Miss Susan—maybe. She is always up to her tricks. But Miss Nancy is an angel if the good Lord ever made one. You can take it from me."

When she had gone Potter stared for some minutes at the door that had closed so emphatically on her exit. What was all this getting him? Beyond a clearer picture of the Gaunts and their servants, not much. A detail here and there. He sighed, and ringing the bell, asked for Hobson.

But the elderly chauffeur could tell him little. Beyond confirming Mrs. Edgar Gaunt's story about the breakdown near The Marmer's on the New Haven road, and a statement that Miss Nancy had taken her car out some time between her return from the club on Friday night and seven-thirty on Saturday morning, he was of little help. Nor was the chambermaid, Gertrude, any more helpful. It was not until he came to Annie, the little kitchenmaid, last on his list, that he got anything of importance, but that brought him up in his chair, alert and eager.

"When was that?"

Annie started and flushed. She was a plain, thin little thing, not more than eighteen, with a rather stupid, empty little face.

"Saturday afternoon, sir—yesterday."

"It couldn't have been Friday? You're sure?"

"No, sir. It was Saturday. The fog didn't come in till Friday night."

Potter nodded. "What time?"

"About five o'clock, sir."

Potter whistled softly. Then he leaned back, finger-tips together, dreamy eyes on the far cornice.

"Let's have it again," he said. "Be as accurate as you can."

"Yes, sir. Do you—do you think it's important, sir?"

"May be very important."

"When I—when I heard about those wet bathing suits on the porch rail, sir, after the explosion, it did seem funny, sir."

Potter nodded, turning his eyes to her flushed, excited face. "Let's have it, step by step. What time did you go down to the store closet?"

"Cook—Mrs. Perkins—sent me down at a few minutes of five to get some of our damson jam to serve with tea. Not that anybody wanted any tea when we sent it up, sir."

Again Potter nodded.

"Say ten minutes of five?" he said.

"Yes, sir."

"Well, I was standing in the store closet with the door open, looking for the jam, when Miss Susan went past to the dryer."

"How do you know where she was going?"

"Well, sir, there was only one place to go, past the store closet, and that's the laundry room where the dryer is. Besides, when I went downstairs, I could hear the dryer going—it makes a humming sound, sir. So I'd looked in to see if someone had forgotten and left it going, because it seemed a funny thing it would be going

Saturday afternoon, and I saw two bathing suits drying there."

"Did you recognise the suits?"

"Yes, sir. They were Miss Susan's and Mr. Carey's, sir."

"Sure?"

"Yes, sir. I'd seen them wearing them only that morning. Miss Susan's was a green-plaid gingham and Mr. Carey's had an orange top."

"But Miss Susan says they hung them on the porch rail when they came in from their swim and that they were still wet, because of the fog, early this morning."

"Well, sir, they weren't, and Miss Susan knew it, because she went into the dryer while I was down there in the store closet. I heard her turn the dryer off and I saw her go upstairs again a minute later with the suits in her hand."

"She didn't see you?"

"No, sir. The closet has a window, so I hadn't turned the light on."

Potter sat up again and looked at her.

"Can you keep a secret, Annie?"

"Y-yes, sir."

"Have you told anyone about this?"

"N-no, sir."

"Then don't—not anyone—not your bosom friend, or your boy friend either, if you have one."

"Oh, sir!" giggled Annie.

He dismissed her then and sat for some minutes drumming his fingers thoughtfully on the desk, before his eyes a vivid picture of Susan's pale defiant face when she declared that she had been standing with her back against the light switch all the time the lights were out and that nobody could have touched it without her knowledge.

When at last he pushed his chair back and rose, his face was grim.

CHAPTER XVII

ON Monday Mrs. Gaunt and her eldest son were buried in the Gaunt lot in the village graveyard. And the next day their names were cut on the big granite shaft under the names of the first Waterman Gaunt and his wife and son.

It was the biggest funeral ever held in Stone Haven—bigger even than the funeral of old Captain Gaunt two years before. The whole town turned out for it and all the shops were closed. Crowds of the curious came from miles around to line the road and stare. There were newspaper men and photographers everywhere.

Ryder had tried to persuade the women not to go to the cemetery, but Susan and Nancy would not listen to him. Heavily veiled, but with heads defiantly erect, they had followed their mother and brother to their graves. The town liked that. "Chip of the old block," they had nodded approvingly, even while they looked with suspicion at the two black-clad figures.

Miss Lucetta Brown went with them. Nancy had sent a note across and she had come at once, her pretty eyes a little puffed with private weeping. She sat between Nancy and Susan on the back seat of the car. Astrid and Elvira stayed at home.

Just before they left the house there had been a difficult little conversation between Daniel and Nancy. He had met her in the upper hall, and she stood before him, flushing painfully. As it happened, it had been their first meeting alone since the ordeal in the library on Saturday night.

Daniel had hesitated a moment; then he held out his hand to her and she laid hers in it.

"I haven't had a chance to tell you—I'm very sorry. You understand?"

"Yes. Oh, yes."

He looked down at the slender white hand he held.

"Ryder's a fine fellow, Nancy. I hope— Oh, hell, I wish you'd told me."

She looked at him miserably. "I'm sorry, Dan."

He looked at her—a strange look that lingered in her mind when he had gone. "You're sure?"

"Quite."

He dropped her hand.

"Well, count on me—any time."

That was all, but she thought of it more than once in the terrible hours that followed.

Sergeant Potter did not attend the funeral. He was otherwise occupied. At nine o'clock he drove up to the public wharf, accompanied by a fingerprint man, a photographer, and a small dark man with a quick, roving glance. There was a police launch waiting at the wharf and in it, beside the pilot, looking very handsome and very sullen, sat Tony Farelli. The three men got in and the launch turned its nose out into the harbour. A moment later it drew alongside the blackened hull of the *Buccaneer*.

The gangway steps had been largely destroyed by the fire and a makeshift ladder had been hung over- side. They mounted gingerly to the after-deck.

This was the only part of the yacht that had not been gutted. The forward part had been burned almost to the waterline and the mid-section was a waste of twisted, blackened wreckage, with only here and there part of a wall or section of flooring capriciously left unburned.

"You'll be smart," grunted Potter to the small dark man, "if you can make anything of that, Mr. Rowland."

The small dark man shrugged.

"Why not? The engine's still there." He stepped cautiously down onto a charred timber and made his way forward.

"Who's he?" asked Tony Farelli curiously.

"Chief engineer of the company that made the engine," Potter informed him. "Thinks he can prove whether it was an accident or not."

Tony looked at him doubtfully. Then his eyes turned to follow the figure of the engineer, climbing gingerly among the debris. "It was an accident all right," he muttered. "Must have been."

"How about that feller you heard swimming ashore?"

"I've been thinking about that," admitted Tony with charming candour. "You know, I'll betcha I imagined that. You know how you will at night—hear a strange sound and your imagination gets working on it—sometimes you think it's a bear—"

"And sometimes you think it's a man swimming ashore and walking on shingle that rattles under his feet," finished Potter.

"Yes," agreed Tony, and glanced at him uneasily.

"So Susan's been getting at you," said Potter dryly.

"What the hell do you mean?"

"I usually mean what I say." He took his pipe out of his pocket and began to fill it carefully. Tony opened his mouth to speak and closed it again. It was very still. The last vestige of the fog had gone and the full length and breadth of the harbour was visible under a mild, clear sunlight. Hardly more than a hundred yards off to starboard the Gaunt house stood, shining white above its terraced garden. Opposite, across the harbour, lay the green mound of Long Point, dotted with summer cottages. Astern the breakwater stretched a low, gray wall, and across their bows lay the inner harbour with its picturesque waterfront: weatherbeaten gray wharves, slender sailboats at anchor, with a background of green gardens, old houses bowered in green and topped with a canopy of arching elms, through which rose three slender white spires. A peaceful scene in which, at the moment, the only movement appeared to be the slow, smooth heave of the unruffled water, the quick, pouncing activity of Mr. Rowland in what was left of the engine-room, and the fingerprint man's slow, methodical progress around the charred and blackened rail. Tony watched uneasily. At last he could stand it no longer. "What's he doing?" he blurted out.

Potter withdrew his pipe from his mouth.

"Looking for fingerprints," he said, and he looked thoughtfully at Tony.

The boy swung on him. There was sweat on his upper lip and on his forehead. "What's the idea?" he asked heatedly. "Why have you brought me out here? What have I got to do with this?"

"That's what I want to know," admitted Potter. "You'll admit it's funny. You tell a story about hearing someone swim ashore to the Gaunt place just before the explosion, and I jug you for knifing Jake."

"Look here, I—"

"All right, all right," interrupted Potter. "Let's say I wanted you for a material witness. Then along comes this Mr. West, who's a beau of Susan Gaunt's, and offers to go bail for you. And I hear he's been calling on Susan just before he does it. Well, I don't raise any objections. I'm naturally curious. I want to see what'll happen next. Next thing I hear is that Susan's sneaked out of the house at six o'clock this morning and met you down at your wharf. And a little later I'm told that you're saying you've decided you didn't really hear anyone swimming ashore. You just imagined it. So I've been wondering whether you hadn't just imagined the whole business."

"You've got a good imagination yourself, haven't you?" jeered Tony.

"Sure," Potter nodded good-naturedly. "I've been using it. I've been trying to imagine what really happened early yesterday morning. Suppose you didn't really go out in the Sound at all. Suppose you came out here, instead. And then, when you got ready, went ashore again, and imagined a man swimming—"

"Why in hell would I want to blow up this tub?"

"I don't know. Perhaps someone hired you to do it."

Tony was thinking fast. At last he laughed with bravado tinged with uneasiness.

"Bologny! You're just trying to make me talk. You can't prove anyone set an explosion. You can't prove it wasn't an accident."

Potter tapped the dottle from his pipe into the bay. "They say Jake will be in the hospital three weeks anyway," he remarked casually. "You ought to lay off that stuff, Tony."

Tony laughed, more naturally, this time.

"You're telling *me!*"

"Personally, I sympathise with you," admitted Potter, "but officially, of course—"

"What the hell good does that do me?"

"It might—it just might—make a difference," said Potter gently, "if you'd come clean."

The face of Susan's field god was full of perplexity. He smiled ruefully.

"You've got me coming and going, haven't you?"

Potter nodded.

"Jake says he doesn't know who attacked him, but if

you admitted it, it might freshen up his memory. He can give the exact time the thing happened. And allowing for the fog, you could hardly have got back to Stone Haven in time to do this job. I'll admit the alibi wouldn't be conclusive, but it would help."

"Sure," said Tony with elaborate sarcasm. "Help to jug me for knifing Jake."

"That's where my personal sympathy comes in," said Potter softly. "If Jake gets well—and he undoubtedly will—we can swear you over to keep the peace and let it go—this time."

"I'm not talking."

"What did Susan give you to hold your tongue?"

Tony flushed heavily and his fingers twitched. He moved uneasily. After a minute, however, he reiterated quietly: "I'm not talking "

Potter nodded.

"All right," he said, "you can go down and wait in the launch."

"What are you going to do about it?"

Potter gave him a long, level glance.

"I don't know—yet."

"Look here, chief!" It was the fingerprint man calling from the head of the charred gangway.

Potter waited until Tony had disappeared over the side into the launch. Then he went over and looked at the section of rail the fingerprint man pointed out to him. On it he saw a perfect set of fingerprints nicely touched up with black film, the prints of all five fingers of someone's right hand.

"Beautiful, ain't they?" said the fingerprint man enthusiastically. "Couldn't have done it better myself."

Potter looked at him inquiringly.

"The smoke did it, see?" he explained. "Laid on a nice thin film, neat as you please. Pretty, ain't it? But I'm afraid that's all, chief—only piece of rail that ain't charred."

"Well, take 'em. Maybe they'll do us some good."

"Oke." He set his camera and Potter went forward to join Rowland in the wrecked engine-room.

Rowland straightened up as he approached and wiped his forehead, leaving streaks of soot.

"Well," said Potter easily, "accident, was it?"

"Accident, my hat!" said Rowland.

He frowned thoughtfully at the grotesque, blackened mass of the engine at his feet. It was set a little forward of amidships, a feed line running along under the flooring from the gas tank in the stern, under the after-deck. The engine had been damaged surprisingly little. Even Potter's inexperienced eye could see that the worst of the fire had been just aft of the engine, under the section where the engine-room had been located. He cocked an inquiring eye at Rowland.

"Well? Make anything of it?"

"Plenty," said Rowland. "In the first place, these engines don't explode accidentally—not much—even when they're running. They're protected in every conceivable way. I've yet to hear of one exploding when it wasn't running and perfectly cool."

"Escape of gas somewhere?" suggested Potter. "Accidental spark?"

Rowland turned a pitying eye on him.

"Before you could get a sufficient quantity of gas vapour to cause an explosion, it would be strong enough to taste. Besides, whoever dropped the spark would have been blown to bits, and I understood you to say nobody was."

Potter nodded. "All right. I believe you. Then how did it happen?"

"That's how it happened." Rowland climbed down from the half-burned floor joist on which he had been standing into the black hollow of the hull. He laid his hand on a section of the feed pipe, half melted and bent by the heat of the fire.

"Cut," he said succinctly. "Not melted—cut. With these, I imagine." He reached down into the grimy bilge that filled the hollow along the keel, picked up an object that projected from the surface of the black, oozy mess, and held it up. Potter took it gingerly and examined it. It was a pair of heavy pliers. He whistled softly.

"Could you cut the feed pipe with these?"

"Certainly. It's three-quarter inch copper pipe. Copper's soft. It's a cinch."

Potter looked from the pliers in his hand to the severed end of pipe. He bent down and felt it.

"Yes," he said. "You're right, of course. It's been cut.

Well, what then?"

"Whoever cut it knew, of course, that the tank would drain out at this point into the bilge. The vapour would seep up through the floor first, and particularly into the cabin directly over the cut—in this case the engine-room. No doubt he left the trap in the floor open. That's how he got at the feed line in the first place."

"All right," agreed Potter, "what then?"

Rowland climbed back on his joist and scratched his head thoughtfully.

"The rest isn't so simple but I'll see what I can do. It's evident that the fire was more intense just here than anywhere else. I can prove that for you, if you like, by the varying melting points of metals—"

"You can save that for the jury," grinned Potter. "I'll take your word for it, for the moment. Let's grant the fire started here. What then?"

Rowland climbed around the charred remains of the engine room, a thoughtful frown on his dark, thin face. The fire, like all fires, had been capricious. One of the ports remained, the glass in place, partly fused and warped. The lower quarter of the closed door into the inner passageway remained in place, charred and blackened, but intact, although the rest of the door had been burned away, and even the hinge was gone.

Rowland studied it carefully, and then lifted it out of its frame. Potter, watching him, saw him bend forward and study the doorsill, by some chance not completely destroyed. The engineer picked up some small object and held it thoughtfully in his palm. At last he set the fragment of door back in place and turned to the detective.

"I've got it," he said. "It's only a hypothesis, of course, but I'll bet that's the way it was done." He stared again at the cut end of the feed line.

"The fellow cut the pipe under the floor, leaving the trap open so that the gas vapour would accumulate in this cabin. No doubt the ports were already closed, but if not, he closed them. You can see for yourself they're very heavy glass and fit tight. Then he went out into the passage and closed this door. He had a piece of hard white cord with him. Either found it on board or brought it with him—say tucked under a bathing cap on his head to keep it dry, if he swam aboard as you suggest.

"Anyway, he had a piece of ordinary hard white cord. He dropped it through the keyhole so that it touched the floor on each side. In fact, although he didn't know it, it did a little better than touch the floor inside. The end of it curled back under the door." He looked again at the object in his hand. Potter found himself getting a little breathless.

"Well?"

"Well, then he was all set. He may have waited a bit till he began to smell the fumes in the passage-way, too. Then he lighted the outer end of the cord, down near the floor, and when it was burning well he went out on deck, closing the outer door behind him, and swam ashore.

"You'll have to try it out to be sure, but I'll bet it would take a good ten to fifteen minutes for cord of that type to burn the three feet from the floor to the keyhole. And that would be all the time he needed.

"I still don't see—"

"When the cord burned up to some point near the keyhole, the weight of the cord inside the door would pull it through. The spark would ignite the dense vapour in the cabin and—there you are!"

He opened his closed hand and extended it to Potter, palm up. On it lay a piece of hard white three-ply cord, about two inches long, and burned at one end.

Potter took it and examined it thoughtfully.

"How in heck did it escape?"

"Caught under the door. The rest of it burned off. Just happened to skip that place. There was a heavy joist underneath."

"Think it would really burn? What I mean is, think that was really the fuse he used?"

"You'll have to try it, but I'll bet you—dollars to doughnuts."

Potter nodded. He slipped the bit of cord into an envelope and labelled it. "I want photographs," he said. "Those fellows over there will take 'em if you'll tell 'em what to take."

Rowland nodded. Potter left him skipping from joist to joist and getting grimier and grimier. He got back into the police boat and had himself taken ashore. Tony Farelli was both disturbed and relieved to find himself completely ignored.

CHAPTER XVIII

DETECTIVE-SERGEANT POTTER, Waiting in Dr. Blake's office for his friend to return from the funeral, was engaged in an odd experiment. He had procured from a hardware store in Massassoit a six-foot length of hard, white three-ply cord and he was trying to burn it. He set fire to one end of it with a match and laid it on the spotless, unused hearth. It burned for a moment, sputtered and went out. Potter sat back on his heels and scratched his head.

Then he moved a straight chair from a corner of the room and turned it with its back to the hearth. He hung the cord over the back of the chair and lighted it again. This time it burned steadily, the flame creeping slowly up the cord leaving a little pile of ash on the bricks.

Potter shook it. It continued to burn. He breathed on it gently. It flickered but continued to creep upwards. He measured out a three-foot length and sat timing the ascending flame, watch in hand. After a while it jerked abruptly over the top, drawn by the weight of the cord on the other side. Sergeant Potter noted the time on his watch, put out the flame, rolled the cord up and put it in his pocket. He restored the chair to its original position and sat down to wait.

Dr. Blake, returning a few minutes later, found him still waiting. It had come on very hot after the fog had lifted and the sergeant was in his shirt sleeves, his feet on the sill of the open window, staring moodily into the neat little vegetable garden that was Blake's pride and joy. He greeted his old friend with a grunt.

"Mrs. Blake got one whiff of my pipe and went to call on the neighbours," he informed the doctor. "Any fireworks at the funeral?"

Blake shook his head. He mopped his forehead with a sodden handkerchief, took off his shabby coat and hung it on the golden-oak clothes tree in the corner.

"Why weren't you there?" he asked. His swivel chair creaked as he sank wearily into it. Potter grunted. "I had work to do."

Blake cocked an inquiring eye, but he said nothing. Potter took his feet down from the windowsill and leaned forward to knock out his pipe in the tin waste basket.

"I don't like the looks of this case," he said heavily. "There's something—horrible about it. Those are nice folks. Oh, I know, I know." He waved a hand to silence Blake's attempted interruption. "They're bad stock. I've been brought up on the story same as you. Their grandpa was a rotter of the worst sort. No, not quite the worst sort because he had guts, but bad enough. Their father was a hard-boiled pirate and their great-uncle was a murderer—probably. But they're nice folks all the same. 'Course Edgar drinks like a fish. By the way, there's a divorce in the making there, all right." He filled his pipe, pulled the drawstring of his pouch with his teeth, and returned it to his pocket. "What a woman! I'd strangle her if she was my wife. Then Carey's a pretty weak sister." He tamped down the tobacco absently. "It's a funny thing about that boy— However, Susan's probably carrying on with that Portygee, but darned if I can think the worse of her for it. He's a decent fellow. And the girl has spunk." He chuckled. "She certainly did give me hell. And Daniel's a decent fellow—hot-headed and all that, but decent. And I'd have staked my life Nancy was the salt of the earth."

"She is," said Blake. "You're not mistaken there."

Potter sighed. "Of course there's always Elvira," he said with faint hope.

Dr. Blake smiled wryly.

"Sometimes I think you took your job because you like criminals better than honest folks."

Potter's eyes crinkled at the corners.

"Well," he said cautiously, "they're sometimes more human." His face hardened suddenly. "But there's nothing human about this crime. It ain't human to kill an old lady in cold blood. Yet I've got to go among these people and pick one of them out and say: 'You did this. You stuck a knife into an old man who was sick and couldn't help himself. You killed an old lady who couldn't lift a finger in defence. You took a third life to save yourself from getting caught and would take a fourth or a fifth for the same reason. You endangered half a dozen innocent people to destroy a paper that would have cost you a lot of money.' It's a damnable business. Murder in a moment of passion you can understand, kinda. But this cold-blooded business—carefully planned, most of it—

"There's only one thing you can say for the feller—that business in the library—the killing of Waterman Gaunt—took nerve and coolness of the highest order. Only three minutes at the outside and hardly a minute's preparation for it, yet it's practically a perfect crime. Not a trace—not a clue. He killed his man and destroyed the incriminating paper in the one safe, final, absolutely simple way. Of course the set-up was perfect for him." Potter laughed ruefully. "Did you know I'd actually wrapped the handle of the knife in my own handkerchief to protect whatever fingerprints might be on it? But still and all, to grasp all the details so quickly—he must have seen the whole thing complete, and located every article before he turned off the light, for he worked in complete darkness. And the only hitch was the ink spilling over the edge of the inkwell. But as it happened that didn't matter, because I'm so used to having my inkwell in a filthy condition I never even noticed it till hours later and by that time he could have got his hands clean if he'd got any ink on his fingers."

He drew thoughtfully at his pipe.

"And when you think that right on top of that he sneaked out of the house under cover of the fog, went out to the *Buccaneer*, got aboard without being seen, went through the complicated business of arranging the explosion and laying his fuse, swam back to shore, got back into the house and got dry somehow without leaving any wet towels or wet clothes around and was dressed in his night things and ready for us when we searched the house after the explosion, well—grandpa himself could hardly have bettered that performance. It's extraordinary."

"But there must have been something wet somewhere," objected Blake.

"There was," said Potter grimly. "There were two wet bathing suits hanging over the rail of the upper porch, and one was Carey's and one was Susan's. They were the suits they had worn swimming the morning their mother died, about eighteen hours before the explosion."

"Well," said Blake, "nothing dries in a fog. They could still have been wet."

Potter nodded.

"So Susan pointed out. She and Carey said the hung their suits there after their swim."

"Well, didn't they?"

Potter stared out of the window a long time before replying. He stared unseeingly at the neat rows of lettuce and radishes and climbing beans. At last he said: "I'll tell you something, but you keep it under your hat. I don't know why I happened to notice it, unless it was because I was puzzling hard over those suits because they were the only wet things we could find in the house and I thought the feller that blew up the yacht must have used one of them. But anyway—" He broke off. "You know how sticky salt water is?"

Blake nodded.

"Well, Collins found the suits and he called me. I felt the first one—it happened to be Susan's—and it was dripping wet, all right. I stood there staring at them, wondering if they proved anything, and sort of rubbing my hands together to dry the palms—you know how you do—and I suddenly realised they didn't stick. They will if they're wet with sea water, you know." Again he paused. Blake waited breathlessly.

"Well, it didn't seem likely that whoever had swum in from the yacht had taken time to rinse his or her suit out in fresh water, yet this suit had been washed in fresh water. I squeezed it out in my hand and tested it and it was fresh. So that seemed to let Susan out. But Carey's suit was wet in salt water."

"Well," said Blake, "then if either suit was used, it must have been Carey's."

Potter grunted.

"You're so smart it hurts," he said irritably.

"What's wrong about that?"

"God knows! The whole business is cock-eyed. It looks as plain as print. They wore their suits in the morning and took showers when they came in, washing off the salt water. They hung the suits on the rail but they didn't dry, owing to the fog. Then along comes the murderer, uses Carey's suit to swim out to the yacht and hangs it up again when he comes back, either forgetting the water would be salt or thinking it wouldn't be noticed, or not caring because we wouldn't be able to prove who wore the suit."

"Well?"

"But the cock-eyed thing about it is that those suits *weren't* hanging on the rail when the murderer started out; they weren't wet—with either salt or fresh water. They were dried in a dryer in the cellar, and Susan knows they were dried because she dried them herself. Annie, one of the maids—saw her and will swear to it."

"Does Susan deny it?"

"She doesn't know I know it—that anybody knows it. She just says—and so does Carey—that they hung their suits there after their swim, and of course they didn't dry on account of the fog."

"Surely you don't think Susan is involved?" exclaimed Blake anxiously.

"Of course she's involved. I must say I can't see her in the role of murderer, although she's probably got more nerve than any other member of the family. But she is certainly protecting someone. If it was only the lie about the suits, it might have been just on impulse to shield Carey because she might think he would be suspected. But she must have wet her own suit and hung it on the rail to give colour to her story—she must have done it. Who else would have known enough about it to figure it out just that way? And then I'm morally certain she was lying when she swore she was standing with her back against the light switch all the time Waterman was being killed. If she was, and had no motive in shielding the murderer, why didn't she turn the light on? She's not a girl to lose her head. She's cool as a cucumber. It doesn't hold water." He paused a moment and then added thoughtfully: "And it's general knowledge that both she and Carey had quarrelled with their mother shortly before she was killed. And Susan admits knowing that her father was planning to make a will in favour of Waterman the night he died."

"It's preposterous."

"I suppose that of all the women found guilty of murder, most of them have been pretty—and many of them have been young."

"But not Susan!" cried Dr. Blake.

"Well, well," said Potter. "She had motive and opportunity and she's told a couple of whacking lies, but we musn't jump to conclusions. She may be shielding Carey, who also had motive and opportunity. The hitch there is that, as I said before, he's a weak sister. And besides he's supposed to have been sick in bed with a heart attack at the time the *Buccaneer* blew up. Not," he added coolly, "that that cuts any ice."

"Ryder says his heart is rotten—same thing his mother had, only worse."

"Oh—Ryder!" muttered Potter impatiently. "And he said Cap'n and Mrs. Gaunt died natural deaths."

"But that was—"

"Look here," said Potter. "We don't need to go over all that again. I've found out some things that will take a lot of explaining. We'll deal with Dr. Ryder later."

Blake looked at his friend with curiosity, but he said nothing. This was not the first time that Potter had used him to talk at when he found himself confused in the midst of an intricate situation, and Blake knew better than to ask questions. It would all come out in good time.

"This Daniel Minton, now," said Potter slowly. "He interests me. He seems to be an able fellow. I've made inquiries about him and they tell me he's done very well these last two years when he's been actual head of the Gaunt Lines. Of course, Mrs. Gaunt has got the credit, but those who ought to know tell me it's Daniel who told her what to do and when to do it. I can't quite get the straight of that situation. On one hand I'm told that she trusted him implicitly and did whatever he told her, and on the other—and Daniel himself says this—that she never liked him and only put up with him at all because she was shrewd enough to see he was useful. Apparently that's the right view, since she intended to leave control of everything to Waterman."

"I don't think Hetty Gaunt ever forgot that Daniel was Sophia's son."

"So Daniel says." Potter smoked thoughtfully for a moment. "Of course there again we have motive and opportunity—if we can break Elvira's testimony. She swears she grabbed hold of Daniel's arm when the lights went out and held on till the lights went on again. On the other hand, I wouldn't believe Elvira on her oath. I betcha she'd lie by preference—and then this gives her an alibi, too." Again he smoked thoughtfully and Blake forbore to interrupt. "I wonder if Daniel really is her lover," he said slowly. "It's a sure thing Edgar thinks so. But I don't think she'd risk her neck for him even if he is.

"I'd love to think Elvira did it," he went on with a grim smile. "She's got the nerve, all right, and she's hard-boiled enough, but I'm afraid she hasn't got the brains. And then, of course, her alibi works both ways. It lets her out, too—unless we can break it."

"Have you thought about Edgar?"

Potter nodded.

"Sure. Edgar's in a bad way. He's lost the money his father gave him when he married. He's sick to death of being dependent on his wife. He's lost a pile gambling and Elvira says some of it is her money and she's giving him hell about it. He had a quarrel with Waterman about the will and was heard to threaten him. And he is the fellow that found Mrs. Gaunt dying. We have only his word for it that there was anyone in the room between the time that Nancy went downstairs, leaving her mother dressing, and the time Edgar shouted out that she was dying. He admits he'd been waiting for an hour trying to see his mother alone. What's to prove that he didn't see her alone, quarrel with her about the will, and kill her? He hasn't any sort of an alibi for any of it."

"Unless it's the fact that he's soused most of the time."

Potter nodded.

"Was he drunk when Wat was killed?"

"He'd been drinking, certainly," said Potter thoughtfully. "But he seemed sober enough then. Mrs. Ingersoll and her brother tried to insinuate that he might have been concerned in that business."

"Do you eliminate them?"

Potter scratched his head perplexedly.

"Certainly not. I'd love to jug those two," he admitted, "but I can't see my way to it. As far as I can prove—so far—Mrs. Ingersoll's association with Waterman didn't begin till a year ago—which is a year after Cap'n Gaunt's death. Of course it's conceivable that he was killed by a different person but, in view of the weapon, it don't seem likely. But there certainly are points—" He glanced across at his friend. "You knew that Waterman left everything to her in his will?"

"No!" Dr. Blake sat up with lively surprise.

"Fact. You should have heard the beehive hum when that got about. If Mrs. Gaunt's will hadn't been destroyed, she'd be the richest woman in the state. And that about lets her out, see? For why in God's name would either Astrid or her brother blow up the yacht under those circumstances?"

"Perhaps someone else blew up the yacht."

Potter nodded.

"I've thought about that, too. They all knew the will was on the yacht. It came out while I was quizzing them all together. Still, there are a good many holes in the theory that Astrid or Rex Olsen killed Waterman. From the little he said before he died, it was quite clear that the letter he found had something to do with the murder of his father. What conceivable interest could that pair have had in suppressing it?"

"Unless their acquaintance with Waterman goes back farther than you suppose."

Potter nodded slowly, his eyes narrowed and thoughtful.

"I'll have Collins check them up. He may be able to turn up something. Certainly they had an enormous stake in two of the murders. And Mrs. Ingersoll was admittedly in a bad way financially."

"What do you know about Olsen?"

"Darn little, now you mention it. He's one of these frank fellers who don't tell you anything. You know the type. Always chatting and telling stories, and when you're all through you're just where you started. He's supposed to paint pictures, but I'll bet he's better at painting the town." He looked across at his friend and grinned. "We'll shave off Mr. Olsen's beard. Maybe we'll find the missing will hidden in his whiskers."

For a moment more he stared out into the garden. There was a perplexed frown on his face.

"There's one thing that beats me," he said slowly. "How in heck did the feller know there was a dagger in that jar? For that matter, how did Mrs. Gaunt know about it? We've been through her room with a fine-tooth comb—through the boxes of papers she had there—old diaries and everything, and there's no reference to anything of the sort. As far as we can prove, they all had a sort of superstitious horror of breaking the seal. They don't call it that, of course, but there it is. Mrs. Gaunt in particular. It seems she delivered blood-curdling lectures to each new parlourmaid on the subject, and she is reported to have thrashed Waterman within an inch of his life when he was a child, because she found him standing on a chair one day examining the seal, and thought he intended to open it. Yet somebody knew there was a dagger there—and Mrs. Gaunt knew it."

"An old letter—" suggested Blake.

"The only letter we can find is one that's framed on the wall in Mrs. Gaunt's room. It's a letter from the first Waterman Gaunt to his brother, describing how a Chinaman whom he called Louis Chen gave him the jar. And in that letter there's no mention of the dagger. It's my opinion he didn't know there was a dagger in it."

"Well," said Blake, "I can't help you. Obviously someone must have opened the thing some time, but they've certainly kept the fact to themselves. It's never been common knowledge. Have you questioned the servants?"

Potter nodded gloomily.

"Sure. But the only ones who've been there long enough to help aren't talking."

Blake sat up suddenly. "Look here!" he said. "How about Lucetta Brown? She and Hetty Gaunt were thick as thieves. Why not try her?"

Potter got to his feet wearily.

"Might as well," he said grudgingly. "Mrs. Gaunt doesn't strike me as a woman who'd be apt to confide much in anyone else."

"After all, every woman has to talk some time—to someone."

Potter grinned. "I'm obliged for the tip, anyway. Let you know how I come out."

"Stay and have lunch," suggested Blake. "From the sounds in the kitchen, I deduce that Mrs. Blake has decided it's safe to return."

"I've got work to do," said Potter for the second time. He settled his limp straw hat jauntily on his head. " 'Work, for the night is coming.' Gosh! What a life!" He went away, walking briskly down the neat path between Mrs.

Blake's flower-beds. The dejection was gone. He moved like a man whose way lies clear before him again.

Mrs. Blake, coming in from the kitchen, sniffed.

"That man's a chimney," she commented with acidity. "The whole house is smelled up. Don't you take to pipe smoking, Eben."

"I haven't his courage, my dear."

"Has he found out yet who did those murders?"

"Not yet."

"If he didn't fuddle his brains with smoke, he'd likely get on faster."

Dr. Blake sighed. His wife looked at him, her sensible, kind face full of the unspoken understanding of a woman who has lived with a man for a great many years and knows him very well.

"I wouldn't worry," she said briskly. "You know neither of those girls had a hand in it."

His face brightened. He got up and went to the window. "Those beets need thinning," he said. "If nothing else breaks, I'll have a go at them this afternoon."

His wife just touched his bent shoulders with her hand as she led the way into the dining-room.

Potter drove to his office in New London and got New York on the wire. He talked to an old friend of his, Detective-Sergeant Hennessey of the New York police. He talked at some length, giving Olsen's clubs and Mrs. Ingersoll's address. His remarks were interrupted and punctuated by fervent ejaculations at the other end of the wire. When he had finished Hennessey chuckled.

"I been thinking I'd hear from you," he said, "ever since I read those names in the paper. They say around here that Gaunt's been buying her lingerie for years."

"Well, she says she only met him a year ago and that they were engaged to be married."

"Oh, yeah? That's what I like about the country; keeps you so innocent-minded."

Potter sniffed. "It's not tittle-tattle I want, but facts. See if you can pin your mind on to that."

When Hennessey rang off, Potter went out into the outer office and found Collins continuing his interrupted slumbers in an inconspicuous corner behind the water cooler. He shook him awake, led him into his private office and shut the door.

Fifteen minutes later Collins emerged looking considerably astonished, went out and got into a small car parked at the curb, and drove away in the direction of New Haven. Shortly afterwards Potter, having sent out for and consumed a hasty sandwich, departed for Stone Haven and the Gaunt house.

CHAPTER XIX

FOR those in the Gaunt house the afternoon passed in a sort of languor of horror, nerves on the hair-trigger, waiting for they knew not what.

They were acutely aware of Potter's presence. They followed with a painful precision his passage through the silent rooms. They were aware of the policemen in the garden and of the reporters outside the fence.

Potter had arrived at two o'clock with a search warrant and two assistants. They had gone methodically through the upstairs rooms. He did not say what he was looking for or whether he had found it. He went doggedly about his task with the air of a man who knows exactly what he is doing, and why. When he had finished, he sent for Reeves and questioned him.

On his return to the kitchen Reeves was met with a salvo of questions.

"What did he want?"

"What did he ask you?"

"Has he found out who did it?"

Reeves winked elaborately at Maggie.

"Wanted to know which of the maids was wearing Miss Susan's nighties."

"Oh, go on with you."

"I told him I hadn't got that far."

Maggie tossed her head. "You don't need ice to keep you fresh," she remarked tartly.

Perkins spoke through the open door of the pantry, where he was polishing silver. His narrow, worn face was pale, his eyes full of anxiety. Hannah, his wife, looked at him with a worried air.

"Did he tell you what he was looking for?" the butler asked.

Reeves took one of Waterman Gaunt's cigarettes from a silver case and lighted it carelessly.

"Ah," he nodded. "He says to me, 'Reeves, you're an intelligent fellow. Perhaps you can help me out.' And then he goes on to tell me what he is up against. And let me tell you, it's a-plenty. This murderer is smart, I'm telling you. But I gave him a couple of good tips."

Perkins gave him a long, steady look, and went back to his polishing.

"Yah!" grunted Maggie disgustedly "He couldn't have told you anything or you'd be bragging about it."

Reeves winked again.

"Oh, yeah? Told me to keep it under my hat. I don't tell everything I know, girlie, without a good reason. But I'll tell you this much: he was looking for a clue—and it's my opinion that he found it."

"What clue?"

Reeves smoothed his lacquered hair thoughtfully.

"A damn funny thing, as a matter of fact. He wanted to know if I'd seen any on the yacht, but I'll swear there wasn't any on board."

"Any what?" asked Hannah Perkins in an exasperated voice.

Reeves looked from face to face impressively.

"Any hard, white three-ply twine."

In the pantry Perkins set down the sugar bowl he was polishing and steadied his trembling hands on the table. In the shining surface of the bowl he could see his own face in distorted caricature. He studied it curiously as though he had never seen it before. Presently his hands stopped trembling and he went on with his work.

Susan spent a wretched afternoon, wandering restlessly from room to room. Carey being up again, her occupation had gone and she did not know what to do with herself. Once she pulled her hat on determinedly, ran down the stairs and flung open the front door. But the sight of three disgruntled reporters playing poker on the sidewalk and a brass-buttoned policeman who cast a discouraging glance at her from across the street made her shut the door again hastily and lean against it for a moment, her knees suddenly weak.

Perkins, hearing the sound of the closing door, came out of the dining-room. Seeing who it was, he came along the hall, glancing into the drawing-room as he passed as though to make sure there was no one there. When he spoke to her Susan felt suddenly as though ten years had rolled away and she was a little girl again, in disgrace for some misdeed.

"Can I do anything for you, Miss Susan?"

She put her hand to her face with a desperate gesture. "I'm so worried, Perkins. Carey flies out at me when I try to talk to him."

"I think, Miss Susan, it would have been wiser to say at once who was in the library with you when you and Mrs. Gaunt examined the black hawthorn."

Susan looked at him with terrified eyes.

"Who was in the library? What do you mean? I didn't know anyone was in the library but mother and me."

It was Perkins' turn to look aghast.

"I thought you knew, Miss Susan. I—I was passing the door and I glanced in. You and Mrs. Gaunt were at the desk. It seemed to me you were about to break the seal of the black hawthorn. I must say I was apprehensive, Miss Susan. Of course, I didn't stop, but I couldn't help seeing that Mr. Carey was standing in the window, watching you."

Susan so far forgot herself as to grasp his arm with both hands. Her face was bloodless.

"Carey! Are you sure it was Carey?"

"Why, Miss Susan, I thought—from your manner—that you knew. I—I assumed that it was Mr. Carey. Of course now you mention it, I'm not sure. He was partly concealed by the curtain and I didn't really look at him anyway, but I'd seen Mr. Carey a moment before on the terrace—"

"Oh, my God!" whispered Susan.

"You didn't know?"

"No, of course not."

"When you told Sergeant Potter that you were standing with your back to the light switch—I thought you must know."

Susan looked at him despairingly. "I had to tell him that, Perkins. I had to. Carey had the most awful quarrel with mother—just the day before—"

"Well," said Perkins consolingly. "If anyone else had seen Mr. Carey, I think they would have said so before now."

"Perkins, do you know that Carey's bathing suit was hanging on the porch rail wet, after the explosion?"

"And yours with it, Miss Susan."

"I—I wet mine and hung it there," whispered Susan miserably, "so no one would know."

A step sounded in the hall above them.

"I've got to see Tony and find out what happened this morning," whispered the girl desperately.

"Might I suggest a swim, Miss Susan?"

"You're a dear, Perkins!" And she dashed upstairs, past Potter, coming morosely down. The detective looked after her thoughtfully.

A few minutes later, clad in a smart green-plaid gingham bathing suit, Susan rang for Maggie.

"Where's my bathing cap?" she asked. "I can't find it."

"On the shelf in your bathroom, Miss Susan."

"No, it isn't. I just looked there."

Maggie went into the bathroom with the patient air of one accustomed to the whims of people who had "just looked" in the places where she had put things away. A moment later she reappeared.

"You're quite right, Miss Susan, it's not there."

"Now that you're satisfied," said Susan tartly, "perhaps you'll look for it."

Maggie had never quite forgotten that Susan, as a naughty little girl, had more than once been spanked under her approving eye. She said firmly:

"Of course this affair is trying to all of us, Miss Susan. I'll look in the drying-room."

"It's not in the drying-room," said Susan.

"I'll just look, Miss Susan."

But the cap was not found. As a matter of fact, it was never found. At last Susan borrowed Nancy's, which was blue and looked horrible with her green suit. She was in a fever of annoyance and impatience when she ran down through the garden.

"Where you going, Susie?" Carey called to her. He was sitting on the sea wall, smoking moodily.

"Swimming," said Susan shortly and unnecessarily, her eyes on the policeman sitting on the wharf. "Didn't Matthew tell you to stop smoking?"

"Oh—Matthew!" said Carey scornfully.

Susan pulled on the blue cap with the deliberate air of one who defies anyone to challenge her eye for colour. She ran down the wharf and dived neatly off the end, swimming out for some distance before she turned casually in the direction of Tony Farelli's wharf. Carey, on the sea wall, watched her moodily. The policeman on the wharf stood up and followed her with disapproving eyes.

About three o'clock Edgar, ejected from his room by Potter's cohorts, lumbered downstairs and searched out Avery in the library. He closed the door behind him and sank into a chair with a groan.

"Good Lord, but I need a drink!" he said morosely.

"Why not have one?"

"Eh?" Edgar looked at him uneasily, and ran a nervous hand over his head. "No. I guess not." He stared into the empty hearth for a moment. "Haven't had a drink since six o'clock last night. First time in ten years."

"On the wagon?" asked Avery idly.

"Eh? Yes, I guess so." Edgar shifted again, uneasily. "That's what I wanted to see you about."

Avery took a cigar from his pocket, looked at it, and put it back.

"Better see a doctor, hadn't you?"

"No," said Edgar. "I want to see you. Want you to get me a divorce."

Avery looked shocked. "My dear fellow—"

"Everybody takes it for granted that I'll be soused every evening from six o'clock on," complained Edgar.

"What's that got to do—"

"I'm telling you. Last night I wasn't soused. I didn't have a drink after six o'clock. And I drank coffee—lots of it."

"Well?"

"I saw him go into Elvira's room about ten o'clock last night and he stayed there until just time to dash for his train."

"Who?"

"Minton."

Avery raised his brows.

"Funny, isn't it? Thought I was drunk—dead to the world. Would have been if Matthew—that is—" Edgar coughed and reddened. "Anyway, I wasn't drunk. Watching for him. I'd turned my light out and left the door open a crack. Saw him go in—and saw him come out. Fact!"

"But—"

"Never mind any buts. This isn't any news. Known it a long time, but no proof before. I'm through."

Avery nodded.

"Better not start anything now," he advised.

"All right," agreed Edgar. "Just wanted to let you know how I stand. How long will it take to clear things up?"

"Several months."

Edgar grinned.

"How does Mrs. Ingersoll come out?"

Avery did not answer for a moment. He stood turning his glasses in his hands, thoughtfully.

"She was asking me that a few minutes ago," he admitted finally.

"I betcha. She and Rex."

"As a matter of fact, Mr. Olsen was present."

"Rather!" nodded Edgar. "Wanted to know when she could collect?"

"H'm! Yes."

"Pretty little woman," said Edgar thoughtfully. "Think she did old Wat in?"

Mr. Avery said nothing. He swung his glasses back and forth on their black ribbon.

CHAPTER XX

AFTERWARDs, in discussing the Gaunt case, Potter was in the habit of saying that it was luck that led to the final solution. He was not a man of great vanity and he was content to let it go at that. But in his heart he knew it was not luck. All through the long hours of that Monday afternoon he was like a man sitting bemused over a picture puzzle, fitting in one improbable piece after another, seeing at first no reason in the preposterous confusion, no coherence in the pattern. Yet gradually the picture began to take shape, the background and surrounding figures fell into place. Only the centre remained a blank with ragged edges. There were pieces missing. But even here an odd piece or two suggested a growing, forming suspicion. He approached it from every direction, arguing against his fast-growing conviction, but the conviction remained. He studied it from all angles and it grew only more substantial. But how to prove it—prove it in the face of all probability—indeed of all possibility? For an hour he sat in the study with the door closed, his eyes on a two-inch fragment of hard white twine, his mind grappling with his problem.

His thoughts came back again and again to Waterman's death and to the paper that had been in his hands when he was killed. An unfinished letter written by Mrs. Gaunt to Avery, he had said, which he had found thrust under the blotter on his mother's desk—a letter so revealing that it betrayed to Waterman the secret of his mother's murder, a letter so dangerous to the murderer that he had taken the incredible risk of killing Waterman on the spot, in the middle of a roomful of witnesses, to suppress it.

Potter groaned, cursing for the hundredth time his own slowness and stupidity. He ought to have realised when the lights went out what was afoot. He had only to put out his hands across the desk, to cover the dagger, to seize the paper from Waterman's hands— But he had been momentarily paralysed with shock and that momentary paralysis had been enough. When he recovered it was already too late.

Yet surely not altogether too late. With what he knew, it should be possible to reconstruct that letter in some fashion. Evidently it had made some reference to the dagger in the black hawthorn jar—"the dagger that leaves no trace." It was safe to assume, then, that the contents of the letter had to do with Captain Gaunt's murder, particularly in view of Susan's testimony that her mother seemed to expect that the seal of the jar had been broken and replaced. It certainly looked as though Mrs. Gaunt had found some evidence that her husband had been murdered, and had, perhaps, written to Avery to ask him to investigate. Perhaps she was writing the letter when the murderer entered her room, and had thrust it under her blotter, out of sight. Did the murderer know she had written it? Probably not, or some effort would have been made to find and destroy it. Potter consulted some of the pieces of his picture puzzle and came to another conclusion. It was possible that the murderer had known nothing of her suspicions, that she had been killed solely to prevent her from making her will in favour of her eldest son, and that the murderer had been in ignorance until afterwards that the will had already been signed.

That supposition involved a rather extraordinary coincidence, however. Much more likely that the murderer knew that the old lady's suspicions had been aroused. It was not impossible that he had been a witness of that scene in the library when Mrs. Gaunt had investigated the black hawthorn. That was something to look into.

Potter smoked and pondered. What evidence could Mrs. Gaunt have found after two years to lead her to suspect that her husband had not died a natural death? But logic did not carry him very far in that direction. At last he shook the dottle out of his pipe and got to his feet. If she could find it, so could he. He slipped his pipe into his pocket and went upstairs. He opened the door of Mrs. Gaunt's room with a key which he took from his key-ring, went in, and closed the door behind him.

The prospect was not hopeful. He had already been through the room with extreme care and had found nothing to excite his particular interest. But he went over it all again, turning over the papers on the desk, looking through the drawers of the old bureau, leafing through the book on her bedside table, which still lay where she had placed it, with her spectacles on top. A blue book with the title in white lettering: *The China Clippers*, by Basil Lubbock. He stared at it a moment impatiently and laid it down. This sort of thing got him nowhere. He had no idea, after all, what he was looking for. For all he knew he might have handled the evidence and not recognised it for what it was. Perhaps it would mean nothing to anyone unfamiliar with the circumstances of Captain Gaunt's death, and what, after all, did he know about those circumstances?

He brought himself up with a start. What did he know? Only what Ryder had told him—that Nancy and her mother had heard a sound in Captain Gaunt's room about two in the morning, had gone in and found the old man dead, and that Nancy had been sent to summon him. Potter frowned at the floor. Nancy and her mother. He went across the room and knocked on the communicating door. After a moment Nancy opened it.

He was startled at the change in her face. She looked as if she had not slept for a week. Her eyes were set in blue shadows and her mouth was pinched. Her dark hair was damp and matted on her forehead, yet in spite of the heat he saw that she was shivering. She spoke with trembling lips.

"Sergeant Potter—you want to see me?"

Suddenly Potter knew what was in her mind. He leapt at his opportunity. "You've been keeping something back from me, Miss Gaunt. Don't you think it is time to tell me what you know?"

"Yes," said Nancy. "I spent last night thinking it over, and I've decided I can't let you commit a horrible injustice. Anything would be better than that."

"An injustice?"

"Carey. You think he did these awful things."

"Perhaps," admitted Potter cautiously.

"I—I—" She put her hand to her throat with a desperate, pathetic gesture. "You must let me sit down. I don't know how I—"

He understood that she did not know how she was to force the words from her lips. He was filled with pity for this racked and tortured creature, but the instinct of the man-hunter was stronger than pity. He could guess what was in her mind, but he had to know. He pulled forward a chair for her. She sank into it gratefully and he gave her a moment's time. Then he said gently:

"Perhaps I can help you. When I knocked on your door just now, I did it with the idea of asking you to help me recreate the night of your father's death."

"Ah!" It was only a suspicion of a breath, but it told him that he had guessed right. His excitement mounted, but he controlled it carefully.

"I want you, if you will, to show me exactly what happened that. night. As I understand it, the room you now occupy was then your father's?"

"Yes." For a moment more she sat quite still. Then she looked up at him. He saw that she had regained control of herself.

"You are right," she said with a faint smile that was curiously touching. "That is what I wanted to tell you about. I will show you exactly what happened and perhaps—" Her lips trembled again and she rose to cover it. She went back into her own room and he followed her.

It was a big room with windows overlooking the harbour, much like the room they had just left in shape and in the ponderous dignity of massive woodwork and corniced ceiling. But in every other respect it was startlingly different. It was papered in a charming French print. The floor was covered with cool summer matting and the thin curtains hung well back to admit the light. The furniture had belonged to Nancy's great-grandmother and dated back, long before the Gaunt affluence, to the time when grace and simplicity were still held in respect by American designers.

"The room looked quite different, of course, when father used it," Nancy explained. "It was furnished much like mother's room. But the arrangement is practically the same. Father's bed stood in the same place with the bedside table, as it is now, to the left of the person lying in bed."

Potter took in the arrangement at a glance, the bed against the inner wall, opposite the windows, and beside the door into the hall; the three other doors, one into Mrs. Gaunt's room, the second into the bathroom, and the third, in the opposite wall, leading into Susan's room. Nancy crossed to this door and opened it.

"Susan's downstairs," she explained.

Potter stood beside her.

"I had this room while father was alive," Nancy told him. "Susan used the room that's now the sitting-room. As you know, father had a stroke about a year before he died, and was very helpless. Perkins used to dress him and move him and that sort of thing, but at night, of course, he was off. Father ought to have had a nurse, really, but he absolutely refused, so I used to leave this door open at night and he'd call if he wanted anything."

Potter glanced at her curiously. "I understood Dr. Ryder to say he couldn't talk."

Nancy's face contracted in a spasm of pain.

"He couldn't," she said in a low voice. "He always had to write down what he wanted to say. But he could make a sound—not very loud, but enough to waken me with the door open—"

"I see," said Potter gently. "You'll forgive me. I want to get every detail straight."

She nodded without looking at him. In everything she said, in every gesture, he was aware of the strain under which she was labouring.

"How helpless was your father?" he asked.

"Pretty bad. His right side was completely paralysed and he was unable to articulate, although his mind was perfectly clear. He could hear and understand what was said to him—perfectly. He had the use of his left hand and he learned to write with it fairly well—well enough to convey his wishes to us."

"Could he get out of bed by himself?"

"No, not without help. Perkins used to get him up in a wheel chair every day, but he practically had to lift him. You see, father was an old man—besides being half paralysed."

Potter nodded. "I have it straight, I think. Now about that night."

Nancy grew a shade paler.

"Father was very excited and wakeful. He'd had a session with Mr. Avery, drawing up his will, and—and—" Her voice sank till it was hardly more than a whisper. "He'd had a quarrel with—mother—" Her forehead was suddenly covered with sweat. She wiped it off with her handkerchief and stood twisting the bit of linen in her hands. "I couldn't help hearing some of it. It was about the will. She resented his handing over all authority to Wat during her lifetime. I was undressing in my room and her voice came through the closed door. She always raised her voice when she was excited." She spoke rapidly, as though eager to get the horrible business over. She looked at Potter with a sort of despairing dignity. "You'll think that I'm committing an unnatural act, Sergeant Potter. I won't explain or apologise. I'm doing it deliberately, because I've decided that I must."

He nodded prosaically. "What happened next?"

"I heard mother go into her own room and slam the door, so I gathered that she had not had her way. A few minutes later I went into father's room. His usual pad and pencil lay on the bed beside him and on the exposed sheet there was a single word written: 'No.'

A growing excitement possessed Potter. Perhaps he caught it from the pale woman beside him.

"Well?"

"When I had made him comfortable for the night I asked him if he would like me to read to him a while. I often did. It helped him to sleep. He indicated that he would, so I got the book and sat in a chair beside the bed where the light was good and read for about half an hour."

"What time would that be?"

"Rather late. It must have been nearly twelve when I stopped."

Potter nodded. "And then?"

"I was going to put the book away, but he held out his hand for it so I gave it to him and left him with the bedside light still on, reading. I never saw him alive again."

Potter gave her a minute. "Yes?" he prompted.

"I went into my room leaving the door open, and went to bed. I was tired and fell heavily asleep almost at once. Some time later I was wakened by something." She turned her troubled eyes to him. "I am trying to be extremely accurate about this."

"I appreciate that, Miss Gaunt."

"I thought at the time that father was calling me, but I was heavily asleep—drugged with sleep. You know how it is when you're wakened suddenly, before you've had your sleep out."

"Why do you doubt that it was your father calling you?"

"Because he was unable to make a loud noise—only a sort of croaking sound. It was sufficient to wake me usually, with the door between the rooms open. But that night, Sergeant Potter, I was very heavily asleep—and when I sat up in bed and looked, the door between our rooms had been closed."

Potter was conscious of a sudden chill in the small of the back. It was her eyes that did it—the horror in them.

"I didn't realise at first that it was closed. I simply thought that his light was out. I sat in bed for a moment or two, trying to collect myself and listening. After a minute I could hear a faint sound in the room as though someone was moving about, and then a bang—not very loud—the sort of sound that would be made by a book falling on the floor. In fact, that was what I thought of at the time. I thought father had gone to sleep reading and the book had fallen to the floor. It didn't seem to make sense, because his light had been turned off, but I was still half asleep. And then I realised that the light wasn't out. There was a thin line of light along the floor on the far side of my room. I stared at it stupidly a moment and then suddenly I was wide awake. I realised that the thin line of light was the light in father's room and it was shining under the edge of the door, and that the door was closed.

"I wasn't particularly alarmed. I thought that perhaps mother had heard him call out and had gone in to see what he wanted and closed my door so that I wouldn't be disturbed. But I thought perhaps she would need me and I'd better see. I felt for my wrapper and slippers. While I was putting them on I heard another sound—as though someone had stumbled against the fallen book and sent it skidding along the floor. That, again, was what I thought of at the time. I had in my mind a picture of my mother moving about beside my father's bed, stumbling on the book he had been reading, which had fallen to the floor, sending it skidding across the room." She looked at Potter. "I don't know whether these details are of any importance."

"They may be of extreme importance. They help one to visualise what went on."

She nodded. "Yes."

And hesitated as though she saw close upon her the climax of horror.

"I couldn't find my slippers at first. It may have been a full minute before I got them on and went across in the dark to that closed door. When I tried to open it, I found it was locked."

She stopped, white to the lips.

"Yes," said Potter. "Suppose you show me exactly what you did." He closed the door leading into the room in which Captain Gaunt had died, now so brightly, so charmingly feminine with Nancy's belongings. "Show me," said Potter.

The girl stumbled to the door and put her hand on the knob. "It was locked. I tried it several times. I couldn't believe it. It seemed impossible. But it was locked. Then I began to get frightened. I don't know why; there's nothing very terrifying about a locked door. But I was frightened. I couldn't understand it. I went out into the hall."

"Show me," said Potter again.

He followed her and watched as she put her hand on the knob of the hall door.

"I tried this door, too, and it was locked."

"Did you hear any more sounds in the room?"

"No. But I might not. I was beginning to be panicky. I went on into my mother's room."

She led the way and Potter followed her. He was consumed with an overpowering sense of climax. Somehow, he could not say how, he knew that the key to his problem was here—here in the mind of this pallid, shivering woman, if he could only find it, if he could only draw it out.

She stood before the door that led from her mother's room back into the room that had been her father's, and turned her stricken face to him.

"It was here," she said, "that I lost my head completely. My mother was not here when I came in. Her lamp was lighted and her bed had been slept in, but she was not here. I tried to open the door to follow her into my father's room, but I could not. It, too, was locked.

"I must have gone out through the window and along the porch, but I don't remember it. I remember standing at my father's window, looking in. The window was open, as I had left it, and I could see my mother standing by my father's bed. He seemed to be asleep, for he lay with his eyes closed. His left arm was flung out and his hand lay across the open face of the book he had been reading.

"It all looked so natural and commonplace that I felt a terrible let-down. I'd been keyed to a great pitch and thought what a fool I'd been. I began to laugh and my mother heard me. She turned with a start and her face—" Nancy faltered, and then went on determinedly, "Her face was terror-stricken. Just for an instant—terror-stricken."

"Show me just where you both stood."

He unlatched the long window and Nancy led the way out on to the porch. She went along to the next window. Potter followed her and stood looking over her shoulder into the room.

"Where was your mother standing?" he asked.

"Over there—near the bedside table."

"Yes?"

"When she saw who I was, she beckoned to me. 'Come here,' she said. I went and stood beside her. I said stupidly: 'I couldn't get in. The doors were locked.' I looked at father. He was lying very still—very peaceful—I thought at first he was asleep. Then I saw that he wasn't asleep. I grabbed mother's arm. 'Yes,' she said very quietly. 'He's dead.'

"I thought I was going to faint but I didn't. Mother held my arm and talked to me quietly. She told me that, after all, father had been ill a long time—that it was only to be expected—that he would have been glad to go—suddenly, like that. I remember saying: 'I must call Matthew.' You knew that Dr. Ryder was in the house that night?"

Potter nodded.

" 'Yes,' said my mother. 'Certainly. Call Matthew at once.' I started for the door. I had to turn the key before I could open it. I looked back at my mother. I think I was going to ask her about those locked doors. But she said quietly, in a matter-of-fact way: 'There's no need to tell Matthew or anyone else—about the doors being locked.' 'All right,' I said. I went along the hall to Matthew's room.

When we got back the doors were unlocked and standing open as usual."

"Didn't that strike you as queer?"

"Not very. To tell you the truth, Sergeant Potter, I thought then, and I have thought ever since, that mother locked them because she wanted to have another talk with father about the will and didn't want to be disturbed. I have even thought that perhaps the excitement and strain were too much for him and he died in the midst of their talk. It was only after I learned that father had been—murdered—" She broke off, trembling so that she could hardly stand. Potter finished for her. He could be cruel, this kind, good-natured fellow. He was cruel now. He had to know.

"It was only then that you knew your mother had killed your father."

She put her hands up with a cry as though to ward off a blow.

"Sit down, Miss Gaunt," said Potter sternly. "There are some things I want to know. First, exactly what happened when you came back into the room with Dr. Ryder?"

"Except that the doors were open, everything was just as it had been. I knew Matthew would want to examine my father and the book, lying under his left hand, was in the way, so I took it up and closed it and put it on the shelf."

Something clicked in Potter's mind. He could never afterwards say what did it—an association of ideas, a sudden glorious hunch. Sometimes, afterwards, he would wake in the night, in a sweat, wondering what would have happened if he had not asked that next question. But he did ask it.

"Do you remember what book it was?"

"Yes," said Nancy, wonderingly. "It was *The China Clippers*, by Basil Lubbock."

Potter stole a glance through the open door into Mrs. Gaunt's room. He saw, in a sudden indelible flash, the big, funereal bed, the teakwood table with the marble top that stood beside it, and on the table, with a pair of spectacles lying on it, a blue book with title printed in white.

He paced the length of the room and back, his mind searching, searching for the lead. Nancy stared at him in rising excitement.

"Is it important?" she asked.

"Do you know where that book is now?" demanded Potter suddenly, stopping before her.

"On that shelf, I suppose; I've never moved father's books."

"It's on your mother's bedside table."

For a moment Nancy stared at him as though she suspected that he had taken leave of his senses. Then she understood. She put out a hand; found a chairback to steady her.

"Come, come!" cried Potter. "Every detail! Search your memory. This sound of a falling book, now—yet you say the book was on the bed."

"It was. Curiously enough I thought of that afterwards. I looked on the floor but found nothing that might have explained the sound."

"He put the book back of course," said Potter. He was back at his pacing—back and forth. "In the struggle—a mild one, no doubt, but a struggle since your father called out—the book fell to the floor. When he was leaving the murderer kicked it inadvertently with his foot. Let us say he had already pulled the bedclothes back in place, but here was the book your father had been reading—out in the middle of the floor, perhaps. There must be no sign of any struggle. He wanted it to appear as though your father had died quietly in his sleep. He picked the book up and replaced it under your father's hand."

"And my mother—"

An incredulous hope lit the girl's strained face "Your mother chanced to be looking through your father's books—did she read books of that type?"

"Everything—any book—every book about sailing ships."

"One more question, Miss Gaunt. You said a few minutes ago that your father kept a pad and pencil beside him."

"Always. It was the only way he had of communicating with us, except by signs."

"Were they on the bed when you found him?"

She shook her head, her eyes widening. Her hand went to her breast as though to quiet the pounding of her heart.

"At night he liked to have his book and a glass of water where he could reach them. The pad was in the way. So I used to put it in the table drawer, and get it out for him when I first went in in the morning. But the pencil—" Her hand went to her eyes for a moment. She was breathing heavily. "Oh, my God! Sergeant Potter, let us look through that book. He used to keep the pencil to make notes in the margins as he read. He did so that night. I took the pencil out of his hand myself—after he was dead."

For a long moment it was so still that the room seemed filled with Nancy's gasping breath. At last Potter said quietly: "I think we have it. I suppose you didn't notice where the book was opened?"

"No, except that it was a picture of a ship, on shiny paper—and towards the beginning of the book. I noticed that because it surprised me. I had read at least three-quarters of the way through when I left him for the night."

"Opened at random," muttered Potter. "It fits, it all fits. It's got to be so."

As though suddenly galvanised into action he hurried through the door into Mrs. Gaunt's room, took the book from the bedside table, carried it to the desk and flipped through the pages carefully, scanning closely each one that faced one of the prints of famous clippers with which the text was illustrated. Nancy stood in the doorway watching him, immobile except for her burning eyes. She saw the look on his face, heard his caught breath, when at last he paused and turned the pages no further.

Before him lay a picture of the *Flying Cloud*, loveliest of clippers, under her towering, cloud-like canvas. There was a wide white margin and across the upper edge of it half a dozen letters, trailing off into indeterminate quavers, were feebly scrawled

"My mother—" whispered Nancy with dry lips.

"You have been distressing yourself needlessly—about your mother," said Potter quietly. "She knew no more about your father's death than you did—although she may have suspected more.

"Oh, thank God!"

Potter turned back a few pages to some notes scrawled opposite the description of the *Staghound*.

"Did your father write this?" he asked.

She looked over his shoulder. "Yes."

"You could not be mistaken? That is his handwriting?"

"Yes. Oh, yes. That is the way he wrote after he was ill, using his left hand."

Potter closed the book. His face wore a look of triumph that she was quick to read.

"Thank you, Miss Gaunt. You've helped me—more than you know."

"But who?" Her face was full of anguished questioning.

"To-night," he said gently. "I promise you shall know to-night.

CHAPTER XXI

WHEN he left the Gaunt house Sergeant Potter stopped in at Miss Lucetta Brown's shop. He was there for perhaps thirty minutes. Then he came out, got into his car, and drove back to New London. He went straight to his office.

Collins had returned and was waiting for him, feet propped on the desk, the evening paper in his hands.

"They're sure giving us a spread," he remarked, flipping the paper round so that Potter could see the two-inch headlines. "Biggest excitement since the Judd affair. New York papers too." He waved a hand towards a disordered pile on the table.

Potter sank wearily into his chair.

"Well, we'll have a bigger story for 'em in the morning," he said, his eyes grim.

Collins removed his feet from the desk.

"No kiddin'!" he said, and there was an odd breathlessness in his voice. "Have you got it?"

"Washed up," nodded Potter with a grim smile.

"Jed you old son of a—Which one?"

At the thing Potter told him Collins' pursed lips emitted a soundless whistle.

"When do we stage the party!"

"I'm staging a party to-night," said Potter grimly. "What a case it's been, Tom! Smart work—smartest I ever saw. Three murders in a row and not a single damn clue—barring a two-inch fragment of common white twine. If it hadn't been for a bit of the wildest and most improbable luck—"

This was the origin of the luck theory. Collins listened with literally bated breath to his chief's account of the events of the afternoon. He examined the entry in the blue book with fascinated eyes.

"Golly!" he breathed reverently.

"Have Henderson look at the handwriting, will you? I should think there was no doubt it was authentic, but considering the old lady's character, we'd better make sure."

Collins grinned. "O.K. By the way, the report came in about those fingerprints—the fistful Peters picked up on the rail of the yacht."

"Yeah?"

"They won't help you. They're Waterman's."

Potter nodded. "Well, can't expect to hit it lucky all the time. Hennessey call?"

"Yep. About fifteen minutes ago. He's got plenty of dirt about Mrs. Ingersoll and Olsen, but it don't seem to fit."

"I'll talk to him."

Potter reached for the phone and spoke into it.

"Get that New York call back, will you?" Dangling the instrument on his knee, he looked across at Collins. "Now let's have your stuff. Get anything this afternoon?"

Potter spent a busy two hours. About eight-thirty he finished his business at the courthouse, ran down the steps, got into his roadster and drove back to Stone Haven.

Potter had done some telephoning before he left New London, so that when he entered the Gaunt house he found an assemblage waiting for him in the library. Besides the members of the household and their shepherding policemen there were several people from outside: Mr. Avery, Jimmy West, Tony Farelli, Melvin Saunders, and Miss Lucetta Brown, who was looking very pretty in soft gray voile; looking also rather flustered and a little frightened.

They had been making some pretence at conversation while they waited, but they abandoned it on Potter's entrance. They were filled with terrified foreboding and they were past trying to cover it. One glance at Potter's face told them that the sword hung over their heads and they watched its ravelling cord with a fascinated horror.

Jimmy West, standing behind Susan's chair, put a steadying hand on her shoulder. She made no attempt to shake it off. Instead, after a moment her own hand stole up and clung to it, hard and desperate. Tony Farelli, sprawled sullenly in the corner of the sofa, glanced at them briefly and looked away.

Susan was trying not to look at Carey, sitting in a low chair by the middle window, crouched forward, his head on his hands. He had not moved since he entered the room. She knew it although she kept her eyes away from him.

When Potter came in with Minton and Avery, Ryder drew his chair nearer Nancy. They did not even look at each other, yet they were bound by that curious mutual awareness known only to lovers.

Astrid Ingersoll and her brother sat together, a little apart from the family, obviously isolated and resentful. She was dressed in ostentatious black, her round, sophisticated face devoid of make-up except for the scarlet bow of her lips.

Edgar, lounging in a deep chair beside the hearth, stared at her appraisingly, his eyes bloodshot and puffy under his heavy brows.

Edgar was showing the effects of a day without liquor. His heavy face was mottled with bluish shadows, the muscles lax and twitching. His hands were unsteady and his temper raw. He was smoking nervously, lighting one cigarette after another and dropping the ashes on the Chinese rug. Behind him, in the corner near the drawing-room door, Elvira sat, nervously twisting a black-edged handkerchief. She was heavily made up and her hair was carefully dressed, but she gave, perhaps for the first time, the impression of a broken middle-aged woman, verging on corpulence, raddled with helpless fear.

Potter took them in at a glance; the servants huddled together near the hall door, anxious and curious; the masters preserving only with difficulty the mask of indifference on the face of their exhaustion and suspense.

He walked to his place behind the desk, glancing as he did so at the black hawthorn jar, now restored to its pedestal on the mantel. He could almost feel the shuddering withdrawal of eyes from the lovely, sinister thing. Then he turned and laid his battered brief case on the desk.

He looked around the room. They wondered what he was waiting for, but in a moment they heard it—the sound of another car drawing up in the street outside. A moment later Collins came in with a small blonde man who drew a chair up to the corner of the desk, took out a black notebook and pencil, and waited.

"There are some questions I want to ask you," said Potter. "I have brought a stenographer to record your replies. I have had enough of evasions and half-truths. Before we leave this room we are going to know who killed Captain Gaunt and his wife and son—and why."

Suddenly Carey raised his head furiously.

"Questions! Questions! I'm sick of them. Why don't you come right out and say you think *I* did it?"

"Carey!" cried Susan desperately.

Potter ignored the outburst. He opened his brief case and drew out some typewritten sheets. For a moment he fingered them absently. Then he looked over them at his audience, glancing slowly from face to face.

Hope came to him. They were near the breaking-point. With any luck he could break them. He glanced again at the reports in his hand.

"On second thought," he said slowly, "I have changed my mind. I am not going to ask questions. I am going to tell you a story. I am going to tell you how these murders took place—and why. I am going to lay all my cards on the table, face up—with one single exception, and that is the name of the guilty person."

There was not even any sound of breathing in the room. After a minute Jimmy West asked quietly:

"Do you know the name of the guilty person?"

"Yes," said Potter.

Carey threw his head up.

"Bluff! He wants us to give ourselves away."

"Shut up!" cried Susan. "For heaven's sake, keep quiet!"

Lucetta Brown leaned forward, her cheeks no longer pink.

"Is the—the murderer—in this room now?"

"Yes," said Potter again. He leaned back, his clasped hands behind his head, his eyes on the painted ceiling. "Are you all ready?" he asked smoothly. "It's not a pretty story, certainly, but it's—interesting." No one answered him. They kept their eyes carefully on his face.

He pulled his head forward for a minute to glance from face to face with a grim smile.

"Stop me if I don't make myself clear," he said pleasantly, "and—correct me if I'm wrong." His eyes returned to the ceiling.

"We'll go back two years, just to begin at the beginning. Almost an even two years, for I understand that Captain Gaunt died on the eighteenth of August?"

"Yes," murmured Nancy.

"Two days before, Mrs. Gaunt, thinking her husband was worse, had sent for Dr. Ryder. Am I correct, Doctor?"

"Quite," said Matthew Ryder.

"Captain Gaunt insisted on knowing the truth about his condition and you were obliged to tell him that he might die at any time. Right again?"

"Yes."

"Now we come to our story. Captain Gaunt, realising that he had not long to live, sent for his lawyer to draw up his will. He had made a will twenty years before, leaving everything in his wife's hands. But his children had grown up meanwhile and he naturally wanted to alter his will in their favour. You were all here at the time—I mean, of course, all the immediate family. Naturally you were able to put two and two together. Evidently you did, for Miss Susan informed me that it was known her father intended to make a new will.

"How it became known that Captain Gaunt meant to leave the greater part of his estate to his oldest son I'm not sure. It is known that he had a quarrel with his wife about it, and I have several times heard it said that Mrs. Gaunt raised her voice when she was angry. It is possible that quarrel was overheard." He paused, but no one spoke.

"At any rate, someone waited until the household was asleep, broke the seal of the black hawthorn jar, took out the dagger that leaves no trace, and went up to Captain Gaunt's room where he lay reading—where he had perhaps fallen asleep with the book in his hand. This person closed and locked the doors of the room to prevent any unlucky interruption. Apparently Captain Gaunt was roused, for he attempted to save himself."

Potter sat upright, his accusing eyes turning from one to another of the white faces before him.

"We must picture an old man, helplessly paralysed, watching the approach of violent death, seeing murder in the eyes of someone standing by his bed. He called out as well as he could—a feeble cry. He threw up his left arm to ward off the blow—and was stabbed—swiftly and remorselessly, high up under the left arm, and through the heart."

Miss Lucetta put her hands to her face.

"Oh!" she moaned softly.

"No doubt the murderer intended to unlock the doors again, but he hadn't time. Someone had heard the cry for help and was trying to get in. He smoothed the bedclothes hastily, replaced the book that had fallen to the floor, and hurried out of the window only just in time." Potter paused and once more reached into his brief case. This time he drew out a book with a light-blue cover, the title printed in white lettering. "This is the book Captain Gaunt was reading, the book the murderer replaced under his hand after he had been killed."

Every pair of eyes in the room swung to the book and lingered there in fascinated horror. Susan sobbed once, and pressed her fingers to her trembling lips. Nancy was shaking from head to foot, but she said nothing.

"In spite of the locked doors," Potter went on, "the murderer got away with it. There was no suspicion of foul play. Mrs. Gaunt no doubt suspected something, but it is certain she did not suspect murder." Potter hesitated. "Perhaps," he corrected himself, "I should not say it is certain. We must remember that she was very unwilling for her husband to change his will."

Carey blazed up again.

"Are you accusing my mother of knowing about my father's murder—and concealing it?"

"Certainly not," said Potter sternly. "Dr. Ryder said that he died a natural death and why should she question it? The only suspicious circumstance was the locked doors. No doubt she was able to find an explanation for that. She must have remembered that there were others besides herself who would have quarrelled with the provisions of the new will."

Avery spoke suddenly from the place he had taken near Nancy on the end of the sofa.

"I must compliment you on the power of your imagination, Sergeant Potter."

"There's not much imagination about it," said Potter grimly. "I can prove it to a jury—step by step—and," he added softly, "I expect to."

Avery shrugged irritably. But Potter was not through with him. "What time was it when you left the house that night?"

"About ten o'clock."

"Did you before you left have any talk with anyone about the will?"

"Certainly not."

"You told no one about Captain Gaunt's intentions?"

"No one."

"Did anyone enter the room while you were with him?"

"I believe Susan came in for a moment."

"Yes," said Susan defiantly, "I did. What of it?"

"Because I wanted to know if father was really making a will."

"Did you learn the terms of the will?"

"No."

"Did you tell anybody about what you knew—that night, I mean?"

Susan's eyes flickered. She hesitated.

"I'd forgotten all about it," she said slowly, "but I did."

"Never mind that now," said Potter quickly. "We'll go into that later."

Susan looked down at the floor, trembling.

"I've already said," went on the detective slowly, "that our murderer got away with that murder. He did. The dagger left no trace—or at any rate no trace was discovered. If that had been all, he would never have been caught. But the same situation arose again two years later—last Friday night." Potter paused and again terror walked in the silent room.

"Our murderer returned to the house about midnight to find that during the absence of the family Waterman Gaunt had been secretly closeted with his mother and Mr. Avery, and that, almost beyond doubt, another will was in process of being drawn.

"There are points about this that remain obscure. I know that the murderer suspected something when Mrs. Ingersoll turned up at the Michitiquock Club. Perhaps it was only a vague idea at that time, a remembrance that Waterman Gaunt had declined to join the party, saying that he was unable to do so. At any rate, our murderer was sufficiently interested, perhaps, to ask questions when the party returned to the house, to learn of the presence of Waterman and Mr. Avery, and to deduce the rest. Whether this came out that night or the next morning—"

Suddenly Reeves, Waterman's man, stepped out from the group of servants near the hall door. He coughed, and winked with a sort of horrible grimace at Potter.

"It came out that night, sir—although I never thought of it until this minute. I met the person you are talking about in the upstairs hall, sir. I had just finished in Mr. Waterman Gaunt's room and was on my way to bed. In answer to a question I mentioned the fact that Mr. Gaunt had met Mr. Avery there that evening."

Avery sat forward. He wore the look of a thoroughly angry man. "This is outrageous, Potter. If you are accusing someone, let us know his name. This hocus pocus—"

Potter broke in. His face was hard as granite, his voice cold and cutting as a knife.

"I am accusing no one," he said. "I am talking about a hypothetical murderer. I am re-creating the way in which these crimes were committed and the reason they were committed. If I know the name of this murderer—if there are others who guess it—that is my affair. I don't accuse without proof. I'm going to have proof that I can take before a jury before I leave this room to-night. And when I leave it, the murderer will leave it, too."

"You've got a warrant, I suppose?" sneered Avery.

"As a matter of fact, I have. Do you want me to serve it now and take a chance? Or do I play it my way?"

Their eyes clashed furiously for a moment. It was Avery who collapsed. He surrendered with a shrug.

"We return then to Friday night," said Potter smoothly. "Our murderer is confronted with a situation that closely resembles the situation he met so successfully before. He can be under no delusions about the provisions of Mrs. Gaunt's will. The secrecy of the meeting, and the fact that of all the children only Waterman was present, admits of only one interpretation. We now come to a point which is not entirely clear. The situation was almost exactly similar to the situation on the night Captain Gaunt was so successfully eliminated. Why didn't the murderer meet it in the same way? Why did he wait until the middle of the next morning, when the danger attendant on his act was multiplied a hundred times! In other words, why didn't he wait till the household had gone to sleep, enter Mrs. Gaunt's room, and kill her then?"

"Because he couldn't."

Potter's eyes swung round to find this new voice. It was Maggie, Mrs. Gaunt's maid. She was white as a sheet, but her face wore a determined do-or-die look.

"Mrs. Gaunt's been sleeping with her door locked ever since Captain Gaunt's death, sir. Not the door into Miss Nancy's room, but the other one. And last Friday night she slept with her windows locked too. Mrs. Gaunt always had her windows closed when it was foggy, she hated fog—always has. She said it spotted the walls. I closed them myself before dinner-time Friday. And when those long windows are closed, sir, you can't open them from the outside. They lock automatically."

Potter brought his hand down with a light, triumphant gesture on the desk.

"That's it!" he said. "That's it, of course. He tried to get in and failed. He was afraid to go through Miss Nancy's room—afraid of waking her. And the next morning Waterman sat with Mrs. Gaunt while she ate her breakfast, and then Miss Nancy. It was not until Miss Nancy went downstairs that the murderer had his opportunity. When it came he seized it. The circumstances made it dangerous, but he couldn't wait; for in the meantime he had been a witness of that scene in the library when Mrs. Gaunt examined the black hawthorn jar and told Susan that it had evidently been opened before.

"That could only mean one thing—that Mrs. Gaunt's suspicions had been aroused. He had no choice but to act as soon as the opportunity presented itself. I have no doubt that as soon as the coast was clear, he reopened the black hawthorn jar, took from it the dagger he had replaced there after the first murder, hid it under his coat and went upstairs. At any rate, with the windows of Mrs. Gaunt's room closed he must, have entered through Miss Nancy's room. Unless," added Potter dryly, "Mr. Edgar Gaunt is mistaken, and he went in from the hall."

Edgar breathed heavily.

"I tell you nobody went in that door for an hour or more before mother was killed."

"Well, then, we must assume he entered through Miss Nancy's room. No doubt he already knew that Miss Nancy had gone out. Perhaps he hid himself in the passageway between the two rooms, or in one of the closets opening from it, and waited for Waterman to leave. One can only imagine the terror with which he listened for the old lady to confide her suspicions, but she did not. I will admit that this is only surmise. But this much we do know: We know that he seized the only possible moment during the morning when the murder was possible: the moment when Nancy went downstairs leaving her mother alone. It is reasonable to assume that he was waiting for it—in Nancy's room."

Suddenly Elvira spoke. Her voice was cracked and hoarse and her eyes, turned on Edgar, were venomous.

"How do you know he wasn't waiting—in the sitting-room?"

"That is also possible," admitted Potter smoothly.

Edgar swung on his wife. His face was suddenly crimson, and the cords in his neck knotted.

"Be careful," he said in a low voice, "or by God—"

CHAPTER XXII

IT seemed to those who listened that Potter's voice would go on forever, that the horror would never be ended. Like the slow dropping of water on a nerve, his words beat down on them, crushing their resistance.

"I needn't trouble you with an account of the death of Waterman Gaunt," he went on smoothly, "you are all too familiar with that already. We can surmise that he would, perhaps, have been spared, if he had not been unfortunate enough to discover a letter his mother had begun to Mr. Avery, conveying her suspicions, and attempted to profit by it. How he was killed, we know, and how the letter was destroyed. But our murderer's problem is still unsolved. He has discovered that Mrs. Gaunt's will, far from being incomplete, has already been signed and that it is in Waterman's custody on the *Buccaneer*. Unless it is destroyed, all the risks he has run are futile, all his efforts are for nothing.

"So we come to what is, perhaps, the most extraordinary feat of all. While the house is full of the police, while, for an hour, our attention is focused on this room, our murderer walks again. He puts on a bathing suit, cuts a length of hard, white three-ply cord from a ball in his desk, borrows a bathing cap and pulls it on with the cord inside to keep it dry, and slips out into the fog. He makes the *Buccaneer*—in itself a difficult stunt in that fog—climbs aboard and gets into the engine-room."

Potter was proving himself a narrator of no mean gifts. He held his audience spellbound while he described, as Rowland had told it to him, the way in which the explosion took place.

"Having lighted his fuse, then, the murderer swims ashore again and reaches the house before the explosion occurs. He hangs the wet bathing suit over the rail and is already in his room, with his night clothes on, when the alarm is sounded. He appears with the rest of the household, is properly horrified, and again flatters himself that he has got away with it.

"But, as a matter of fact, there were two slips, infinitesimally small but sufficient to point unmistakably the path he had gone. The first was that it never occurred to our murderer that any part of the fuse he had used could escape the fire, so he made no effort to get rid of the ball of twine from which he had cut it—and this was subsequently discovered in a desk in his room."

Once again Potter had recourse to his brief-case. This time he took out an envelope and drew from it a two-inch piece of white cord. He laid it beside the blue book on the desk. "This was found jammed under the engine-room door, unburnt. Not much, you see, but sufficient to hang him."

Astrid Ingersoll sobbed hysterically.

"The other slip," Potter went on, "was not his fault. Correct me if I'm wrong, Miss Susan, but I think you heard a sound on the porch when the murderer was removing his bathing suit. I think you went out to investigate and found nothing but the wet suit on the rail. I think that at that moment the explosion occurred—the moment in which you realised that the wet bathing suit was Carey's."

"No! No!" cried Susan, on her feet, swaying.

"Yes, said Potter sternly. "You lost your head. You knew that Carey's suit had been dried after your morning swim because you had dried it when you dried your own. You already feared that Carey was involved in the murders. So you rushed back into your room, took your own bathing suit from the closet in the bathroom where it is kept, wet it and hung it on the rail beside Carey's. And afterwards told the story of your swim and said that the suits had not dried. You thought in the disturbed state of the household no one would notice. You did not know you had been seen bringing the suits up from the dryer."

Susan looked at the point of collapse.

"It's not true—any of it."

"It's time," said Potter sternly, "for you to come out in the open. You've been obstructing this inquiry from the beginning. Why? Were you afraid someone would find out about Carey's quarrel with his mother? If you hoped to conceal that you have a touching faith in the discretion of this household. It was one of the first things I was told when I began my investigations."

"You're a—devil," whispered Susan.

"I'm going to have the truth. Why did you lie about the light switch when your brother was killed? Were you actually standing with your back against it?"

"Yes."

"What's the use, Susan?" cried Carey suddenly. "Why don't you tell him? She wasn't anywhere near the light switch. She hasn't the foggiest notion whether I touched it or not. In fact, I believe she thinks I did." Brother and sister looked at each other then—a look of agonised questioning. Then Susan sat down again and looked at the floor.

"And the morning of your mother's death—why did you say there was no one else in the room—that no one overheard you?"

"Because no one did. We were alone." Her voice was full of bitter exhaustion.

"Didn't you know that Carey was seen on the terrace—that he was seen looking in at the window?"

Susan cast a swift, reproachful look at Perkins, almost wringing his hands.

"It wasn't me," he said wretchedly.

His wife spoke then, her comfortable voice sounding like the voice of the one sane person in a mad-house. "It was me, Miss Susan," she said. "I know Mr. Carey hadn't anything to do with the murders, but I thought he might have told somebody else."

Carey was looking at Potter with an odd, concentrated look.

"We'll come back to that point later," said Potter. "Mr. West"—and now for the first time the detective took cognizance of Jimmy West's presence in the room— "why did you offer to go bail for Tony Farelli?"

West hesitated. Susan was looking at Potter curiously.

"Go on and tell him, Jimmy," she said softly. "Tell him anything he wants to know."

"I did it," said West pleasantly, "because Susan asked me to."

"Did she give any reason for her request?"

"Yes. She said Farelli had only been arrested because he had—very decently—given evidence about hearing the man swim ashore from the yacht and she didn't want him to suffer for it."

"Anything else?"

"Yes," said West, after a glance at Susan. "She said she wanted to see him and asked me to arrange it."

"And you did so?"

"Yes. I called her later and told her if she could manage to slip out of the house early next morning, Tony would meet her at his wharf."

Potter transferred his eyes to Farelli's face.

"Did you meet her?"

Tony looked at Susan. "Ask her," he said.

"Yes," said Susan. "I met him. I told him I was worried about Carey and he agreed to say he wasn't sure about hearing anybody swim ashore. I thought maybe you wouldn't be able to prove that the explosion wasn't an accident."

Potter looked his exasperation. "Well," he said, "anyway, we have it straight now. You did hear someone swimming ashore?" he asked Tony.

Susan's field god cast her a reproachful glance.

"Sure," he said.

"You're certain of it?"

"Of course I'm certain. Think I'm a dumb-bell? And I'm certain he climbed ashore at the sea wall down at the foot of this garden. I could hear the shingle rattle."

"Swear to it?"

"On the Bible," nodded Farelli.

Susan seemed hardly to breathe. Her eyes never left Potter's face. "All right," said Potter. "Now there's something else I want to know. Dr. Ryder, when Carey wired you that his mother was dying, what train did you take?"

"The twelve-ten."

"Close work, wasn't it, Doctor? She only died at eleven and you got the telegram in time to pack your bag and get the twelve-ten."

Ryder frowned suddenly.

"What are you getting at?"

"I'm curious to know why your car is now parked in a garage near the station at New Haven—and was parked there by you at about two o'clock on the day of Mrs. Gaunt's death."

"I never said that I took the train in New York," said Ryder evenly.

Potter sat forward, squaring his shoulders.

"Now we're getting somewhere," he said. "Just where did you take the train?"

"At New Haven, naturally, since I left my car there."

"That is, you took the train that leaves New York at twelve-ten?"

"Yes."

"And simply allowed it to be assumed that you had come through from New York?"

"I don't know what you mean. The question never came up."

Potter turned on Nancy.

"Miss Nancy, when did you leave the house on the morning of your mother's death?"

She was pale to the lips. "About seven o'clock."

"Did anyone see you go?"

"Not that I know of."

"You slipped out quietly?"

"Not particularly. It happened that no one was up."

"And you drove—where?"

Nancy looked at Ryder.

"To The Mariners, just beyond New London."

"And met Dr. Ryder?"

"Yes. We had breakfast together."

"What happened then?"

"I returned—here." She grasped the arms of her chair to steady the shaking of her hands. Ryder laid a hand on hers.

"I returned with her," he said gently. "That's what you wanted to know, isn't it? It was very foggy, and I was nervous about her driving by herself, so we left her car at The Mariners and I drove her home."

"What time did you get here?"

"About ten o'clock."

"Of course you came in and spoke to the household?"

Matthew Ryder smiled grimly.

"A rhetorical question. I did not, as you know."

"Why not?"

"Two reasons—neither of them very good. One was that we knew that Mrs. Gaunt resented any obvious attentions to Nancy so that we avoided all appearances of an understanding between us. The other was that I had to return to New. Haven immediately anyway. I had come up, as I frequently do, to see a patient."

"You can give me his name and address?"

"Certainly."

"And you did not enter the house?"

"I did not."

"Very well. What did you do then?"

"I drove to New Haven. It was one o'clock when I got there, for I had to drive cautiously because of the fog, and I'd had some engine trouble too. I stopped for a bit of lunch and went round to my patient's house. There I was told that my office had been trying to reach me. I put through a New York call and my secretary told me a telegram had come, saying that Mrs. Gaunt was dying and asking me to go at once. I knew that I could get back much faster by train, so I wired I was coming, left my car in a garage, caught the train, and Carey met me in the New London Station. If he'd bothered to look, he would have seen that the wire was sent from New Haven."

"You are certain that wire was sent from New Haven?"

"Of course I'm certain. I sent it myself."

"And you are prepared to swear you didn't enter this house on Saturday morning?"

Nancy was on her feet, her eyes blazing.

"It's outrageous!" she flashed at Potter. "Of course he didn't come in. He left me at the door and drove straight away."

"Did you tell him that your mother was making a will in favour of Waterman?"

"I told him we suspected it."

"Was it before or after you told him that he offered to drive you back to Stone Haven?"

"It was just as I was preparing to leave that he said he would drive me back."

"After you told him about the will?"

"I suppose so."

"And it's possible, isn't it, that when he left you at the door he might have driven down the street a little way, returned through the garden in the fog, entered by way of the porch—"

"Stop!" cried Nancy. "It's insane."

"He was in the house when your father was killed. And he, better than anyone else, would be in a position to know that wounds made with a long, narrow instrument don't bleed externally—much."

The room was full of a mounting hysteria. Elvira giggled suddenly, and pressed her black-bordered handkerchief to her mouth to silence the sound. Only Dr. Ryder seemed not to be caught in the common mood. His plain, sensible face remained composed. "Do you accuse me of these crimes?"

Potter suddenly did a surprising thing. He smiled.

"No," he said, "I don't. You've hit on the one unanswerable argument. If you'd been guilty, you'd have asked your secretary to wire. You couldn't have known that no one would notice the wire was sent from New Haven."

CHAPTER XXIII

POTTER looked down at the notes that lay before him on the desk.

"We have a singularly complete picture of these murders. If the actual facts vary from the account I have given you, it can only be by a hair's breadth. I am in a position to prove, step by step, beyond any reasonable doubt, the truth of the story. But, so far, the personality behind these manifestations has remained a shadow. I will name the shadow for you presently. But, meanwhile, I would like for a moment to use what Mr. Avery calls my imagination."

He leaned back in his chair, hands clasped behind his head, eyes again on the painted ceiling. His craggy face was grim and thoughtful. His listeners waited in an almost unbearable suspense.

"We'll begin by drawing a picture of our murderer—we'll begin by saying that he is a man. We'll assume that. It's perhaps not certain from the facts as I've given them to you. There's nothing about these crimes that—technically speaking—a woman couldn't have done. But I think you'll agree it's improbable. They're essentially masculine crimes.

"We'll begin, therefore, with a man—a man of physical strength and dexterity, a good swimmer and one who is thoroughly familiar with the harbour. But, above all, a man of really extraordinary nerve and smartness. And we must add to these characteristics a motive strong enough to outweigh the almost incredible risks of the enterprise. We must assume that our murderer had much to lose as well as much to gain.

"Very early in this inquiry I looked about for such a man. You all had something to lose by the change in Mrs. Gaunt's will, but, after all, there was no question of her leaving any of her children penniless. I began to question whether, after all, that motive, plus the very evident dislike in which most of you held your mother, was enough. I doubted it. The risks were enormous—the sort of risks that are taken deliberately only by a desperate or a very determined man. It seemed to me that only one man now in this room had the motive I was seeking—the motive that involved fear of extreme loss as well as hope of gain.

"I was left with a picture taking shape in my mind. There were difficulties in my way—difficulties that at times seemed impassable—yet the conviction continued to grow and strengthen in my mind.

"I pictured a boy growing up more or less under a social cloud. An ambitious, smart boy, less favoured than his fortunate cousins. I pictured him filled with the old tales of the buccaneering Gaunts—his great-uncle and his grandfather. I pictured his eagerness to follow in their footsteps, his soreness, his resentment at being shut out of what he felt to be his rightful place. Then came the healing of the breach and, at last, his opportunity. He was given a place in the offices of the Gaunt Lines.

"This boy had inherited a genius—a genius that had skipped the third generation in the direct line—the hard, ruthless genius for success. Ships were his natural medium as paint is the natural medium for a painter. He knew how to use ships for the making of fortunes. Before long he had become a forceful influence. And before much longer he had become dominant. Old Captain Gaunt was failing. His sons were indifferent. This man seized his opportunity.

"And then he discovered that it was to be snatched away from him. That because of a mere sentimental relationship and the accident of birth he was to lose not only the labour of twenty years, but his future as well, for he had no illusions about what would happen with Waterman in control.

"I have already said he was a ruthless man, as all gifted money-makers have been ruthless. He was prepared to take by any violence the thing that he considered his own."

Potter kept his eyes carefully on the ceiling.

"I'm a native of these parts," he said slowly, choosing his words. "I was brought up on the story of the Gaunts. I guess I know as much about the first Captain Waterman Gaunt as his grandchildren do. And about this time in my thinking I began to see a curious thing. I began to see that old fellow had handed down something besides his money. I began to see he'd handed down an idea—a point of view—character, if you want to call it that. There's been a lot of talk about the 'curse of the Gaunts.' *That's* the 'curse of the Gaunts.'

"The second Waterman Gaunt had it and his wife, too. Hard people they were. Unscrupulous, too, and strong. In their own way, in their own times, they followed the sea for the same reason the old man did—because there was money to be wrung from it, fortunes to be made sending grimy freighters here and there over the globe.

"And then I took the last step in my thinking: I saw that a funny thing had happened. Instead of following down in a straight line, this idea—this character—whatever you want to call it—this thing that had made the first two Waterman Gaunts the men they were, had missed the third generation—skipped it entirely, and cropped up again, not in the sons of the second Waterman Gaunt, but in his nephew. I am speaking, of course, of Daniel Minton."

They had kept their eyes carefully from Minton's face but now they turned to him, where he sat immobile at the corner of the desk like a man in a dream. A few moments before he had been one of them, together against a common enemy. Now he was alone—terribly alone.

He seemed to rouse himself with an effort.

"Very pretty," he said. "Very romantic. No doubt you are not depending entirely on your imagination?"

"I have already said," murmured Potter, withdrawing his gaze from the ceiling and fixing it to Minton, "that imagination has nothing to do with it. I'll go back now and check a few points."

He looked across at Susan. "Perhaps," he said acidly, "you're willing to talk now?"

Susan was frankly clinging to West's hand. She looked at the point of collapse.

"Yes," she whispered.

"You have already told us that, after you had seen Mr. Avery with your father on the night he died, you told someone that they were drawing up a will. Who was that someone?"

Susan's lips tried to shape a name and failed. She tried again. "Daniel Minton."

Potter looked at Perkins, the butler.

"I am told " he said, "that at eight o'clock on the morning of Mrs. Gaunt's death you passed the door of the library and saw Mrs. Gaunt and Miss Susan examining the black hawthorn jar?"

Perkins wet his dry lips with his tongue. "Yes, sir."

"And that you saw someone else watching them from the window?"

"Yes, sir."

"Who was it?"

"Well, sir, I didn't really get a good look at him, but my impression was that it was Mr. Carey, because I had seen him only a minute before walking up and down the terrace."

"And this was at eight o'clock?"

"Five minutes to eight exactly, sir. I had just looked at the hall clock."

Potter turned to Miss Lucetta Brown. She started visibly. "Miss Brown, at what time did you leave your house on Saturday morning?"

"At ten minutes to eight. I always do. I like to get the shop opened by eight o'clock precisely."

"And you started promptly on Saturday morning?"

"Yes, sir."

"Tell us what you saw when you came out of your house."

"Well, it was very foggy. I stood a minute on my back porch, trying to see the *Buccaneer*, but I couldn't even see as far as the end of the garden."

"But you could see the Gaunt house?"

"Oh, yes."

"And the terrace along the back of the house?"

"Yes."

"Did you see anyone on the terrace?"

"Yes. When I first came out Mr. Carey was walking up and down. And a few minutes later Mr. Minton came out and joined him. I could hear them talking for a moment and then Carey left and went down through the garden."

"Did Mr. Minton leave too?"

"No."

"Tell us what happened."

Miss Lucetta glanced quickly at Minton and quickly away again. "He stood smoking for a moment," she said faintly. "Then he seemed to hear something. He threw his cigarette away and went quickly along the terrace to the library window. He stood there for a while looking in—several minutes. Then he looked round over his shoulder quickly as if to see if anyone was watching, and went in through the window."

"Was that all?"

"N-no, sir," murmured Miss Brown in some confusion. "I—I knew I ought to be getting along to the store, but it was kind of funny and I waited just to see if anything happened. He was in there maybe three or four minutes and then he came out again. He looked around, but he didn't see me. I have a moonflower vine on my porch and it hid me some. He came quickly along the terrace and slipped in the back door. And that was all."

"You have no doubt at all that it was Minton you saw?"

"Oh, no. I'm certain. I saw him clearly."

"And you're willing to swear that it all happened just as you say?"

Miss Lucetta's eyes filled with nervous tears.

"Oh, yes. It happened exactly that way."

Potter picked up the bit of white cord on the blotter and returned it to its envelope.

"We can dispose of this. The ball from which it was cut—or, at least, the only ball in the house that exactly resembles it—and Reeves swears there was none on the yacht—was found in a drawer in the desk in Mr. Minton's room."

He took the blue book in his hands, weighing it idly, but he made no reference to it.

"In building up a case where the evidence is largely circumstantial," he said slowly, "one must cover three points. The first one—motive—we have already dealt with. But besides motive, we have two other points to consider: the weapon, and the opportunity—which includes, of course, the question of alibi, if any. I'll confess that, for a long time, the weapon stumped me. It seemed fairly obvious that the dagger in the black hawthorn jar was the weapon used in all three murders. We know it was used to kill Waterman Gaunt III. We have every reason to believe it was used to kill his mother and father. Yet everyone in the house claimed to be ignorant of the contents of the jar. Obviously someone was lying, but who?

"After a very little questioning, I realised that, while you were all too sophisticated to admit it, nevertheless you took the tradition of the jar too seriously to open it lightly. Yet one of you had opened it. I thought about the implications of that idea for a while and again I began to see something. I began to see that, if no member of the family would open the jar just as a matter of curiosity, without a reason, it was still possible that some member of the family might have opened it deliberately, for a reason. But this, in turn, brought me up against improbability. If, on the one hand, none of you could quite dismiss the idea of 'the curse of the Gaunts' from your subconscious minds, it was highly improbable that any one of you could take it sufficiently seriously to believe that you could bring disaster on the family by removing the seal on the black hawthorn jar.

"And then I began to see something else. I began to see that this reasoning only held good as applied to your present point of view. Go back far enough, to a more credulous age—I began to see again, as I saw before, an ambitious, brooding boy, bitter about his exclusion from the family fortune and his rightful place in the sun. He was aware of the story about the black hawthorn. No doubt he believed that, if he could only break the seal, the ghosts in the jar would avenge the wrong that had been done him. I set about it to see if I could prove that he had, indeed, acted upon this belief. It was my good fortune that led me to Miss Lucetta Brown."

Miss Lucetta started and paled as their eyes swung round to her. She looked at Nancy. "My dear, your mother made me promise I'd say nothing about it, but as things are—it seemed best—"

"I'm sure mother would want you to tell—anything you know."

Miss Lucetta looked at Daniel Minton. For a moment She had a curious illusion. She seemed to see his face as it had been when he was a boy—sullen, secret, yet oddly touching. Her eyes filled.

"I—I can't do it," she muttered. Then suddenly she straightened and her hands clenched on the limp handkerchief in her lap. "I hope you'll forgive me, Sergeant Potter. I—I—I suppose you want me to tell what I told you this afternoon. It happened years ago—thirty years ago. I'd forgotten all about it. I'd never have remembered if you hadn't almost described it to me and then asked me if it had ever happened." She wiped her eyes. Her pretty mouth was grim. "The children were all small then. Wat was fourteen and Edgar twelve and the others, of course, all younger. I was staying in the house because Captain Gaunt was away on a business trip and Nancy'd been ailing. I'd come to keep Hetty company.

"Hetty's sister, Sophia, was dead then, but Hetty still refused to speak to Mr. Minton or to let her children play with Daniel. I used to tell her she was foolish, but you might as well argue with a stone wall. There it was.

"Hetty used to be nervous at night when Captain Gaunt was away. She wouldn't admit it, but she was. I used to hear her walking round at night, looking for burglars. Well, one night I heard her go past my door about twelve o'clock. I didn't think anything of it, but I listened, and presently I thought I heard raised voices downstairs. I couldn't be sure, but I put on my wrapper and opened my door and listened, and sure enough, Hetty was talking to someone down in the library. I knew that, because I went to the head of the stair and I could see the band of light streaming out through the library door. I could tell she was angry, because she always raised her voice when she was mad.

"I couldn't hear what she was saying, but after a minute I heard a sound like a slap and a boy blubbering, and then running feet and the bang of a window being closed. I went downstairs to see what was wrong and when I got to the library door I could see Hetty with her wrapper on, bending over the desk. She jumped when I spoke to her and then, when she saw who it was, she began to cry. I've never seen Hetty cry before or since." Again Miss Brown dabbed at her eyes with her handkerchief.

" 'Just look, Lucetta!' she said to me. 'Just look!'

"Well, I looked, and there was the black hawthorn jar standing on the desk with the seal cut open and the stopper all askew. I was startled, because I knew how Hetty felt about it.

" 'What did you open it for?' I asked her.

" 'Open it?' she cried. 'I didn't open it. That brat of Sophia's did it. Forced up the lock of the window with a knife and got in like a burglar and opened it. Told me he hated us all and wanted to bring trouble on us. I thought I heard a noise and came down to see. When I got here he'd already done it.'

"She was crying terribly—as much with rage as with fright, I thought. I tried to soothe her.

" 'You don't really believe in the curse, do you?' I asked her.

"She looked at me in a very funny way.

" 'I don't know,' she said. 'Of course, when you ask me flat out like that, I'd say no, but—I'm not so sure.'

"However, she'd stopped crying, which was something. She got some red wax out of the desk and I helped her seal the thing up again. I guess she was a little ashamed of herself by then. Anyway, she made me promise never to tell what had happened. And I never have," finished Miss Lucetta, "until now."

"Did you see the dagger?"

"No. She must have already put it back before I got there."

"But you think she knew it was there?"

"I'm sure of it. There was a lot of cotton wadding scattered on the desk and she slipped her hand into the jar and packed it in very carefully before we sealed it. I thought then there must be something inside, but she was so upset I didn't like to ask her."

Potter nodded, his eyes again on the blue book in his hands.

"So we have motive—and weapon," he said. "Now—opportunity. And here we come to the one serious hitch in our line of argument: Our whole story hinges on the premise that one man committed all these crimes. And Daniel Minton has an alibi covering the time when Waterman Gaunt was killed. Mrs. Edgar Gaunt swears that she grasped his arm when the lights went out and did not relax her hold until the lights were turned on again. If this alibi holds, our whole edifice falls to the ground. I must ask Mrs. Edgar Gaunt to consider carefully whether she may be—mistaken."

All eyes swung now to Elvira. She returned Potter's stare defiantly.

"Of course I'm sure."

"There is, of course, one hypothesis left to us," said Potter. He turned the blue book over, his eyes following idly the printed title. "We may assume that Mrs. Edgar Gaunt has also a motive for suppressing the truth—that she is, in fact, an accessory to the crimes."

Edgar laughed grimly.

"That's good!" he said. He looked at Potter as though about to speak, but he changed his mind with a shrug. After all, she was in up to the neck already.

Elvira was on her feet now, swaying.

"That's a lie," she said hoarsely. "Heaven knows I think they all got what they deserve, but I had nothing to do with killing them. Edgar's already told you that I was in my room at the time his mother was killed."

Potter looked at her now: at her raddled face upon which the powder had clotted, at the terror in her eyes.

"I don't say you used the dagger, Mrs. Gaunt. I say you know more than you have told. Once again: is it true that you had hold of Minton's arm all the time the lights were out?"

Minton had got to his feet. He was looking at Elvira. Her eyes went past Potter and clung in fascinated, horrified questioning to Minton's face. She did not answer Potter's question. After a moment he spoke again.

"Which is it going to be, Mrs. Gaunt? Are we to bill you as an accessory or are you going to talk?"

Suddenly Elvira broke. She put up her hands as though to shield herself from Minton's look.

"Of course I didn't have hold of his arm. It was he that said it first anyway—not me. I don't know where he was when the lights were out."

Potter laid the blue book on the desk. He got to his feet.

"I do," he said. He walked around the desk. "Daniel Minton, I arrest you for the murder of Captain Waterman Gaunt and his wife and son."

He drew an official-looking paper from his pocket.

"If you care to have Mr. Avery examine the warrant," he added dryly, "he will find it is quite in order."

He was forced again to admire his adversary's nerve. Minton faced him with a grim smile.

"So you think that's a case?" he asked. "Good God, man! Don't you know that a good trial lawyer would make hash of it in an hour?"

"I don't think so," said Potter quietly. "Particularly as there's another point I haven't mentioned yet."

He picked up the blue book from the desk and opened it at the picture of the *Flying Cloud*.

"I am told," said Potter, "that death from the sort of wound we have been considering would probably not be instantaneous. Certainly Mrs. Gaunt lived for some moments after she was stabbed. Death occurs from internal bleeding, and that takes a certain time. Captain Gaunt, like his wife, did not die at once."

He looked over the top of his book at Minton.

"He lived to attempt an accusation of the man who had killed him. It was not completed, but it is sufficient.

"Old Captain Gaunt was in the habit of annotating the books he read. On the night he died he was so engaged and had a pencil in his hand for that purpose. This pencil the murderer either overlooked or assumed to be of no importance. When he thrust this book, opened at random, under the dying man's hand, he was, in effect, signing his own death warrant. For Captain Gaunt, at the point of death, found strength to scrawl on this open page the name of his murderer. You will see it here on the upper margin: 'Dan sta—' "

Susan moaned once, her hands to her throat, swaying.

"How about it?" asked Potter.

"A plant," said Minton.

Potter nodded to Collins, who stepped forward and slipped the handcuffs, one on Minton's wrist and one on his own.

For a moment Minton stood like an animal at bay, four-square. He looked at their hostile faces. He looked around the room with a strange look, as though he was taking his farewells. Then he looked at the black hawthorn jar.

He said nothing, but his look was freighted with so strange a meaning that those who saw it shivered as at the passing of a ghost.

Then he left the room with Collins. After a few words with Potter, Avery followed them.

It was when the door had closed on them that it happened. Susan Gaunt, white to the lips, pushed past Potter, circled round the desk, and pulled the black hawthorn jar from its pedestal. It crashed to the hearth—crashed into a thousand fragments. Susan turned and looked defiantly from one stunned face to another. Then, putting her arms on the mantel, she bent her head on them and burst into hysterical tears.

It was Carey who went to her. He put his hand on her shoulder and stood beside her awkwardly.

"It's over, my dear," he said gently, his voice shaking a little. "It's all over."

"Yes!" cried Susan. She threw her head back, disdainful of her tear-reddened lids. "The tradition's smashed—gone. All our ghosts out in the sunlight."

The room was quiet. The walls seemed to lean together, listening. Susan's eyes sought Jimmy West's. There was still the shadow of fear in them. They seemed to ask him:

"Surely this—is the end?"

THE END

RAMBLE HOUSE's

HARRY STEPHEN KEELER WEBWORK MYSTERIES

(RH) indicates the title is available ONLY in the RAMBLE HOUSE edition

The Ace of Spades Murder
The Affair of the Bottled Deuce (RH)
The Amazing Web
The Barking Clock
Behind That Mask
The Book with the Orange Leaves
The Bottle with the Green Wax Seal
The Box from Japan
The Case of the Canny Killer
The Case of the Crazy Corpse (RH)
The Case of the Flying Hands (RH)
The Case of the Ivory Arrow
The Case of the Jeweled Ragpicker
The Case of the Lavender Gripsack
The Case of the Mysterious Moll
The Case of the 16 Beans
The Case of the Transparent Nude (RH)
The Case of the Transposed Legs
The Case of the Two-Headed Idiot (RH)
The Case of the Two Strange Ladies
The Circus Stealers (RH)
Cleopatra's Tears
A Copy of Beowulf (RH)
The Crimson Cube (RH)
The Face of the Man From Saturn
Find the Clock
The Five Silver Buddhas
The 4th King
The Gallows Waits, My Lord! (RH)
The Green Jade Hand
Finger! Finger!
Hangman's Nights (RH)
I, Chameleon (RH)
I Killed Lincoln at 10:13! (RH)
The Iron Ring
The Man Who Changed His Skin (RH)
The Man with the Crimson Box
The Man with the Magic Eardrums
The Man with the Wooden Spectacles
The Marceau Case
The Matilda Hunter Murder
The Monocled Monster
The Murder of London Lew
The Murdered Mathematician
The Mysterious Card (RH)
The Mysterious Ivory Ball of Wong Shing Li (RH)
The Mystery of the Fiddling Cracksman
The Peacock Fan
The Photo of Lady X (RH)
The Portrait of Jirjohn Cobb

Report on Vanessa Hewstone (RH)
Riddle of the Travelling Skull
Riddle of the Wooden Parrakeet (RH)
The Scarlet Mummy (RH)
The Search for X-Y-Z
The Sharkskin Book
Sing Sing Nights
The Six From Nowhere (RH)
The Skull of the Waltzing Clown
The Spectacles of Mr. Cagliostro
Stand By—London Calling!
The Steeltown Strangler
The Stolen Gravestone (RH)
Strange Journey (RH)
The Strange Will
The Straw Hat Murders (RH)
The Street of 1000 Eyes (RH)
Thieves' Nights
Three Novellos (RH)
The Tiger Snake
The Trap (RH)
Vagabond Nights (Defrauded Yeggman)
Vagabond Nights 2 (10 Hours)
The Vanishing Gold Truck
The Voice of the Seven Sparrows
The Washington Square Enigma
When Thief Meets Thief
The White Circle (RH)
The Wonderful Scheme of Mr. Christopher Thorne
X. Jones—of Scotland Yard
Y. Cheung, Business Detective

Keeler Related Works

A To Izzard: A Harry Stephen Keeler Companion by Fender Tucker — Articles and stories about Harry, by Harry, and in his style. Included is a compleat Keeler bibliography.

Wild About Harry: Reviews of Keeler Novels — Edited by Richard Polt & Fender Tucker — 22 reviews of works by Harry Stephen Keeler from *Keeler News.* A perfect introduction to the author.

The Keeler Keyhole Collection: Annotated newsletter rants from Harry Stephen Keeler, edited by Francis M. Nevins

Fakealoo — Pastiches of the style of Harry Stephen Keeler by selected demented members of the HSK Society.

RAMBLE HOUSE

Fender Tucker, Prop.

www.ramblehouse.com fender@ramblehouse.com

318-455-6847 443 Gladstone Blvd. Shreveport LA 71104

RAMBLE HOUSE's OTHER LOONS

The Organ Reader — A huge compilation of just about everything published in the 1971-1972 radical bay-area newspaper, THE ORGAN.

Dr. Odin — Douglas Newton's 1933 potboiler comes back to life.

The Chinese Jar Mystery — Murder in the manor by John Stephen Strange,1934

The Julius Caesar Murder Case — A classic 1935 re-telling of the assassination by Wallace Irwin

The Contested Earth and Other SF Stories — A never-before published space opera and seven short stories by Jim Harmon.

Freaks and Fantasies — Eerie tales by Tod Robbins, collaborator of Tod Browning on the film FREAKS.

Vixen Scandal — Two sleaze masterpieces from the 60s by Jim Harmon: *Vixen Hollow* and *Celluloid Scandal.*

Maniac Siren — Two more sleaze marvels by Jim Harmon: *The Man Who Made Maniacs* and *Silent Siren*

West Texas War and Other Western Stories — by Gary Lovisi

Marblehead: A Novel of H.P. Lovecraft — A long-lost masterpiece from Richard A. Lupoff. Published for the first time!

The Secret Adventures of Sherlock Holmes — Three Sherlockian pastiches by the Brooklyn author/publisher, Gary Lovisi.

The Universal Holmes — Richard A. Lupoff's 2007 collection of five Holmesian pastiches and a recipe for giant rat stew.

Tales of the Macabre and Ordinary — Modern twisted horror by Chris Mikul, author of the *Bizarrism* series.

The Gold Star Line — Seaboard adventure from L.T. Reade and Robert Eustace.

The Werewolf vs the Vampire Woman — Hard to believe ultraviolence by either Arthur M. Scarm or Arthur M. Scram.

Black Hogan Strikes Again — Australia's Peter Renwick pens a tale of the outback.

Four Joel Townsley Rogers Novels — By the author of *The Red Right Hand: Once In a Red Moon, Lady With the Dice, The Stopped Clock, Never Leave My Bed*

Killing Time — New collection of short novels by Joel Townsley Rogers

Night of Horror — A short story collection of Joel Townsley Rogers

Twenty Norman Berrow Novels — *The Bishop's Sword, Ghost House, Don't Go Out After Dark, Claws of the Cougar, The Smokers of Hashish, The Secret Dancer, Don't Jump Mr. Boland!, The Footprints of Satan, Fingers for Ransom, The Three Tiers of Fantasy, The Spaniard's Thumb, The Eleventh Plague, Words Have Wings, One Thrilling Night, The Lady's in Danger, It Howls at Night, The Terror in the Fog, Oil Under the Window, Murder in the Melody, The Singing Room*

The N. R. De Mexico Novels — Robert Bragg presents *Marijuana Girl, Madman on a Drum, Private Chauffeur* in one volume.

Two Hake Talbot Novels — *Rim of the Pit, The Hangman's Handyman.* Classic locked room mysteries.

Two Alexander Laing Novels — *The Motives of Nicholas Holtz* and *Dr. Scarlett,* stories of medical mayhem and intrigue from the 30s.

Two Wade Wright Novels (and counting) — *Echo of Fear* and *Death At Nostalgia Street*, with more to come!

Three Rupert Penny Novels — *Policeman's Holiday, Policeman's Evidence* and *Sealed Room Murder,* classic impossible mysteries.

Five Jack Mann Novels — Strange murder in the English countryside. *Gees' First Case, Nightmare Farm, Grey Shapes, The Ninth Life, The Glass Too Many.*

Four Max Afford Novels — *Owl of Darkness, Death's Mannikins, Blood on His Hands* and *The Dead Are Blind* by One of Australia's finest novelists.

Five Joseph Shallit Novels — *The Case of the Billion Dollar Body, Lady Don't Die on My Doorstep, Kiss the Killer, Yell Bloody Murder, Take Your Last Look.* One of America's best 50's authors.

The Best of 10-Story Book — edited by Chris Mikul, over 35 stories from the literary magazine Harry Stephen Keeler edited.

The Anthony Boucher Chronicles — edited by Francis M. Nevins
Book reviews by Anthony Boucher written for the *San Francisco Chronicle,* 1942 - 1947. Essential and fascinating reading.

A Young Man's Heart — A forgotten early classic by Cornell Woolrich

Muddled Mind: Complete Works of Ed Wood, Jr. — David Hayes and Hayden Davis deconstruct the life and works of a mad genius.

My First Time: The One Experience You Never Forget — Michael Birchwood — 64 true first-person narratives of how they lost it.

The Incredible Adventures of Rowland Hern — Rousing 1928 impossible crimes by Nicholas Olde.

Don Diablo: Book of a Lost Film — Two-volume treatment of a western by Paul Landres, with diagrams. Intro by Francis M. Nevins.

The Charlie Chaplin Murder Mystery — Movie hijinks by Wes D. Gehring

The Koky Comics — A collection of all of the 1978-1981 Sunday and daily comic strips by Richard O'Brien and Mort Gerberg, in two volumes.

Gamefinger — Incredible 1966 sado-sleaze from Clyde Allison (William Knoles).

Dime Novels: Ramble House's 10-Cent Books — *Knife in the Dark* by Robert Leslie Bellem, *Hot Lead* and *Song of Death* by Ed Earl Repp, *A Hashish House in New York* by H.H. Kane, and five more.

Stakeout on Millennium Drive — Indianapolis Noir — Ian Woollen.

Dope Tales #1 — Two dope-riddled classics; *Dope Runners* by Gerald Grantham and *Death Takes the Joystick* by Phillip Condé.

Dope Tales #2 — Two more narco-classics; *The Invisible Hand* by Rex Dark and *The Smokers of Hashish* by Norman Berrow.

Dope Tales #3 — Two enchanting novels of opium by the master, Sax Rohmer. *Dope* and *The Yellow Claw.*

Tenebrae — Ernest G. Henham's 1898 horror tale brought back.

The Singular Problem of the Stygian House-Boat — Two classic tales by John Kendrick Bangs about the denizens of Hades.

The One After Snelling — Kickass modern noir from Richard O'Brien.

The Sign of the Scorpion — 1935 Edmund Snell tale of oriental evil.

The House of the Vampire — 1907 thriller by George S. Viereck.

An Angel in the Street — Modern hardboiled noir by Peter Genovese.

The Devil's Mistress — Scottish gothic tale by J. W. Brodie-Innes.

The Lord of Terror — 1925 mystery with master-criminal, Fantômas.

The Lady of the Terraces — 1925 adventure by E. Charles Vivian.

My Deadly Angel — 1955 Cold War drama by John Chelton

Prose Bowl — Futuristic satire — Bill Pronzini & Barry N. Malzberg .

Satan's Den Exposed — True crime in TorC New Mexico — Award-winning journalism by the Desert Journal.

The Amorous Intrigues & Adventures of Aaron Burr — by Anonymous — Hot historical action.

I Stole $16,000,000 — True story by cracksman Herbert E. Wilson.

The Black Dark Murders — Vintage 50s college murder yarn by Milt Ozaki, writing as Robert O. Saber.

Sex Slave — Potboiler of lust in the days of Cleopatra — Dion Leclerq.

You'll Die Laughing — Bruce Elliott's 1945 novel of murder at a practical joker's English countryside manor.

The Private Journal & Diary of John H. Surratt — The memoirs of the man who conspired to assassinate President Lincoln.

Dead Man Talks Too Much — Hollywood boozer by Weed Dickenson

Red Light — History of legal prostitution in Shreveport Louisiana by Eric Brock. Includes wonderful photos of the houses and the ladies.

Gadsby — A lipogram (a novel without the letter E). Ernest Vincent Wright's last work, published in 1939 right before his death.

A Snark Selection — Lewis Carroll's *The Hunting of the Snark* with two Snarkian chapters by Harry Stephen Keeler — Illustrated by Gavin L. O'Keefe.

Ripped from the Headlines! — The Jack the Ripper story as told in the newspaper articles in the *New York* and *London Times.*

Geronimo — S. M. Barrett's 1905 autobiography of a noble American.

The Compleat Calhoon — All of Fender Tucker's works: Includes *The Totah Trilogy, Weed, Women and Song* and *Tales from the Tower,* plus a CD of all of his songs.

The Naked Trocar with **The Best Revenge** — Two misdemeanors by Fender Tucker from 2007

www.ingramcontent.com/pod-product-compliance
Lightning Source LLC
LaVergne TN
LVHW091642100826
845152LV00006B/140/J

* 9 7 8 1 6 0 5 4 3 0 1 5 7 *